Stolen Memory

SHARON JOHNSTON BACON

WESTBOW
PRESS®
A DIVISION OF THOMAS NELSON
& ZONDERVAN

WestBow Press books may be ordered through booksellers or by contacting:

WestBow Press
A Division of Thomas Nelson & Zondervan
1663 Liberty Drive
Bloomington, IN 47403
www.westbowpress.com
844-714-3454

ISBN: 978-1-6642-6982-8 (sc)
ISBN: 978-1-6642-6983-5 (hc)
ISBN: 978-1-6642-6981-1 (e)

Library of Congress Control Number: 2022911445

Print information available on the last page.

WestBow Press rev. date: 07/26/2022

Chapter 1

My head hurt, my wrists were on fire, and my arms throbbed. My entire body ached, but the ropes wouldn't give so much as a quarter of an inch, no matter how hard I struggled. We were lying on a dirt floor. I tried not to think about spiders. Dim light barely penetrated the grimy little windowpanes high above our heads so most of the room was shrouded in shadow. I turned my head toward my sister, but I could barely see her tear-streaked face.

"Do you think they'll come back soon?" Panic had turned Stormy's voice into a high-pitched squeak.

"Don't know."

She started to wiggle caterpillar-like, slowly inching toward me, scooting closer and closer until we were practically nose to nose before she asked, "But they won't hurt us, will they, Delilah?"

"Of course not. They stuck a gun in our backs, shoved us into a van, hog-tied us like calves in a rodeo, drove us to this godforsaken place, and locked us in a cellar, so whatever gave you the idea that they might hurt us?"

Maybe it was the fear and the exhaustion that got to me, but those words fell from my lips before I had a chance to catch them. Now I looked into Stormy's terrified eyes and wished I could stuff everything I had said back into my mouth and swallow.

"We're gonna die, aren't we?"

"No, we aren't, Stormy. It's going to be OK."

Our ride in the van had seemed to go on forever but probably hadn't lasted more than thirty minutes or so. Yet it's hard to make an accurate guess when you are tied up and bouncing around in the back of a van amid a bunch of junk. Frankly, you're terrified out of your mind and can't think straight … or at least I was. I remembered that the last part of the trip was especially bumpy and then I heard bushes scraping along the side of the van. I'm guessing we had turned onto a very narrow dirt road and then an even narrower driveway. That's why I figured we were far away from any kind of civilization. Now we were left isolated, alone, and defenseless— with no idea where we were or even why we were here in the first place. Yep. We were in big trouble.

I shoved the growing dread back down my throat and attempted to scope out our surroundings. But I was bound with ropes, tied tight as a tourniquet, and could barely manage to move my head side to side. The only thing I could tell for sure was that we were in a cellar, with a dirt floor, high windows, and old stone walls. The whole place smelled deserted, but I'll tell you what, it was the silence that scared me most. Gut-twisting reality hit me. There probably wasn't a house or even a car within ten miles, which meant that not a single soul would hear our cries for help. Nope, there was nobody else to help us, so getting us out of this mess, preferably all in one piece, was up to me.

With a whole lot of grunting and strained muscles, I tried to roll over and sit up. All I managed to accomplish was to get myself into an even more uncomfortable position. As a reward for my efforts, the ropes around my wrists and ankles tightened, digging even deeper into my skin. Best of all, my jeans had twisted themselves into a knot, and I had managed to tear my good T-shirt.

"Crud!"

"Can't you get loose?"

"Of course I can," I snapped. "I just don't want to."

With that, Stormy scrunched up her face, and I braced myself for a flood of tears. "Don't let them see you cry," I hissed at her. "They'll think you're afraid."

Her voice trembled. "I *am* afraid!"

2

"Yeah? Well, big deal, so am I, but we can't let *them* know that."

She sniffed a few times and finally seemed to get ahold of herself.

We lay there, close together, each of us lost in our own thoughts. I guess we were just too scared to carry on a conversation. To keep my mind from exploring the dark realities of our present situation, I concentrated on watching dust mites dance on the sunrays that managed to pierce those filthy cellar windows. But when we heard a car pull up and heard the front door creak open, I forgot all about dust mites.

I swear, my heart stood still as heavy footsteps sounded across the room above us and then paused. The harsh bark of laughter sent a wave of terror washing over me as the cellar door opened. My underarms were soaked and sweat ran down my back. The sour smell of fear stung my nose. Then Stormy started to moan.

"Shh! Get a grip." My voice was raspy and creaked like an old screen door.

Stormy bit her lip and grew quiet while we waited, completely helpless, as someone pounded down the basement steps. There was an ominous pause in the murky shadows. Everything was quiet except for my heart, which now was thudding like a bass drum in my ears. Then we heard breathing coming in short, tight whistles as another person shuffled down the stairs.

The overhead light was switched on, and we blinked in the sudden blinding light. As our eyes adjusted to the glare, the men stepped into view. They hadn't bothered to cover their faces—probably not a good sign. Apparently, they weren't the least bit worried we could ID them, and that spooked me.

An old man hobbled down the last couple of steps and stepped onto the dirt floor. He paused and narrowed his eyes, staring at us for a long minute before heading our way. His left leg dragged a bit, stirring up a small cloud of dust as he painfully crossed the cellar until he reached the spot where we lay.

He reminded me of a shriveled-up string bean: long, thin, wrinkled, and bent. His white hair looked as if it belonged to some Angry Bird on a bad hair day. His nose overpowered the rest of his face, and his eyes were a washed-out blue. His suit looked three sizes too big, which gave the impression that he had lost a lot of weight recently. He seemed unsteady on his feet, swaying a bit as he flexed his hands into fists. Hovering over us, he studied Stormy and me like a vulture.

A few steps behind him, the same Neanderthals we had the pleasure of meeting during our ride here stood, watching him warily, waiting for their instructions. Regardless of all his frailties, he still was downright menacing and was obviously the head honcho. All eyes were on the old man when he narrowed his eyes and growled, "You girls wanna go home?"

Stormy answered in almost a whisper. "Yes, please."

"Yes, *please*?" He hunched over, laughing and wheezing, until a violent coughing fit turned his face a dusky shade of purple. The third thug, one we hadn't seen before, slapped the old man on his back until he stopped hacking and was able to catch his breath. He slowly straightened up as best he could and jerked his head toward us while wiping his mouth on his sleeve. "Stand 'em up."

The hairy hulk who held my shoulder in a bone-crushing grip was the epitome of Sasquatch. His ill-fitting suit seemed to be near the bursting point under the strain of his bulging muscles. He was handsome with chiseled features and a mane of blond hair, but his blue eyes were ice-cold. They met mine for a moment before he pulled a knife out of his pants pocket and slashed through the ropes tied around my legs.

Then he flipped the knife to his cohort who snatched it in midair and skillfully cut through Stormy's ropes. This dude, shorter and more compact, was built like a fireplug. Somehow, he was even more menacing than my captor. His skin was sallow, and his hair hung in long dreadlocks, but his most striking feature was a long, angry-looking scar that snaked its way down his face from just below his left eye all the way to his chin. He wore a black suit with a black shirt and tie to match. Yikes. Watching how expertly he handled that knife and the cruel expression on his face, I figured that, more than likely, his soul was even darker than his outfit. He grabbed Stormy by the arm and yanked her to her feet.

Stormy and I teetered back and forth, attempting to gain our balance on numb legs that had been tightly bound at the ankles for hours. When it seemed like we were going to topple over, the thugs jerked us up by the hair in order to keep us on our feet. Stormy gave a short yelp when her ponytail got yanked, but I gritted my teeth against the pain and kept quiet.

That third member of this gang of "Robin Hood's Band of Merry Men" was apparently the old guy's right-hand man. Impeccably dressed in an expensive suit, he was massive, even compared to his muscular colleagues. Built like a tank and just as intimidating, he just stood by the old man's side, impassively watching the proceedings.

The old man sort of stumbled over to me and came so close that his rancid breath nearly made my eyes water. "You want out of here?"

I straightened up to my full height of five foot two and glared at him. "Yeah," I snarled, hoping to sound a lot tougher than I felt.

"Then find that wacko you call 'mother,' get it from her, and bring it back to me."

"B-bring what back?"

"My books!"

With a quick jerk of her head, Stormy pulled her hair out of her captor's grasp and stuck her nose in the air, full of phony bravado. She attempted to stomp her foot. Not easy when your legs are numb. "Our mother doesn't have any books. She's always moving around, so she can't be dragging a bunch of books with her." My little sister was impetuous, she was obtuse, she was mistaken, and I was proud of her.

The big kahuna's bulbous nose flared. "Not those kinds of books, meathead! You think I have my own personal library or something? You think maybe I got a bookmobile following me around, huh? Not books, books, you knucklehead. I want my stick back!"

Stormy's voice shook, and she looked considerably less confident than she had a moment ago. "Your stick? What stick?" she asked.

"For my computer, you numbskull!"

Then came the great dawn. My epiphany moment. "Our mother copied your ... uh ... company's files onto a memory stick and then stole it?"

He flashed what could be interpreted as a grim smile. "So, your sister is the beauty, and you're the smart one, huh?" That was a left-handed compliment if I'd ever heard one. "Yeah, that's what she done, and then she wiped my computer clean as a whistle." He shook his head and snarled, "And she's gonna pay for what she done too."

He stared up at the grimy windows and moved his jaw back and forth like he was chewing on his words before he pointed a gnarled finger at me and said in a thin, reedy voice, "You go; she stays. Find the stick and bring it back to me. Then both you and your sister can go home."

I glared at him. "I'm not leaving without my sister."

He shrugged. "Well, then, I guess we'll have to kill you both right now."

"Then I guess you won't ever recover your memory stick," I shot back. Sometimes my stupidity masquerades as courage.

He scowled at me and sighed. "So, maybe we'll do it the hard way if that's what you want. My boys can be very persuasive, you know? Maybe Shirley would get motivated if she started receiving little presents of her daughters' body parts wrapped up in gift boxes with pretty bows just like Christmas ... a finger here, an ear there ... gets a little messy though." He nodded toward my sister. "I'd hate to cut up a beautiful dame like her, but yah gotta do what yah gotta do. Know what I mean?"

As I suppressed a shudder, Stormy took a deep breath and launched into one beaut of a screaming tantrum. She'd had years of practice to perfect her craft and had become quite an expert at it, although she hadn't pulled one of her hysterical conniptions in a good, long while. When she was a lot younger, she could rev it up and work herself into such a full-blown hissy fit you'd swear that she could shatter glass. I guess the terror of what was happening to us kind of short-circuited her brain so now she was like a little kid again. Her shrieks bounced off the walls and rattled around in our brains. I just couldn't help myself and glanced up to see if the windows were intact, but amazingly enough, they were still in one piece.

One of the men yelled, "Make her stop! Shut her *up!*"

I shrugged. "I don't know how to," I shouted over the din. "Once she gets going, there's no stopping her. She can't help it; she's only a kid, and when she gets scared, it just takes over. She just can't control herself."

The old man rubbed his face and looked over at the guy who still had a death grip on my arm. He nodded, and the next thing I knew, the gorilla's hairy paw lifted me as he pressed a huge gun to my temple. My knees went weak, but I didn't go down. Instead, he effortlessly held my 140 pounds up in the air, and I dangled there like a grotesque marionette.

"Okay, kid," the old man growled. "Yah wanna see your sister's brains splattered all over the walls? Or, are you going to shut up?"

Stormy's eyes grew wide, but she gulped several times, stopped screaming, and then thankfully managed to muffle her sobs.

He got right into her face. "Any more noise, and your sister's minus her head. Ever see what a Magnum can do at point-blank range? Makes a real big mess. Wanna see?"

Stormy began shaking her head and whimpering like a puppy. "No, no, please don't. Please don't!"

"Okay, so now we understand each other." He stood for a long while and seemed deep in thought, and then he sighed and pointed toward the cellar steps. "I changed my mind. Boris, you and Razor take 'em back."

"Take 'em back? But, boss, after all the trouble it took to ..." His mouth clamped shut like a snapping turtle, and he shriveled under the godfather's relentless glare.

The old man turned to me, poked his bony finger in my chest, and snarled, "And get that stick back to me if you know what's good for you and your cute little sister. That goes for your weirdo mother too! There ain't no place you can hide from me." With another jab of his finger, he added, "The next time we have a discussion, I won't be so nice." He narrowed his eyes. "Need I tell you that it's best not to mention this little meeting to nobody 'cause I won't like it. And if *I* don't like it, *you* won't like it."

"But ... h-how will I let you know?"

"Don't worry about it. I'll be in touch."

They loaded us back into the van and once again trussed us up like Thanksgiving turkeys. It didn't seem possible that our nightmare had only begun this morning, just a few short hours ago when they snatched us from our quiet little Georgia town of Brenville. But sure enough, here we were back in the van and starting back home. Since we were tied up and couldn't brace ourselves, Stormy and I had another rough trip down that dirt road, ricocheting off boxes, tools, and other various sharp objects. Then they drove down a curvy road so fast that we were slung back and forth along with all the rest of the stuff until they pulled onto a highway and the ride finally smoothed out.

After what seemed like an eternity, the van stopped, and our two chaperones heaved themselves out of the front seats and ambled to the back of the van. They were none too gentle when they cut our ropes, slid open the side door, and shoved us out onto the sidewalk. We had barely hit the ground when they took off, tires squealing. By the time I got my blindfold off, all I could see were taillights disappearing around the corner.

While I staggered to my feet and stomped around to get my numb legs functioning again, I looked over at Stormy. "Are you okay?"

She stood up, dusted off her jeans, and tucked in her T-shirt. She was shaking and wide-eyed, but otherwise seemed okay, although her voice wobbled a bit. "Who were those guys?"

"I don't know, but they sure meant business."

It was getting dark when we started walking down the crumbling sidewalk toward our run-down apartment building. We were battered and bruised, but all-in-all, none the worse for wear.

Our two friends were standing on the street corner and trying to drum up business. They waved as we passed by, but since Stormy and I were still deep in a serious conversation, we just waved back and didn't stop to chat.

I guess they noticed that we were a bit disheveled because Ebony hollered after us, "Hey! What happened to you?"

"Later," I called and kept on walking.

Stormy glanced over at me as we made our way home. "So, we better get the memory stick back to them real quick, that's for sure."

I raked my fingers through my hair and glanced over at my sister. "Yeah, but the problem is, our mother has the memory stick, so if we want to retrieve it, we've got to find her first."

Neither of us mentioned the obvious, but the trouble was, we hadn't seen her in months. And if that wasn't bad enough, we had no idea where to even start looking for her.

Chapter 2

WE DIDN'T EXACTLY HAVE A NORMAL CHILDHOOD, MY SISTER AND ME. Yeah, I know that compared to the fate of lots of other street kids, it could have been a lot worse. After all, we both survived with our lives, and thank goodness our ... um ... innocence remained intact. But if you really want to get right down to it, I hardly had any kind of a childhood at all.

First of all, there's the matter of my name, Delilah, that Mommie Dearest saddled me with. And wait, it gets even better; my last name is Sampson. What mother in her right mind would name her daughter Delilah Sampson? Well, yeah, there it is right there. My mother's mind hasn't been right since she was a teenager. She tripped out on drugs regularly until her ticket had been punched one too many times. Ever since then, she has had only a passing relationship with reality.

When I was about seven years old or so, I noticed that my mother's tummy was getting real fat. Then one day, she locked herself in a bedroom with a couple of her girlfriends, and after a whole lot of screaming, my sister made her appearance into the world. At first, she was named Summer Rain, but after my mother and her friends discovered how she would pucker her face up like an apple doll and then let loose with ear-shattering screeches that would make a Banshee proud, she was renamed Stormy. She's been stuck with that label for the past sixteen years, but to tell you the truth, it's a name that's worthy of her.

Our mother was never exactly a poster child for motherhood. She instructed us to call her by her given name, Shirley, and told us just to treat her like a big sister. She said not to let anybody know she was our mother because she didn't want people to think of her as 'old'. If that wasn't damaging enough, she also informed us that she had never wanted to be a mother in the first place. Talk about giving your kids a complex! Apparently, she had quickly concluded that since she had given birth to us, her contribution to our upbringing had been fulfilled. And I guess since she had decided she didn't need to help raise us, she also felt that there was no need to become any further involved in our lives.

So, at a very tender age, I inherited the responsibility of caring for my infant sister. Somehow, we both survived. Our meals were haphazard, sleep was only on an "as-needed" basis, and formal schooling was nonexistent. But since neither of us was born in a hospital and therefore was unencumbered by a birth certificate, being harassed by social services or even coming to the attention of a truancy officer was never a problem.

I never had a formal education, but somewhere along the way, I received my schooling from a woman I knew as "Subway Sally." She was homeless, filthy, smelly, and strung out, and I adored her.

Years ago, Sally had appropriated a shopping cart from a local grocery store. She was fiercely protective of it and never allowed it out of her sight. As a child, I half-believed the tales she spun that transformed her rusty old cart into a magical carriage. She kept a dazzling collection of treasures hidden deep within its dark interior, such as priceless jewels, a dragon egg (she said it only seemed like it was made of wood because a fairy had put a spell on it), and other mysterious riches that boggled my young mind. Yet it was the old, dog-eared textbooks tucked away among all her other valuables that intrigued me the most.

At first, Sally would sit me on her lap and trace the words with a dirty finger as she helped me sound them out. She gave me the gift of reading. She also gave me fleas and head lice. Over time, using those old textbooks, she taught me English, math, history, and even some rudiments of science.

I suspect she had once been a teacher, but she never mentioned her former life or why she had left Atlanta and ended up on the streets of Brenville. Yet, over the years, she instilled a fierce love of learning within me. Thankfully, once Stormy was older, I was able to pass on this insatiable hunger for knowledge to my younger sister.

Under Sally's watchful eye, I developed into a voracious reader. She helped me get a library card, and because of her influence, I came to realize that this little rectangular piece of cardboard was a golden ticket to the world.

Subway Sally was a vital part of my life for a long time, until the day she just disappeared and never came back. My heart was broken, but that's what happens on the streets. Life is hard, so friendships are few, often temporary, and rarely permanent.

Stormy learned at a very tender age how to wield her tantrums as a deadly weapon. She would begin to scream, and everyone would turn on me and yell, "Shut her up if you know what's good for you!" And since I knew what was good for me, I would shut her up. That almost always consisted of giving her whatever she wanted ... immediately.

One vivid memory of mine was when a beautiful Barbie doll somehow found its way off the store shelf and under my shirt. I loved that doll and tried to keep her secret from my little sister. But, of course, despite all my precautions, she found me out one day, and nothing would do but I give it to her. Reluctantly, I handed over my ill-gotten spoils that she so passionately coveted. Then I watched her slowly destroy my treasured doll as she toted her around until Barbie's clothes were ragged and her hair became matted. Sadly, when Stormy got tired of my once beautiful doll, she just tossed her aside. Such is life.

But believe it or not, my sister is a good girl, even if she is spoiled. I did the best I could raising her, but then again, I was just a child myself and cast into an adult role that I was totally unprepared for, without any good role models to help me figure things out. Looking back, there's a lot of things I should have done differently, but as they say, what is done is done.

Despite everything, or maybe because of it, I still feel compelled to take care of my little sister, and I will do anything to keep her safe. So, I guess that's what made me determined to clean up this mess no matter what.

Chapter 3

HARDSCRABBLE. THAT'S A GOOD DESCRIPTION, AND IT ABOUT SUMS UP our life. The one good thing that came out of our dysfunctional childhood is that my sister and I are close … real close. Come to think about it, that's about the only good thing that came out of our unconventional upbringing or rather, the lack of any so-called "upbringing" at all. Oh, yeah, and it also taught us to be self-reliant. Or, at least, *I'm* self-reliant, and Stormy relies on me. Our mother never really factored into the equation, other than birthing both of us. She just kind of drifted in and out of our lives, a sort of a benevolent, insignificant presence.

So, naturally, that means I'll have to straighten up this current mess by myself. I'm barely twenty-four, but I have been on my own for as long as I can remember. So, I'm old enough and possess enough survival skills to know it's not a good idea to get mixed up with a bunch of Mafia wannabes. And let's get real. Any kind of interaction with them sure isn't good for your health, or your life span either. But this wasn't my call. As a matter of fact, this whole thing wasn't even my mess. But thanks to our mother, we were up to our necks in it, and believe me, it stunk to high heaven.

Stormy and I had never been coddled like most kids, so we didn't fall apart just because we had been kidnapped by some two-bit Al Capone who now wanted to kill us. Once we got home, we just washed up and made ourselves a couple of sandwiches. We sat across from each other at our rickety kitchen table on our two chairs, which were even more wobbly than the table, and calmly ate our meal.

The only other "furniture" we own are a mattress on the floor and several pilfered plastic milk crates laid sideways and stacked on top of each other to serve as a dresser to hold our clothes.

Our apartment, drolly described by our landlord as a "studio apartment," comes with both complimentary roaches the size of house cats and rats so big they would give a pit bull a run for its money. We both work at a local greasy spoon where the pay is lousy, and on the rare occasion that someone leaves you a tip, it's only chump change. So, this dinky little fifth-story walk-up apartment is the best we can afford. But at least it keeps us dry and relatively warm. Although it isn't much, it's ours, and it sure beats living on the streets.

At any rate, Stormy and I decided to try brainstorming in order to figure out what to do. We agreed to consider all the different angles and see if we could come up with a plan to solve our rather complicated dilemma; namely, how were we going to locate our mother. And once we found her, how in the world would we get back that missing memory stick?

Anyway, I figured this whole scenario was a little like writing a novel or something. Years ago, back when I was an aspiring, although spectacularly unsuccessful, young author of detective stories, Subway Sally taught me to ask myself the "five questions" before starting to write. So, now I was going to apply those principles to real life.

I took a bite of my sandwich, picked up a pencil, opened my notebook, and looked over at my sister. "Okay, so that we can look at this in an organized, logical manner, let's try to figure everything out by asking ourselves these five questions: who, what, when, where, and why. Namely: "Who" had our mother download the 'godfather's' books? "What" was she planning to do with all that dirt she got on Stanley? "When" did she manage to steal the information? "Where" did she find Stanley to connect up with him in the first place? And maybe most important, "Why" did she steal the memory stick and wipe his computer clean after she downloaded all the information?"

I drummed my fingers on the table with one hand and bopped my pencil against the notebook with the other. Nervous energy, I suppose. "I think our priority is to find Shirley and shake her until the stick falls out of her ... whatever. Once we get the memory stick, I'll take it back to the old guy and then everything will be okay." *Sure, it would.*

Stormy frowned as she bit into her sandwich and then waited to make any comments until she finished chewing and swallowing the mouthful. Then she asked, "How did she get her hands on that guy's stick in the first place?"

"Probably by getting her hands on his ..." I ducked my head. "Never mind."

She grinned and shook her head before coming up with another idea. "Blackmail?"

"Shirley's not that dumb. Too dangerous." I sighed as I pushed my empty plate away. "What we need to do is to look at this situation from all possible angles and try to make some sense of all this mess."

Stormy wiped her mouth with the back of her hand and glanced down at what she had written in her notebook. "Okay, first off, where would she get a memory stick?"

"That's easy. Just about any store around here." I gnawed on my fingernails to help me concentrate. "I think we better figure out how she got together with the godfather in the first place and how she managed to get close enough to him to access his computer."

"Bet it was through drugs. She probably was a customer who caught his eye."

"Or she was working as one of his dealers."

Stormy shrugged. "In any case, she captured his heart, so to speak."

We both knew that at the age of forty, our mother lived hard and played harder. Even so, Mother Nature had been very kind to her. Although she was way too thin and had a trace of that haunted, strung-out look of an addict, she was still beautiful. And she was also alluring in an exotic kind of way, with a lovely face, straight, shiny black hair that almost reached to her waist, a smoky voice, come-hither violet eyes, and a Dolly Parton figure.

Stormy had taken all our mother's attributes and run with them. She was knockout gorgeous with raven hair, the same violet eyes, a lot taller than me (most people are), and curves in all the right places. I, on the other hand, must have taken after my father's side of the family ... whoever he might be and whose identity, by the way, was a mystery to everyone, including my mother. But in any case, he mustn't have been particularly attractive. Apparently, I inherited all his "ugly genes" with my mousy brown hair, plain old boring brown eyes, a butterball body, and a face that didn't exactly stop a clock, but sure didn't turn any heads, either. Life is not fair.

I pulled myself out of my reverie and turned back to the business at hand. "Okay, she met him, became involved either buying or dealing, and then they, uh, became close."

"Hard to imagine she would be anything but eye candy for him though. I doubt that the old guy was able to do anything with her."

I felt my eyebrows practically shoot all the way up to my hairline. "Stormy!"

She put her hands on her hips. "Well, you saw him. After just walking down the steps, he could hardly breathe. And remember how he couldn't catch his breath when all he did was laugh? I thought he was going to drop dead right in front of us. He's old, he's sick, and I'll bet he won't last much longer."

"Hah! That kind lives forever. Apparently, they must make a pact with the devil." Shaking my head at my little sister's know-it-all attitude, I skimmed through what I had written in my notebook and considered what she had said. I glanced at Stormy as I picked up my glass of water and drained it before continuing our conversation. "Well, she had some kind of hold on him, though. Have any idea what it might have been?"

"Besides sex?"

I shot her a look.

"What?" She stuck out her bottom lip in a pout. She looks so cute when she does that, and she knows it. But as she paused to think, she frowned and said, "Well ... maybe she has some dirt on him, like who supplies his drugs, or where he hides the bodies."

I grunted and checked my notebook again, hoping some answers would magically appear on its pages. No such luck. "Okay, suppose that's all true. How could she get access to his computer? Wouldn't the old guy be suspicious and make sure she didn't get within fifty feet of the thing?"

She thought a moment. "I bet he sleeps a lot, being old and sick and all, so she probably waited until he was conked out. Maybe she even slipped him an extra pill or something. Then, while he slept it off, she copied the stuff off his computer."

Our eyes locked for a moment, and then I returned to the questions at hand. "Okay, somehow Shirley gets to his computer and copies his files. So, how did she know what to look for and how to download it?"

"Easy. She was hired and then trained to do the job. Probably was told to get on his good side, get the info, and then split."

I sat up a little straighter and focused my attention on what Stormy was saying. "Who hired her?"

"Somebody very ambitious. They wanted to take over his business."

"Password?"

"Inside job."

I pondered all this for a while. "Okay, so, somebody on the inside wanted to take over the business. They hired Shirley to cozy up to him and get the information they needed. They're the ones who gave her the password and taught her how to do the job."

"Yeah. They wanted to replace him as top dog in the organization. Or maybe they just wanted to get all the dirt and then blackmail him instead."

"But then Shirley skips. Why?"

"Maybe she wanted a bigger piece of the pie."

"Or the whole pie."

"Or she finds out that whoever hired her decided to eliminate all the witnesses?"

My sister and I stared at each other.

Stormy shook her head. "She's in big trouble."

I ran my hand through my hair. "That's not completely true. If we don't find both her *and* that memory stick real quick, we're *all* in big trouble."

Chapter 4

I WORRIED ABOUT TAKING STORMY WITH ME, YET I WAS AFRAID TO LEAVE her alone, so in the end, I decided to bring her along. I figured it was the lesser of two evils. We dressed in baggy jeans and big old sweatshirts that covered all our feminine attributes. Of course, with me, there weren't all that many attributes to hide. We tucked our hair into ball caps and pulled them down on our foreheads to complete our ensembles.

First, we hit the various crack houses that we knew our mother patronized from time-to-time, but naturally no one knew where she was. Just what I expected. There's a kind of "honor code" among addicts: Nobody knows nothin' about nothin'. Period. End of story. But we had to start somewhere.

Next on our agenda was to visit the bars, all located on the seedier side of town. No one had seen Shirley in months and not a single person had any idea where she might be. You can take that bit of intelligence for what it's worth. Drunks aren't particularly known as trustworthy sources of information, not to mention that the reliability of conversations with bartenders tends to have a direct correlation to how many twenties you slip them. Since we had exactly zero dollars with which to bribe them, the quality of the data they supplied was somewhat suspect.

"Look, kid," one of the bartenders told me, "Barflies like your mother are a dime a dozen. They're always coming and going, and I can't keep up with them. You know what I mean?"

Unfortunately, I did.

After exhausting all of Shirley's usual hangouts, we were up against a brick wall. No one had any idea where she had gone or who she might be with … or at least that's what everybody told us. Supposedly, she hadn't been seen or heard from in months. We looked everywhere we could think of until we ran out of ideas of where she could possibly be. Finally, we gave up and started back toward the apartment.

When we reached our neighborhood, we stopped and chatted with our friends who were working their street corner near our home. As we considered our next move, Stormy stared off into the distance. "Nobody has seen her in a long time. Do you think she's dead?"

Ivy, dressed for business in six-inch heels, a skintight, very low-cut top, hot pink short-shorts and hair dyed to match, patted her arm. "Don't worry, honey. She ain't dead. We'd hear about it through the grapevine, and we ain't heard nothin."

"But that's just it. Nobody's heard anything at all. She just disappeared."

Ebony, tall and voluptuous with dark skin the color of mahogany, shared the street corner with Ivy. She listened to us talk for a while before she chimed in. "Somebody would'a run their mouth if sumpin' had went down. People don't keep no juicy news like that to themselves for long. If somebody offed your mother, you can bet the word would be out on the streets by now."

I glanced over at my sister. We didn't have much of a relationship with our mother, yet there still was … something. Kind of like how you feel about that stray dog that hangs around the neighborhood. You don't love it. You don't even like it. But you sure would hate if something bad happened to it. Stormy looked a little worried, but not especially upset, so I figured she was more concerned about finding the memory stick than what might have happened to Shirley.

I shaded my eyes with my hand and looked down the street. "Well, we tried looking in all her regular haunts, and there's no trace of her. Now what?"

"Yah want us to keep our ears to the ground and see if we can turn up something?"

"Yeah, Ivy, that would be great. Thanks."

Ebony gave us a sympathetic smile as we turned to leave. "Keep safe, girls."

We walked through our decaying neighborhood until we reached our ancient brick apartment building and started to trudge up the stairs to our fifth story walk-up. "I hate to say this, Stormy, but maybe we should check the morgue."

She kind of stumbled on the steps and made a strangled sound. "I couldn't. I can't. I just can't."

"That's okay. I won't expect you to go. But I think I'd better do it ... just in case."

We reached our apartment, and as usual, I started to jiggle the key, but before I could get it turned in the lock, the door swung open. We froze in the doorway, and just stared at the mess. Clothes were slung all over the room, the mattress was slashed with its guts hanging out, dishes were smashed, and food was scattered all over the floor.

Stormy spoke first, her voice sounding hollow. "Guess they were looking for the stick."

"Yep. And I'll bet you that they got annoyed when they couldn't find it."

I was right. It was even worse than it looked. They had cut and torn most of the clothing we owned and attempted to destroy everything else they could get their hands on. Just pure meanness.

Stormy's eyes filled with tears that threatened to overflow. "What are we gonna do?"

"Clean it up and start over," I said, pushing past her to walk through the room and survey the damage. I felt strangely calm. After all, how could I get all *that* upset over "stuff" when my little sister was safe? I was so grateful that I had taken her with me to search for our mother. My skin crawled when I thought about what might have happened if she had been home alone when they broke in.

Stormy followed me around the room, looking like a little lost lamb stumbling through the debris and trying to take it all in.

After checking the bathroom to make sure our company had indeed left, I slammed the apartment door shut, locked it, and jammed a piece of one of the broken chairs under the doorknob. Then I grabbed the broom and a couple of garbage bags and started to attack the wreckage.

Sniffling a little, Stormy watched me for a while, and then wiped her nose on her sleeve, snared a bag, and joined in.

We worked silently for a while, finding some items of clothing and a few dishes we could salvage. I could only manage to cobble together enough usable wooden pieces to put together one of the chairs. Pitiful. We shoved as much of the stuffing back into the mattress as we could, and duct-taped up the hole. Then we toted a load of laundry down to the basement to wash the few clothes we had left.

When Stormy and I got down to the so-called laundry room, we discovered that somehow, we had been foolish enough to leave a load of our clothes in the dryer. I guess I was so worried about finding our mother that I forgot to retrieve them before we left. It's a wonder one of our fellow tenants didn't help themselves to our wardrobe, but thank goodness nobody did, so our laundry was still there. At least *that* was a plus.

After we went back upstairs and had done as much as we could, we took stock of what remained of our "worldly goods." I put my arm around Stormy and tried to comfort her. "Well, I have to admit, our choice of attire has really taken a hit, but at least we still have our waitress uniforms and the other clothes that were downstairs in the dryer." I sighed. "Guess we'll probably have to kind of ration our food for a while, and it looks like our mattress will be lumpier than ever." I forced out a laugh that sounded phony even to my ears, but hey, that was the best I could do. I gave Stormy an awkward squeeze. "Well, all things considered, I guess it's not so bad."

My sister pulled away and looked at me like I had two heads. "Not too bad? Are you kidding? Most of my clothes are ruined! They even cut up my favorite Mickey Mouse T-shirt. And what if they come back? That lock didn't stop them from breaking in." Her voice shook. "We need to get a dead bolt!"

I crossed my arms and leaned up against the wall. "Yeah. Let's go down to the hardware store, charm them into giving us a dead bolt, and then maybe even convince them to install it for us, free of charge. Think about it, honey. We used the last of our change to do the laundry, and now we can't buy a dead bolt 'cause we're dead broke."

Stormy's lip started to quiver again. "So, what do you suggest? Just sit here and wait until they come back?"

I considered the problem for a while. "Let's go back down to the basement. I think I noticed some pieces of boards lying around."

As luck would have it, in the corner of the cellar, there were some two-by-fours leaning up against the wall. A few had been cut at an angle that made them perfect to wedge against the door. We confiscated a couple of short lengths and lugged them up all five flights of stairs from the basement to our apartment. We managed to wedge them at an angle against the door and stepped back to survey our handiwork. "That should work. It's not too convenient when we're coming and going, but it's sure effective in keeping unwanted visitors out."

"Yeah, and we're five stories high, so they won't be climbing in the windows." She made a noise that sounded like something between a half sob and a giggle as she flipped a strand of hair out of her face. "I can't believe I'm saying this, but for the first time in my life, I'm glad I live in a fifth-story walk-up."

Chapter 5

As we walked down the sidewalk, Ivy and Ebony were waving at us from their regular corner.

"Hey, come here," Ebony hollered. "We wanna tell yah sumpin'."

We hurried toward them. "What's up?"

"We heard ..."

Just then, our conversation was interrupted when Ebony was distracted by a potential customer. She sashayed over to his car, and they argued for a bit, but since they couldn't agree on a price, he drove off.

She shook her head and growled, "Cheapskate," and then turned back to us. "Like I was saying, we heard sumpin'. The word is that Shirley hooked up with Stanley the Swindler for about three months. She worked for him as a secretary or a bookkeeper or sumpin' like that, and then she quit, sudden like. Nobody knows where she went after that."

Another epiphany hit me. "Is this 'Stanley the Swindler' a scrawny old guy with a big nose?"

"Yeah, that's him. Stanley Barron, a.k.a. Stanley the Swindler, is a small-time, second-rate gangster. Vicious and mean as a snake. Got some bad muscle working for him too."

Great. That sure made me feel better. "What's the word on when Shirley disappeared?" I asked. "And is the street saying that Stanley had anything to do with it?"

Ebony shrugged. "Just know that Stanley wasn't too happy about her vanishing like that, so he's lookin' for her. It's been a couple five months, I think."

Wonderful.

"Do you think he killed her?" Stormy's face was white. The thought crossed my mind that she might be worried about our mother, but I dismissed the idea as ludicrous.

Ivy put her hands on her hips. "Think about it, honey. If he had killed her, he wouldn't be looking for her, would he?"

Stormy relaxed a bit and smiled. "No, I guess not."

I pretended to be hunting for something in my purse so my little sister wouldn't catch me studying her. I just *knew* she couldn't be upset about Shirley 'cause she sure shouldn't care what happened to her. After all, *I* was the one who raised her. *I* was the one who changed her poopy diapers and wiped her snotty nose while other girls my age were happily playing with dolls. *I* was the one who scrounged around to find food when she was hungry. And *I'm* the one who found her a safe place to sleep and stayed awake all night long to make sure nobody hurt my baby sister. And in the meantime, our mother was who knows where, doing who knows what. My childhood was stolen from me while our so-called mother was flying high on the newest "designer drug." Let's face it; most of the time, she hadn't realized that either of us even existed.

I gave myself a mental shake, pushed those raw memories to the back of my mind, and rejoined the discussion. "So, you're telling me that she's been missing for about five months, and Stanley really doesn't know where she is."

Ivy nodded and started to say something when a truck slowed down and stopped. She went over, and after spending a few moments talking to a guy who looked like a young version of Willie Nelson, she climbed in the pickup and took off.

Ebony cussed under her breath. "That should'a been *my* john. Ivy ought'ta know better."

"Don't worry," Stormy said. "You'll get the next one."

We exchanged glances, and then both of us looked over at my sister.

Ebony grinned at her. "Thanks, Stormy. But best you back away from the curb a bit so they don't think you're lookin' to turn a trick, too."

My little sister's face turned red, and she made a hasty retreat.

"I don't think Stanley did your mama in, but if I were you, I'd steer clear of him. He's a bad one."

I snorted. "Too late for that." I filled her in on all the stuff that had happened in the past few days.

As she listened to me chatter, she waved and smiled at the passing traffic, calling out to any occasional motorist who seemed to show some interest. But she wasn't having much luck.

Ebony shook her head in disbelief after I finished talking. "Um, um, um! That's bad, kid. *Really* bad. Maybe you should lay low for a while."

"We can't. We've got to work at the diner tonight or there's no job, which means there's no money for rent or food or anything else. It's not like we can find another place to work. Connie doesn't ask questions and pays us under the table, so we don't need social security cards or IDs or any other stuff like that. So, as long as we show up on time, stay sober while we're at the diner, and do our jobs, she's happy. The pay's not great, but we really don't have any other options."

She gave me a sad smile. "It sure beats turning tricks."

Just then, a luxury car pulled up. Ebony leaned into the window and talked to the driver, who was dressed in an expensive business suit, complete with power tie. Then she opened the door, gave us a quick wave, and drove off with her customer.

As the car disappeared around the corner, I thought about how ironic it was that once that man completed his business with Ebony, he'd be going home to his wife and kids. I figured it was more than likely that he and his family lived in some fancy-dancy gated community. And I'd bet everything I own (I know, it isn't much) that he feels superior to the likes of us. Life stinks sometimes.

Then, adding insult to injury, my sister; my little, innocent sixteen-year-old baby sister, watched them drive away and said wistfully, "I wonder how much she makes in a day. I bet she makes *real* good money."

I grabbed her arm and propelled her down the sidewalk toward home. "Don't even let it cross your mind!" It made me so mad just thinking about it. "That holier-than-thou guy looks down his nose at a woman like Ebony and thinks that she's just a piece of trash even while he's using her. He thinks he's better than all of us just because he has some cushy job and a trophy wife. There are things in this life that are more important than money, girl."

Stormy yanked her arm from my grip, practically sprinted down the sidewalk to our building, blasted through the entrance and stomped up the stairs in a huff.

I followed her, with my rotten mood accelerating with every step I took. Apparently, the same was true with Stormy because after we walked into the apartment, she spun around and got into my face. "Stop treating me like a child!"

"You *are* a child! You're barely sixteen, and believe me, you don't want to work the streets. Don't be so naive! It's dangerous work, and not only that, that lifestyle will ruin you. It would just be a matter of time."

Well, by this time, I was yelling. *How very mature of me.* Then Stormy turned on the water works, which made me even madder.

Then, once again, I ran my mouth before my brain got in gear first. "After all I've done for you, you owe me!" I screamed.

As soon as I said it, her eyes got wide and the hurt I saw reflected in them stabbed me in the heart.

"I'm sorry, Stormy. I didn't mean it. You know I didn't mean it. I'm just stressed out and worried, that's all."

She turned her back, went into the bathroom, slammed the door, and locked it with a decisive click. I just stood there, feeling like the worse kind of worm.

After a while, I knocked on the door. "Come on, Stormy. Let me in. It's almost time to head for the diner, and I've got to get ready."

Silence.

I knocked harder. "Open up! We can't be late, or Connie will have our hides."

Not a sound was coming from the other side of the door. I was about ready to rip the doorknob out by its roots when the door opened, and she sashayed out, dressed in her waitress uniform and ready to go. Cussing, I dove into the bathroom, did my thing, and slung on my clothes. By the time I came out, she was gone.

Panic-stricken, I tried to think where she would have gone, until I realized that since she was dressed in her uniform, she probably intended to go to work. I flew down the stairs, busted my tail moving down the sidewalk, got to the diner in record time, and clocked in with three minutes to spare. My heart was in my mouth as I grabbed my apron and went out front to see if Stormy was there. Sure enough, there she was, flirting with a good-looking guy while she took his order. When I saw her, my knees went weak with relief. But for the rest of our shift, she pointedly ignored me, and afterwards we walked back home in silence.

I tried talking to her but got the cold shoulder right up until we went to bed when she turned her back on me and went to sleep ... or at least pretended to sleep. It proved to be a very long night. I don't know how long our feud would have lasted if it hadn't been for what happened the next morning.

Someone was pounding on our door. I rolled over and squinted at the clock. 6:30 a.m.! *Who in their right mind would be at our door at this hour, knowing we worked the night shift?* I dragged myself off the mattress and staggered across the room. "Hold on! I'm coming!" I hollered as I started to remove the two-by-fours braced against the door.

"Shouldn't you find out who's on the other side of the door before you open up?" Stormy's sleepy voice penetrated my brain and brought me to my senses.

"Who's there?"

"It's me, Ebony. Let me in!"

She burst through the door as soon as I got it opened. For as long as I've known her, I'd never seen her like this. Her hair was a mess, her clothes were disheveled, and tears were streaming down her face. She was sobbing so hard I couldn't understand a word she was saying.

"What happened?"

She took a few shaky breaths before attempting to speak again. "It's Ivy. That john in the pickup truck hurt her. Hurt her bad. *Real* bad. Like to cut her to pieces ... her face ... they found her in a ditch. He threw her away like a piece of garbage. She might not make it." Ebony covered her face with her hands and bent over. "She might not *want* to make it! I saw her in the hospital. She looks like something out of a horror movie." Then Ebony stopped and stared at me before her eyes got wide as she slapped her hand over her mouth. "It was my turn to turn a trick. He should'a been my john. That should'a been *me* whut got cut!"

As I guided her over to our only chair and sat her down, I glanced over at my sister. She was sitting on the mattress looking like she was going to get sick. "Get up and bring her a glass of water," I snapped.

Stormy padded over and grabbed one of the few cups that had survived our visit from Stanley the Swindler's goons. It was missing a handle, but since all our glasses had been smashed, it was the best we had to offer. She filled it from the tap and shoved it toward Ebony. "Here."

Ebony gripped the mug with both hands, but she was shaking so hard that she slopped most of the water down her ample cleavage. "Look at me. I'm a wreck. Wouldn't think I'd be so shook up 'cause this kind of thing comes with the territory, you know? But she was cut up so bad ..." She was trembling as she raised her eyes and met my gaze. "My pimp is going to beat the snot out of me for leaving my corner and staying at the hospital all night, but I had to be with Ivy. Now I just got to talk to somebody. I ain't got no other real close friends, and I just got to talk to *somebody*."

I pulled her into a hug. "We *are* your friends, Ebony. I'm glad you came." I held her tight and rocked her like an infant until she cried herself out.

After a while, she quieted and sat up straight. "I gotta pull myself together and get back to my corner. Can I use your bathroom?"

Stormy looked horrified. "You're not going back out there, are you? What if that guy comes looking for *you?*"

"Honey, if I don't go back, my pimp will do me 'bout the same as Ivy. And besides, I'm not dumb enough to get into that sick dude's truck. I got a good look at him, so I'll recognize him if he ever comes around again."

"Which hospital is she in?" I asked.

"Central Hospital, room 373. Don't know how long they'll keep her, though. They usually don't want the likes of us around, dirtying up their pretty little hospital room, especially since we ain't got no insurance. They'll kick her out as soon as possible."

"So, she'll need a place to stay," Stormy said, and then her face brightened. "She can move in with us."

I glanced around our minuscule apartment, looked at the mattress on the floor, and then stared at my sister in disbelief. "Where would she sleep?"

I turned toward Ebony for backup, but to my horror, she smiled in agreement with Stormy. "She won't be turning tricks no more, so our pimp will throw her out on her rear." She shrugged. "Sleeping here on the floor is better than out on the streets. It's safe, and it's dry. But maybe you should look at her face before you make any decisions."

My little sister set her jaw and stared me down. "I don't care what she looks like. She's our friend, and she needs help."

Once again, she made me proud.

Chapter 6

EVEN THOUGH WE HAD BEEN WARNED, SEEING IVY'S FACE WAS A SHOCK. I'd never seen anything like it. Ebony was right; she looked like something out of a horror movie. I had the sinking feeling that either the doctor who stitched her up had a bad attitude or was spectacularly incompetent. I'm guessing he probably figured that she was nothing but a prostitute, so why should he take the trouble to do a good job? Or maybe he just was a lousy doctor. In any event, it was a case of Betsy Ross gone mad. Surgical thread was sticking out everywhere, and the swelling and bruising were terrible. Frankenstein never looked so bad. It made me furious to see such a botched job. But what can you do? What's done is done. That's life.

So, I took a deep breath, plastered a smile on my face, and walked toward the bed. "Hey, Ivy! How are you doing, girl?"

Her eyes were dulled by drugs and pain ... and hopelessness. "What are you doing here?" she asked in a flat, almost monotone voice.

"We came to see you."

"Why? Were you curious how bad he done me?" She turned her face away from us. "I'd be better off dead."

I bit back a reply, but then Stormy stepped closer and gently kissed her on top of her head. "You're going to be okay, Ivy. You're just hurt. We love you, and when you're well enough, we want you to come home with us."

"I don't need your sympathy. What I need is a mirror." She rolled over and sat up. "They won't let me see a mirror." Her voice kept rising until it reached near hysteria. "Why won't they let me look in a mirror?"

I expected the nurses to come running to see what was going on, but nobody showed. I guess they were used to people going bananas and yelling.

She was so pitiful, and she didn't seem to be listening even when I tried to soothe her. So, I decided to give it to her straight, though I did try to soften it a bit. "To tell you the truth, Ivy, you look a little rough right now. It would be better to wait a while until the swelling goes down and some of the bruising goes away."

"No! I want to see my face, and I'm gonna see it right now!" Stormy and I tried to talk some sense into her, but she didn't seem to even hear us. Suddenly, Ivy yanked out her IV, flung the blankets back, and struggled out of bed. I tried to grab her arm, but she jerked away, staggered across the room, and headed towards the bathroom as relentless as a runaway train.

I sprinted around the bed and chased after her, but she was moving amazingly fast. "Please, Ivy, get back in bed" I pleaded.

"No!" She yanked open the bathroom door and slammed it behind her. After a few seconds, an ungodly keening erupted, and then there was a crash, followed by an ominous silence.

I jimmied the door open just as several nurses came running. We stared down at Ivy stretched out on the floor. She had fainted dead away.

The nurses got her settled back into her bed and managed to get ahold of the doctor who ordered a sedative that knocked her out cold. That was a good thing.

The only one who was truly sympathetic toward her was an older nurse: a hefty dark-skinned woman with snow-white hair. She apparently had seen it all, over the years. "That poor lost soul," she crooned. "What a terrible thing to happen." She shook her head as she motioned for us to step out into the hall. "Thank the good Lord she has you." She nodded toward me as she reached out and took both of Stormy's hands in hers. "Listen to me, sweet girl. That poor woman will probably lash out at anyone who tries to get close, but you can't give up on her no matter what she says or does. She'll say hurtful things and try to push everybody away, but she needs you, whether she knows it or not. You and your sister are the only ones she has left in this world. Don't know how she'll earn a living now, neither. It's gonna be a rough row to hoe to try to deal with her, I know, but just hang in there. God will help you along the way and get you all through it, and He'll surely reward you for your kindness."

Stormy nodded as she gazed toward the hospital room where Ivy was sleeping. "What will she look like after everything heals up? Will she be even close to normal?"

"She'll be pretty scarred up, honey. But I'm far more worried about the inside than I am of the outside. She's hurt bad, on the inside … much worse than on the outside. You understand? And only God can fix her."

"I … I don't know. God and I aren't exactly on speaking terms, you know?" She glanced over at me. "We don't go to church or anything. I really don't know much about God."

The nurse patted her arm. "That's okay, honey. He knows everything there is to know about you and He's just waiting for you to turn to Him. All you have to do is reach out, and He'll be right there."

Stormy looked confused and seemed to want to ask her some questions, but then, someone buzzed their call button. "Gotta go and take care of my other patients now, sweet girl. Maybe we can talk later." With that, she bustled down the hall.

The nurse had said that Ivy would sleep for hours until the medication wore off, so we left her room and walked out to the elevator. After we pushed the down button, I turned to my sister. "I hope we're not biting off more than we can chew. This isn't a fairy tale, you know. It's real life, and Ivy is going to be hard to handle. She's bitter, and angry, and …"

"And she needs us. Please, Delilah, I want to help her."

"But what if she doesn't want our help?"

"Who else does she have? And where will she go? She'll probably end up killing herself if nobody helps her. Do you want that to happen?"

I sighed. I had lost the argument, and we both knew it. "Come on. Let's go home," I growled. "We've got to figure out the sleeping arrangements."

31

Chapter 7

WE MANAGED TO COMMANDEER A MATTRESS FROM A BUSTED COT THAT one of our neighbors was throwing out. Then we slid things around to make enough room to walk a narrow path that wove from the front door to the "bedroom" where our mattresses were, to the kitchen area, and to the bathroom. Now everything is so crammed together that there isn't room for much else, so I guess we won't be doing line dancing in our apartment any time soon. Home sweet home.

Ebony was right. Ivy moved in with us after only staying in the hospital for three days. Apparently, they pushed her out as soon as they could. She came home with a mess of instructions on how to take care of her face and a bunch of bottles and tubes of stuff to treat her wounds. Just as soon as she walked in the door, she pitched the whole shebang into the garbage, but I retrieved it all and then laid down the law. "Look, Ivy, this is how it's going to be, for long as you stay here with us. We're following these instructions to the letter 'cause I don't intend to deal with your face getting all infected."

"What difference would it make?"

I gritted my teeth and tried to keep my voice calm. "Honey, we care about what happens to you. We're gonna look after you and help get you well."

"Are yah gonna fix my face, too?"

I held her gaze and didn't waver. "We are going to make sure it heals up as best it can. Then we'll help you deal with it."

"Great," she snarled as she flopped down on the cot's mattress and yanked the blanket over her head. "Now that's a *real* comfort."

Well, I was right about a couple of things. Yes, Ivy was hard to handle, and another yes, we didn't have enough room to add another person. And one more great big yes; we had bitten off a lot more than we could chew. Swell.

That Sunday afternoon, Ebony came to visit and brought Ivy some of her clothes. "I snuck out as much stuff of yours as I could, but Dutch was watching me real close."

Ivy crossed her arms across her chest and glowered. "What do you expect me to do with these? You know I can't turn tricks no more with a face like this."

"So, wear them around the apartment. You ain't planning to go around nekkid, is you? These girls sure don't want you flashing yer bare keister at 'em. 'Sides, the stuff you can't use, you might could sell to one of the other girls or trade 'em for sumpin' else. Look, Ivy, I took a big chance smuggling this stuff out right under Dutch's nose, and yah know what he would'a done if he'd caught me." Ebony stood in the middle of the room with her hands on her hips, seething with anger. "Yah know I done you a big favor, so don't get smart with me, girl."

I held my breath while the two of them glared at each other. All I needed was a hair-pulling catfight right in the middle of my apartment. But I guess Ivy must have thought it over and decided she should be at least a little grateful to her friend.

"Yeah, guess you're right, Ebony," she muttered. "I 'preciate it."

Ebony nodded. "You're sho' 'nuf right about that. And I'm right, so listen to me, girl. Yah either got to go on livin' or else just curl up and die." She laughed and pointed her finger at Ivy. "And you're just too ornery to give up and let that slimeball win. Yah gotta fight, and yah gotta keep on fighting, girl."

With that, she apparently had finished saying her piece. With hands still on her hips, Ebony slowly turned and surveyed our apartment. Looking around, she asked, "What do you girls do for entertainment around here? There ain't no room to move, and you ain't got no TV, no Nintendo, and most important, no men ..."

Then she glanced over at Stormy and realized she was listening, so she dropped the subject like a hot potato. She cleared her throat and steered the conversation in an entirely different direction. "Stormy, you girls got any leads on what's happenin' with yo mama?"

My sister shook her head. "No. We haven't found out a thing."

"I've been thinkin'. Have you tried checkin' out the churches 'round here?"

My jaw dropped. "You got to be kidding."

She turned to Ivy. "Member the last time we saw her, Ivy? She was excited about the 'new life' she found. Talked about how God would forgive all our sins so we could start over and how Jesus loves us and all that kind of garbage."

"Yeah. She kept blabbering on and on about being 'born again' and nutty stuff like that. We figured she was on some new drug or somethin'. You know how she loved experimentin' and was always popping anythin' and everythin' she could get her hands on."

Stormy's eyes got wide. "You don't think she's turned into some kind of religious fanatic, do you?"

I ran my hand through my hair and sighed. "Sure hope not. That's all we need." I shrugged. "Anyway, I can't follow up on that angle and find out 'cause I wouldn't know where to begin. I've never even been inside a church much less have a clue about how you're supposed to act." I snorted. "They would probably throw me out on my ear before I even had a chance to sit down."

Ebony shook her head. "Well, don't look at me. They wouldn't even let me get near the front door of their precious church. Them holier-than-thou churchgoers in their fancy dresses and big 'ol hats think they're soo much better than me." She laughed. "They'd probably get the vapors and faint dead away if I told them the truth about how their pious husbands spend good money so I can show them a fine time and give 'em what they ain't gettin' at home."

"Ebony, watch your mouth around the kid," Ivy said.

"Sorry. It just makes me so mad when they look down their noses at us." She shook her head at me. "But I still can't believe that a smart cookie like your mom would fall for sumpin' like that."

I shrugged again. "I sure hope not, but stranger things have happened."

Chapter 8

A FEW DAYS LATER, WHEN IVY WAS FEELING A BIT STRONGER, SHE AGREED to stay with Stormy while I checked out the hospitals and the morgue.

There were only three hospitals with morgues in our general area, but after checking them out, I hadn't uncovered a single clue to help me find our mother. It was like she had vanished into thin air.

And, since I dreaded it so bad, I had saved Brenville's police department morgue for last. Once I got there, I found out that it was every bit as gruesome as I had imagined, and it really left me shaken.

They had only one Jane Doe who fit Shirley's description. But there was a problem. Before she ended up in the city's morgue, she had already been in the dumpster for several days before the neighbors found her and called the cops. She wasn't a pretty sight, believe me. I was able to tell it wasn't our mother although it would be a long, long time before I would get the picture of that rotting corpse out of my mind. I stared down at her, unable to pull my eyes away from the grotesque form that used to be a woman, and then I finally shook my head. "That's not her," I whispered.

I started to get light-headed, and the old cop who oversaw this "Rocky Horror Picture Show" took my arm to steady me. Then he led me out of the morgue though the double doors to a long hallway lined with uncomfortable metal folding chairs. His face was emotionless, but I suppose he had witnessed so many devastated people breaking down after identifying their loved ones that it no longer had much effect on him. I guess the only way he could manage to keep his sanity was to ignore all the pain that swirled around him.

"Sit down," he told me in a flat voice, "and put your head between your knees until you feel better." I wanted to tell him that it would take a lot more than that to make me feel better, but I decided to do what he told me instead. He made sure I was seated, then began to whistle as he turned, pushed through the swinging doors, and returned to his work.

As my head cleared, I noticed a hand near my face, holding a paper cup. I slowly sat up straight and found myself gazing into a pair of warm, dark brown eyes.

"Are you okay? Was she someone you knew?" he asked.

I shook my head as I took the cup and sipped some water. "No, I was looking for my mother, but it wasn't her. It's just ..." The hallway started to go black again, so I lowered my head back down.

He took the cup from me, stretched out his legs, crossed his ankles, and started to talk as if it was a normal conversation. "It's hard to have to go in there and identify someone, especially under these particular circumstances because I know she's in pretty rough shape."

I sat back up, and he handed the water back to me and paused to study my face. "I'm sorry about your mother."

"It's okay. I really didn't expect to find her here, but I had to check anyway."

"How long has she been missing?"

"Five months," I answered. Even as I was talking, in the back of my mind, I couldn't get over how I was talking to a stranger ... and an adult male stranger at that.

I leaned back and scrutinized the man sitting beside me. He was a big man, probably in his late twenties with a rich baritone voice. Tall, muscular, and somewhat chunky, he was built like an athletic teddy bear. His face was a kind of homely in a cute sort of way. He had a broad forehead, a slightly flattened nose, a mustache parked over full lips, and a bushy beard that covered a strong jaw. Desperately in need of a haircut, he kept pushing back the hank of dark brown hair that hung in his eyes. Instead of a uniform, he was decked out in "civvies" ... faded jeans, a wrinkled flannel shirt, and muddy sneakers. Guess this must have been casual Friday.

Yet, for some strange reason I couldn't even begin to understand, I felt comfortable being with him. That was a first for me.

He stuck out his hand. "I'm Mutt."

"Mutt?"

He gave me a crooked grin. "That's not my given name, but considering the name my mother saddled me with, I prefer that my friends call me Mutt."

"Okay ... but what is your real name?"

He sighed deeply. "You really want to know?"

I nodded.

"It's Clyde."

"Umm ... that's not so bad."

His face was solemn. "Last name is Dale."

I thought about it for a moment, and then it came to me. "Clyde Dale?"

"Yep."

"Oh." I mean, what can you possibly say to a man whose name is Clyde Dale? My own name didn't seem quite so bad anymore.

"I think we have something in common," I said as I grinned at him.

"Your name is also Clyde?"

I giggled. I giggled! Here I was, sitting in the cellar of a police station just outside a morgue, and flirting with a strange man. What was wrong with me?

"Nope. It's Delilah. Delilah Sampson."

"Whew. Soo, it's safe to say that both our mothers had a sense of humor?"

My face fell. "Something like that."

"I'm sorry. That was an insensitive thing to say while your mother is missing."

I shrugged. "We weren't that close anyway. I just need to find her."

We sat together in companionable silence for a while, and then he turned to me and flashed another one of those cute, lopsided smiles. "I'm Detective Clyde Dale with Missing Persons, among other things. You might say I'm the Brenville Police Department's jack-of-all-trades. Anyway, I can help search for your mother ... if you like."

My suspicious nature took over, and I frowned. I guess he realized I was skeptical, so he pulled out a badge from his jeans pocket and showed it to me.

I studied it for a while before I looked up and asked, "What are you doing down here, anyway?"

"This is a police station, and I'm a cop." He grinned at me and shrugged. "So, here I am."

"But why are you here in the basement? I wouldn't think that a morgue is exactly a place where you guys usually hang out."

"The grapevine told me that someone was here trying to ID my Jane Doe, so I came down in case there was a positive identification." Our eyes met, and he held my gaze. "Honestly, I really would like to help you."

"Oh." I ducked my head. I was torn. We sure needed help, but how could I trust a cop? And if being a cop wasn't bad enough, he was a stranger. And besides, if you get right to it, I didn't even know if he was who he said he was or what his real motives were. For all I knew, he could be impersonating a cop and be working for Stanley the Swindler.

Yet the more I thought about it, his explanation for being here sounded reasonable, and the badge did look genuine to me, although my expertise in that area was sorely limited to say the least. He probably was legit, yet I still couldn't be completely sure.

I didn't know what to do. It felt as if the weight of the world was crushing me as I slumped down in the chair and tried to figure out my next move. I was stressed to the max and felt as if my head would explode. And as I kept thinking about all the problems I was facing, my throat just kept getting tighter and tighter until, to my horror, two big tears escaped my eyes and slid down my cheeks.

"It's going to be okay, Delilah. I'll help you."

Those few kind words did me in. I hadn't had anyone try to comfort me since … I don't remember when. Probably never. I was overwhelmed that a stranger cared that I was upset and would take the time to try to help me. Pressure kept building up in my chest, and my emotions ran amok. Then, suddenly, the floodgates opened, and tears erupted.

He patiently sat beside me, waiting for the storm to pass, not saying a word until I finished blubbering.

I gradually got ahold of myself and sat up straight. I was mortified when I thought about how I must look. I always cry ugly.

He reached over to snare a box of tissues sitting on a nearby chair seat and handed it to me. "Feel better?"

I nodded, pulled out some tissues and noisily blew my nose.

"Want to tell me about it?"

My instincts told me not to tell him anything. But then I figured, what have I got to lose? I'd always tried to use common sense and look where it's gotten me. At this very moment, I'm being hunted by a crazed two-bit gangster and his goons, not to mention that I had also become a den mother to a rebellious teenager and an out-of-work, suicidal prostitute. And, of course, there was the fact that the three of us were stuffed together like sardines into a tiny apartment, but I won't even go there. To top it all off, I'm searching for a mother who had never been a mother, ever, and who, if truth be told, I really didn't want to find in the first place.

I was between a rock and a hard place with no place to turn. It hit me all at once and shattered my natural reserve. The next thing I knew, I spilled my guts.

He listened intently, only interrupting to ask an occasional question. Then he sat back and stared at me. The only comment he made was "Wow."

That's when I got buyer's remorse. I knew I shouldn't have told him anything, much less everything. "Look, Detective Dale—"

"Please call me Mutt."

"I thought only your friends called you that."

"With you, I'll make an exception."

"Okay. Look, Mutt, this was all off the record, right?"

"Well, it can be, if that's what you want. But keep in mind, Stanley Barron doesn't play games. You and your sister are in real danger. Yeah, he's a bungler, but he does get lucky occasionally. He's a nasty piece of work, and he hires vicious thugs who enjoy performing stuff that a normal human being wouldn't even think of doing. Every time you step out your door, you become fair game to him … plus he enjoys the hunt. I really think you could use my help."

When I began to shiver uncontrollably, he gave my shoulder a gentle squeeze. I blew a strand of hair out of my eyes and sighed. "I'm sorry. I don't know what's wrong with me. I'm usually able to keep things under control."

"That's okay, Delilah. You've been through a whole lot more than most people could handle. And considering what you had to witness in there," he nodded toward the double doors, "it's no wonder you're having a delayed reaction. Afterall, you're only human."

He leaned back and pulled out a small notebook and a pencil from his pocket. "Okay," he said. "So, let's get started. You'll have to repeat everything you told me so we can go over it all and see if we've missed anything. And I'll need you to answer my questions as honestly as you can." He paused and met my gaze. "If we work together, we'll find her, Delilah. Trust me."

It made no sense, but I did trust him. Who would have thought?

Chapter 9

It wasn't until I started talking to Mutt that I realized just how little I knew about my mother. It was kind of sad ... pitiful, actually.

He would occasionally glance at me and then scribble something in his notebook while I prattled on about everything I knew about Shirley, the sum total of which was woefully limited. As I ran out of things to say, I gradually wound down and then stopped talking.

He focused on his notebook for a while before looking up at me.

I shrugged and muttered, "Well, I guess that's all."

Mutt gave me a quick smile and then gave his notebook another hard look before he cleared his throat and twisted around in his chair to face me.

"Well, looks like you covered all the bases in your search, Delilah, but maybe we should make the rounds again and ask some more questions. It might make a difference if a cop was doing the inquiring."

I raised my eyebrows at him. "If they smell a cop, most of the people I've talked to will scatter like roaches when a light is switched on."

Mutt grinned and made a show of sniffing his armpits. "Didn't think I smelled that bad."

"You know what I mean."

He immediately sobered. "Yeah, I do. Guess I could do my undercover cop thing. Let me go home and change into more appropriate clothes, and then we can fraternize with the natives."

Glancing at his current relaxed outfit, I wondered what he considered "appropriate clothes" for undercover work. Smiling, I asked, "Are you sure you want to do this?"

"Of course. I already told you that I want to help."

I stood up and got ready to leave. "Where shall we meet?"

"How about I drop you off at your house, and then I could come back and pick you up."

Panic washed over me. Was all this just a way to find out where I lived?

Mutt must have seen the fear on my face because he sighed. "Okay, not such a good idea. Where would you feel comfortable meeting?"

I thought a moment. "I'll be waiting outside Connie's Home Diner on Manchester Street. Do you know where that is?"

"I've heard of it. I'll be there in thirty minutes."

Twenty-five minutes later, I was standing in front of the diner when a rusted-out hatchback pulled up. I watched as the driver parked and then struggled to extricate himself from the car. He was a big guy, dressed in an oversized hoodie, with sagging pants hung so low that his tighty-whities showed for all the world to see. His ragged sneakers completed "the look." When he started toward me, I eyed the diner's door, trying to decide whether I should duck inside or not, but then I recognized him.

"Mutt?"

"Yep. It's me in the flesh. Ready?" He gestured toward his car. "My chariot awaits, my lady."

I laughed. "Are you sure that rust bucket is going to even make it down the street?"

He clutched his chest. "Are you disparaging my wheels? You wound me to the core."

After I got in, I roared with laughter when he had to slam the passenger door three times before it stayed closed. He walked around the car and folded himself up like a contortionist and wiggled to get behind the wheel. Finally, he managed to get settled into the driver's seat. While I wiped tears of laughter from my face, he glared at me. "Are you enjoying yourself?"

"Yes, immensely."

He grinned. "Good." Then he threw the car in gear, and we chugged away from the curb.

When we checked out the first crack house, I immediately recognized the piece of slime who answered the door. The curtain of stringy hair hanging down and nearly covering his face couldn't disguise that his pupils were mere pinpoints. His filthy clothes were typical of all the drugged-out losers who populated the neighborhood, and not only that, he stunk. He looked me up and down with a lewd smile on his face. "Hey, sweetheart, whut up?"

"Hey, Randy. Still looking for Shirley. Heard anything?"

"No, sweet mama, but why don't you step in here, and I'll show you something real good."

Mutt stepped out of the shadows and put his hand on my shoulder.

"Whoa." Randy took a step back and craned his neck to look up at Mutt who was a good foot taller than he was. "You're one big dude," he croaked. He turned back to me. "Didn't know you had a boyfriend, Delilah." Then he shot a nervous smile in Mutt's direction. "Sure didn't mean to horn in on your territory, bro."

Mutt nodded. "It's all good. Now yah wanna answer the lady 'bout her mother?"

Randy shrugged. "Why should I?"

In an instant, he was pinned against the wall. By the time Mutt's hand was removed from the unfortunate punk's throat, we had learned everything Randy knew about Shirley, which was pitifully sketchy and nothing new.

I guess Randy expected to be paid for his information since he had the chutzpah to stick out his palm. But when he saw the murderous glare Mutt gave him, he quickly shoved his hand into pocket. I had the sneaking feeling he was very lucky that the only thing he got from our little chat was a sore throat.

We made the circuit of all the other crack houses I knew my mother had patronized at one time or another. Since Mutt knew the talk and could walk the walk, I doubted if anyone even had a clue that he was a cop. But despite his considerable persuasive powers, we didn't find out anything else that was useful.

Next, we toured the bars. This time, he let his Jacksons talk because once he slipped a bartender a twenty, they became a lot friendlier to Mutt than they had ever been to Stormy and me. Unfortunately, we didn't uncover anything new or even interesting from any of them.

We climbed back into the slum-mobile and headed toward the diner. "You spent a lot of money back there. I don't know how I'm going to repay you."

"Don't worry about it. I'll put it on my expense account."

"Okay, thanks." I slumped into my seat and sighed. "But I still think it was a big waste of time and money."

"Are you kidding me? We learned a lot."

"Like what?"

"Like she's still alive, or someone would have heard about it by now."

"That's what Ivy said."

I chose to ignore his questioning raised eyebrows, so he paused for just a moment before he said, "Okay. Number one, she's alive. Number two, she's been out of the action for about five months. Number three, she worked for Stanley Barron for approximately three months until she disappeared, and he's been looking for her ever since."

"We figured that out already."

Glancing at me, he continued driving down the street. "Number four, she hasn't had the chance to unload the memory stick or sell the information."

"How do we know that?"

"Because Stanley is still alive, but his tail isn't in jail yet either."

"Oh, okay. So, what's number five?"

"Ahh … number five …" He thought for a while. "Number five, nobody knows where Shirley is."

"*That's* Number five?"

He shrugged and gave me that crooked grin of his. "I admit that one's a little lame."

Swell. My very own, modern-day Sherlock Holmes with a touch of Jay Leno thrown in. I glared at him. "So, now what?"

"So, now we dig a little deeper. Give me a day or two, and I'll get back with you."

Chapter 10

I REALLY HADN'T EXPECTED TO HEAR FROM HIM AGAIN, BUT TWO DAYS later, there was a knock at our door. I squinted through the security peephole and saw Mutt. My first thought was, *Wow, he kept his word!* My second thought was, *How in the world did he find out my address?* He raised his hand to knock again just as I cracked open the door.

"Hey, Delilah. I was beginning to wonder if you were home or not."

"How did you find out where I lived?"

He grinned. "I'm a cop in Missing Persons. That's what I do best: find people." He was wearing a flannel shirt and jeans again. I guess it must be his unofficial uniform. There was an awkward pause, and then he laughed. "Well, are you going to invite me in, or are you coming out?"

Just then Stormy came and stood behind me in full pit bull protection mode. "Who is this guy?" She turned her attention on Mutt and snarled, "What do you want?"

Ivy's voice was as hard and unwelcoming as Stormy's when she called to us from inside the apartment. "He's a cop. Don't let him in. I ain't done nothin' wrong."

Mutt raised an eyebrow and looked at me.

I sighed in defeat and swung open the door. "Come on in." I nodded toward my sister. "This is Stormy, and over there is our friend Ivy."

He smiled. "Glad to meet you, Stormy. Delilah has told me a lot of nice things about you."

That wasn't the best thing to say, given how I always stressed how important it was to keep to ourselves and not share any information, ever. Oh, boy, was I ever busted.

She glared at me and crossed her arms over her chest. If steam could come out of someone's ears, it sure would have been coming out of hers.

Ivy was sitting at the table with that deer-in-the-headlights look.

Mutt wove his way around all the clutter until he reached her chair and stuck out his hand. "Hey, Ivy, glad to see you up and about. We're still looking for that creep who attacked you. When you feel up to it, I'd like you to come in and take a look at some mug shots."

She just stared at his hand without making a move until she slowly raised her head and met his gaze. "Why should I come to the police station? I ain't putting on no show for you pigs so you can take pictures and have some laughs."

Mutt reached out and grasped her hand, caressing the top of it with his thumb. "Ivy," he said softly, "I promise you that the entire police department takes your attack very seriously. Believe me, we won't stop hunting for that monster until we find him and put him away for a long, long time."

She yanked her hand away. "What do I care? It don't matter whether he's caught or not, and it sure ain't gonna help my face none."

Mutt crouched down in front of her, his voice gentle. "Of course, it matters. You didn't deserve this. And besides, don't you want to keep him from doing this to someone else? I'm going to find him, Ivy, if it's the last thing I do. And you're going to help me."

"Why do you have your nose stuck in this? This ain't no missing person case."

He shrugged. "Well, I occasionally like to do a little moonlighting on the side. Besides, Brenville's police department is a small one, so we all have to multitask, you know?" His face was grim. "When I heard what the sick punk did to you, I had to pursue this case. That monster needs to be put in prison for a long time."

Ivy's eyes shimmered with tears as she studied his face. Then she bent her head and seemed to be thinking while her fingers played with her pajama buttons. Mutt patiently waited as she chewed her lip for a while, but when she lifted her head, her expression was determined. She gave him a quick nod. "Okay. I'll help."

"Good. We're going to put him away until his grandchildren have grandchildren." He stood up and grinned at her. "And, Ivy, I'm betting you've got the guts to make sure that it happens."

He put out his hand, and they shook on it, and then he turned to me and asked, "By the way, Delilah, have you ever heard of Preacher John Robinson?"

"No. Should I?"

Ivy snorted. "He's the one whut holds them church services in that old, abandoned warehouse on Powell Street, ain't he? He's something else. A real religious fanatic. Always trying to get us girls to go to his church service. Says we could get washed clean 'in His blood.'" She gave a little shiver. "Sheesh! He sure is one weird dude. Haven't seen him in a while, though."

"Yep, he's the one. My sources tell me that Shirley attended his services. You know anything about that?"

"Our mother went to church? You've got to be kidding!" Stormy sounded horrified.

Ivy crossed her arms over her chest and scowled. "John Robinson ain't nothing but a con artist."

Mutt shook his head. "Actually, I think he's the real deal, and he preaches a good message. I haven't been able to dig up any dirt on him at all. Both he and his organization seem to be on the up-and-up." He studied Ivy for a moment. "And what Preacher John's talking about is having your sins forgiven through the cleansing blood that Jesus shed on the cross."

We all stared at him while we digested this information until I finally found my voice. "Well, what has that got to do with Shirley's disappearance?"

"Preacher John only comes to the city a few times a year to hold revivals. The rest of the time, he is a pastor at a megachurch upstate, about a hundred miles from here. I was wondering if your mother could have followed him up there."

I could feel my blood pressure rising. "Are you out of your mind? Shirley would never take a preacher for her sugar daddy, so unless he was supplying her with drugs, she wouldn't have anything to do with him."

He shrugged. "Okay. I was just wondering. As far as I could tell, she vanished about the time that he finished his revival and went home. But I wasn't thinking that there was anything unsavory going on between those two." He paused and then seemed to choose his words carefully. "This church has an excellent drug rehabilitation facility there, and I was wondering if your mother had entered their program."

I shook my head. "She would never have anything to do with a bunch of religious fanatics. Not unless pigs fly." I narrowed my eyes at him. "You sure seem to know a lot about this preacher."

He grinned. "I'm a cop, so I attended his revival meetings to investigate and make sure he wasn't a charlatan. Like I said, Preacher John has a good message and I enjoyed his church services. Everything I've uncovered shows that his ministry does good work, and their finances are rock-solid. They reach out to people who are down-and-out, and their drug rehabilitation program seems to be very effective. Honestly, I was impressed with the man and the infrastructure he and his people have set up."

"Well, Shirley wouldn't be caught dead in any church, so there's no way she's involved with this so-called "Preacher John" or his organization."

"Are you sure?"

"Absolutely positive!"

Chapter 11

THE TRUCK CRUISED BY AS STORMY AND I WERE WALKING HOME FROM the diner. We were dead tired and didn't pay much attention until it drove under the streetlight, and I caught a glimpse of the driver's face. I froze in horror when I realized it was the Willie Nelson look-alike. Suddenly, he sped up and roared down toward the intersection, squealing his tires as he made a U-turn. I could hear the truck barreling back down the street toward us. Survival mode kicked in as I spun Stormy around, gave her a push, and screamed, "Run!"

The next thing I knew, we were caught in its headlights, making us a beautiful target. We took off like a pair of scared jackrabbits with a pack of hound dogs at our heels, but I knew we could never outrun that truck and it would be only a matter of seconds before that maniac flattened us. I shoved Stormy when we reached an alleyway and yelled, "This way!" We made a sharp right turn, sprinted down the alley, and slid to a stop in front of the eight-foot-high chain-link fence that blocked our way. We could hear the truck back up, turn, and begin to creep forward, blinding us with its headlights.

Panicking, I spun around and noticed a door almost hidden in the shadows. I yanked on the doorknob, and to my amazement, the door swung open. I pushed Stormy into the pitch-black space, dove in after her, and slammed it shut. Feeling around, I found a dead bolt and slid it into place. As we cowered in the dark, we could hear an engine idling, and then the truck door slammed shut. The driver's heavy footsteps echoed in the alley as he came closer and closer, and then we heard the heart-stopping sound of him rattling the doorknob.

My mind screamed at me to move, so I grabbed my sister's arm, and we shuffled through the darkness, bumping into stacks of boxes as we made our way toward the weak shaft of light shining from under a door.

Our stalker was getting serious, and it sounded like he was trying to pry open the door.

I made a quick decision. We had the choice of either facing the devil we knew or facing the devil we didn't know. I already knew what the one who was trying to bust his way in was capable of, so I pulled the door open, and we stepped into the room.

As our eyes adjusted to the bright light, we stared into the faces of a bunch of surprised card players seated at a scarred poker table littered with stacks of money and bottles of hooch.

Everyone paused for a split second before the circle of hands that had been holding cards just moments before suddenly bristled with handguns, all very big and all looking unquestionably lethal.

"Whut up, ladies?" A muscular, olive-skinned man with black hair pulled back in a ponytail and a face covered with gang tattoos slowly stood up. He crossed his arms over his chest and glared at us.

I pulled Stormy behind me and straightened up to my full, very intimidating, five-foot-two height. "Hey."

"Whut'cha doing here? Don't remember invitin' no entertainment." He grinned and took a step toward us. "But it's all good."

One of the men sitting at the table leaned back in his chair. "Hold on, Snake. Ain't them the gals whut took in Ivy?"

He narrowed his eyes. "That right?"

Oh boy! I had never met Snake face-to-face before, but I sure had heard plenty about him, and none of it was good. As I withered under the glare of this clearly unwelcoming gathering, I wasn't sure whether harboring a retired prostitute would be counted as a plus with these men or not. But considering what was probably waiting for us in the room we just exited, I decided we had a better chance with the card players. I tried to keep my voice steady but didn't have much luck. "There's this guy ... the one who hurt Ivy ... he ... he chased us down the alley, so we came in here to get away."

Snake glanced over at the door and worked his jaw. "He still there?"

I shrugged.

Then, right on cue, "Willie Nelson" burst into the room. He took quick stock of the situation, cursed, spun around, and ran back out, slamming the door behind him. Instantly, the room erupted in shouting and cussing.

Stormy and I dove under the table and huddled together while the men rushed out like a hoard of bloodthirsty orcs, hot on their quarry's trail. We both jumped at the sound of gunfire while we hunkered down in our not-so-perfect hiding place. Then we heard the truck roar away, more gunshots, and finally, silence.

After a while, there were heavy footsteps and a lot of creative language in both English and Spanish as the men made their way back into the room. They had obviously failed in their hunt.

It seemed prudent to remain hidden, but a couple of seconds later, I found myself staring at a pair of Air Jordans.

Snake bent down, looked me in the eye, and jerked his head toward the room. "C'mere."

We were cornered. I figured we'd have a better chance if we came out from under his table voluntarily and stood on our own two feet rather than refusing and getting dragged out, so I scooted toward the Nikes. Stormy followed me, dusting herself off as she stood up.

I straightened up, faced the one they called Snake, and attempted to pull off my best tough gal impression. I failed miserably. Of course, it didn't help that I was trembling so hard that my teeth were chattering. I glanced over at my sister, but she wasn't in any better shape than I was.

Snake studied us for a while before shaking his head. "Whut you doin' walking the streets this time of night?"

"We were coming home from Connie's Home Diner. We work the night shift."

"You ignorant or something?"

"No. Just broke and gotta work. It's the only gig we can get, and we need the money."

"What time you get out?"

"About one. We have to clean up after we close."

"You ain't gonna walk by you selves like that no more."

"But …"

He held up his hand to silence me. "One of my boys will walk youse home at night. What's the schedule?"

"Ahh … it changes every week."

"Don't matter. I'll know when you're there." He scowled at me. "You two don't walk alone no more. Hear me?"

"But I can't pay you for…"

"It ain't for you. It's for Ivy." He jerked his head toward the door. "Buster, you and Jose take 'em home."

"Thank you."

"Don't mention it." He smiled. "And don't crash none of my parties no more, neither."

Chapter 12

MUTT SHOWED UP AT OUR DOOR EARLY THE NEXT MORNING. HE WAS showing up at our doorstep fairly often now, although usually not *this* early.

"What are you doing here?" I snarled as I opened the door. "We work the night shift, you know."

"So I heard. But word on the streets is that you girls ran into some trouble last night. You shouldn't be walking home alone so late, especially in this neighborhood."

I bristled at his obvious slur about my neighborhood but decided to ignore it. "Well, we won't be walking by ourselves anymore. Not that it's any of your business, but we've got ourselves an escort now."

I attempted to close the door, but he was too fast and stuck out his foot to keep me from shutting it. "Who's the escort?" he growled.

"Like I said, it's not any of your business." I pointedly looked down at his foot. He wasn't impressed. By this time, I was grinding my teeth. "Why are you doing this?"

All the cockiness drained out of him, and he met my gaze with solemn eyes. "I don't know."

Crossing my arms over my chest, I blew some hair out of my eyes and continued to stare him down. "That's no answer."

He lowered his eyes and sighed. "I know." Pacing back and forth in the hallway, he ran his hand through his hair and looked so pitiful that I felt myself softening, just a bit. Then all of the sudden, before I could even react, he pulled me out of the doorway and into the hall. My first thought was, *Ooh, crud, I'm wearing my pj's!*

Here I was with my short, mousy, brown hair, nondescript brown eyes, and a somewhat chunky body that was more lumpy than curvy, wearing faded Snoopy pajamas and ratty fuzzy slippers. *Yep,* I thought, *I am the epitome of an irresistible sex goddess.*

My next thought was that I remembered I hadn't brushed my teeth, and I panicked. Spinning around I tried to scoot back into the apartment, but he gently held on to my arm.

"Please, Delilah, I won't try anything. I promise."

I angrily yanked out of his grasp. "Look, I've got enough people trying to hunt me down and kill me. I don't need another stalker."

Mutt jerked back as if he'd been hit with a stun gun. "Is that what you think I am? A stalker?"

I closed my eyes and sighed. "No. No, I don't think of you that way at all." I gave a helpless shrug. "It's just that I don't understand why you're here."

He studied my face for a moment, and then he chuckled. "I don't understand why I'm here, either." He stood in front of me, and I couldn't help noticing how his eyes were the color of melted dark chocolate. *Yum.* I got kind of lost in my thoughts for a moment before I turned my attention back to what he was saying.

"When I saw Harry helping you out the morgue's door that day, something inside me just … you looked so … I don't know … All I wanted to do was to hold you and comfort you … protect you. I … I can't explain it. You're so pretty. And then, after we spent time together … the more I got to know you, the more I … I don't know … Argh! I'm not explaining this very well."

I tried not to grin because I felt a little sorry for him. Then it hit me. Did Mutt really say I was pretty? Me? He actually thought I was *pretty*? I was contemplating this amazing development when the door was yanked open. Stormy stood there, holding a frying pan, and Ivy was beside her, gripping a butcher knife. They were loaded for bear.

Mutt took a step back.

I put my hands on my hips and faced them. "What do you think you are doing?"

"It's not what *we're* doing," Ivy snarled. "It's what this pig thinks *he's* doing."

Mutt tried to placate her. "I just wanted to talk to Delilah for a few minutes … in private."

Ivy's hand tightened on the knife. "You dragged her into the hall dressed only in her pajamas, so you could just talk to her? You think I was born yesterday?"

"Look, I was worried about what happened last night, and I wanted to check on her."

She stared at him. "Whaddayah mean, 'What happened last night'?"

Mutt glanced from me, to Ivy, and then back again to me with a raised eyebrow.

I cleared my throat. "Um, Ivy was asleep when we got home, so she doesn't know anything about it."

"Know about what!" She lunged toward Mutt, but Stormy managed to intercede before she committed murder right in our hallway.

"Wait a minute, Ivy," she said. "Let's hear what he has to say."

Mutt raised his hands in surrender. "Yeah, and how about we continue this conversation inside in your apartment?" Mutt gently guided me back through the doorway, and Stormy and Ivy followed close on his heels.

I reached over and touched Ivy's arm. "Maybe you should put that knife down."

She narrowed her eyes, put her hands on her hips, and stood her ground, still gripping her weapon. "Okay, let's hear it."

A nervous giggle bubbled up from my throat. "Well, you see, Stormy and I were walking home from work, and this truck came by."

Ivy hitched up her sagging pajama bottoms and glared at me. "And?"

"And all of a sudden, I recognized the driver, and well, he must have noticed that I recognized him, or maybe he recognized Stormy and me from the other day, or maybe …"

"Just get on with it, Delilah!" she snarled.

"Well, he chased us with the truck, so we ran into an alley, but there was this big old chain-link fence." I knew I was jabbering, but I couldn't help myself. Retelling what had happened brought last night's terror back in full force. "He tried to follow us, so we ran into this warehouse and ended up in this room full of poker players. Then they all went out and they started shooting, and they chased the driver. And Snake said …"

"Snake!" she said. "You talked to Snake?"

"Yeah," Stormy interrupted. "He was mad at us at first until somebody told him that you were staying with us. Then he said that we shouldn't be out that late all by ourselves, so he was going to have one of his boys walk us home from now on."

Mutt looked grim. "That Snake is one bad hombre. I can't believe that you were foolish enough to barge right into his card game. It's a wonder you weren't shot!"

I put my hand on my hip. "Well, we didn't mean to. We were just trying to get away from Willie Nelson."

Mutt looked really confused. "*Who* were you trying to get away from?"

"The guy in the truck looks like Willie Nelson, only younger, and he was doing his best to run us down, so we were trying to get away."

Mutt looked like he needed to sit down.

Ivy gestured toward the chair. "Park it before you fall on the floor."

He ignored her. "Let me get this straight," Mutt said as he counted down our talking points on his fingers. "Someone who looks like Willie Nelson was attempting to mow you two down in his truck and chased you down an alley."

Stormy and I both nodded.

"So, you ducked into a building and found Snake and his buddies playing poker."

We nodded again.

He rubbed his face. "Then, the men all chased the driver and shot at him, but he got away. And this is the same guy who cut up Ivy. Is that right?"

Stormy picked up the story. "Right. So, that's when Snake said he'd have his guys take us home and that they would be walking us home from now on."

Ivy finally laid the knife down on the table and smiled. "Snake and me go way back."

"Yeah," Stormy said. "He was a little scary at first, until one of the other guys told him who we were. After that, he was real nice."

"Honey, Snake don't do nice. But since he said he'll protect you, he'll do it." Ivy laughed and shook her head. "Who would'a thought?"

Chapter 13

A FEW DAYS LATER, MUTT SOMEHOW PERSUADED IVY TO COME DOWN TO the police station. It was the first time Ivy had left the apartment since she came home from the hospital, and Stormy and I decided to go with her to provide moral support. Before she left, she pulled on a hoodie and yanked its strings as tight as she could to cover most of her face. Then we all shoehorned ourselves into Mutt's rattletrap of a car and headed downtown.

Ivy was shaking when she walked through the station's door, but she relaxed a bit after a couple of the cops gave her a friendly welcome. A female officer even came over and gave her a hug. Stormy and I must have looked a little surprised at her reception until Ivy gave us a wobbly smile and explained, "I was a regular here."

Mutt took her to a private room and pulled out several notebooks filled with mug shots. He seated Ivy at the table and dumped the stack in front of her, and then he gestured towards a couple of folding chairs. "Come over here, ladies, so you can take a look, too. You both saw the guy when Ivy got into his truck, and you might be able to help ID him." He grabbed a chair, turned it around backwards and straddled it. "Take all the time you want. There's no hurry."

Ivy just sat there, staring at the pile, seemingly unable to move.

Mutt put his arms across the back of the chair and rested his chin on them, patiently watching her.

She was trembling when she finally reached over, took the top book off the stack, and opened it. We all leaned forward so we could see the photos better as she methodically began to turn the pages. She was halfway through the second book when the three of us all gasped at the same time.

"That's him," Ivy said, tapping the photo.

Stormy and I grimly nodded.

"Are you sure?"

"Yeah, I'm sure. I have nightmares about him every night. I'll never forget that face."

Mutt turned the book around and examined the photo. "You know, he does look like Willie Nelson." He read us the information printed beneath the photo. "Rodney Butler a.k.a. the Slasher." He glanced up at us. "I had a hunch he might be the one, but he went underground and has been quiet for a while." He summed up the information for us as he continued to read. "Served time for rape and aggravated assault. Got out of prison six weeks ago." He looked up at me and scowled. "What I don't understand is what gave Butler the idea that Ivy was involved in all this and why he thought she knew where Barron's memory stick was."

"Well, he did ask if Delilah and I were friends. When I said yes, he asked where the stick was. When I said I didn't know what he was talking about, he went berserk."

Mutt met Ivy's troubled gaze and seemed to think about what she had said for a while before he nodded. "So, now that we know who we're looking for. Ivy, I promise you we're going to catch that scumbag. He's going to do some hard time; I'll personally make sure of that."

Ivy nodded. "Yeah, but only if I don't kill him first."

Mutt reached over and took her hand. "He's not worth it, Ivy. Just let the law take care of him."

She wouldn't meet his eyes as she pushed back her chair. "Take me home. I'm tired."

The ride back to the apartment house was tense. Mutt glanced over at Ivy several times and seemed to want to say something, but he apparently thought better of it. When he pulled up to the curb, she got out and slammed the door.

Stormy and I wriggled out of the car just in time to watch Ivy blow up at Mutt. "How do you keep this piece of junk together? It's more rust than metal. Why don't you get yourself a decent car?"

He grinned. "Cops don't get paid much."

"Yeah, but you get paid enough to get some wheels that ain't falling apart. You risk your life just getting into this thing." Her face was flushed with anger as she put her hands on her hips. "And if you can't afford to buy a drivable car, it sure makes me wonder what you do with all your money."

He just shrugged.

"I mean it. What do you do with it? You need decent wheels."

He smiled. "I've got better things to do with my money than to spend it on a car when I have one already."

"You call this pile of dog turds a car?"

"It gets me to where I want to go."

She narrowed her eyes at him. "Well, I still would like to know what you do with all your money." She glared at him and then sneered, "Maybe you're a dirty cop." Then she spun around and bolted up the steps and into the building without another word to any of us.

Stormy watched her go. "She's really upset."

Mutt leaned up against a dented fender. "Can you blame her, Stormy? Seeing his picture probably brought it all back to her. Got to admire her though. It took guts to walk into the station and go through those mug shots." He shook his head. "But it's going to take even more courage for her to begin a new life. Ivy's lucky to have you two helping her."

After he said goodbye and drove away, Stormy and I trudged up the stairs to our apartment. It was a shock to see Snake slouched against the table, talking to Ivy. He flicked his eyes towards us and then jerked his thumb in the direction of the door. "Out."

If you're smart and Snake tells you to leave, you leave. And even if you aren't the sharpest tool in the shed, when Snake tells you to leave, you leave. Stormy and I backed out and headed downstairs then we sat down on the stoop and waited.

"What do you think he wants?" Stormy whispered.

"I have no idea."

"He won't hurt her, will he?"

"I don't think so. Ivy didn't seem scared, and besides, I get the feeling that they're old friends." I checked my watch. "Hope he leaves soon. We need to get ready. We have to head for the diner in less than an hour."

Stormy sighed. We worked long hours for little pay, and I knew it was hard on her. She never got to have fun or even get the chance to just be a kid. She didn't have any friends her age, either.

When we were younger, thanks to our mother's lifestyle, we always had to scrounge around, fighting and scratching just to survive. Our life is still hard, but at least we work at the diner, so we always have enough to eat and can live in our own apartment. But after paying the rent and buying a few essentials, there isn't anything left over for luxuries. In fact, we don't even have a TV.

Books are our greatest source of entertainment. Ever since we were little, we haunted the library. Reading was the kind of thing we could afford since library cards were free, and we enjoyed reading to each other. Also, one of our neighbors gave us some board games that her adult kids didn't want any more, and we would spend hours playing Monopoly, Scrabble, and Parcheesi. Oh, and we sang. We still love to sing together.

So, anyway, that's the way we entertain ourselves. Oh yeah, we used to sneak in the side door of the old theater down the block to watch a movie. But then it closed last year, and that ended that. So, all in all, it's not exactly a great life for a sixteen-year-old girl. Such is life.

We sat on the stone steps for what seemed like hours until my tail went to sleep. Finally, Snake sauntered out the front door and down the steps without so much as a glance our way. His fancy black car with its tinted windows was parked in front of our building. He slid behind the wheel, and the engine roared to life. Instantly, the rap music blasting from his stereo rattled windows for blocks around. It was so loud that I could feel the thump of the bass in my chest.

After Stormy and I watched him leave a streak of rubber behind as he drove off, I stood up, brushed myself off, and headed for the door, "Well, I guess it's time to get dressed for work."

When we walked into the apartment, Ivy had on a pair of jeans and was pulling a decent looking shirt over her head.

"What's going on?" Stormy asked.

"Getting ready for work. Snake said the cook at the diner quit and now I've got the job. He said I could stay in the kitchen and didn't have to see nobody."

I managed to find my voice. "That's … uh … that's great! So, now you'll be working with us. But I didn't know you could cook."

"I can't. But Snake said it won't be a problem." She glared at us. "Hurry up and get ready. I don't want to be late."

Okaay. Ivy got a job at the diner as the cook, yet she can't cook. Swell. Then again, if Snake says it won't be a problem, then it won't be a problem. But it's a safe bet that, from now on, eating at Connie's Home Diner would prove to be an adventurous culinary experience and probably an interesting one too. And come to think of it, it could even turn into a dangerous one. Oh, boy.

Chapter 14

FOR THE PAST FEW WEEKS, MY LIFE WAS GOING FAIRLY SMOOTHLY FOR A change.

The cook at Connie's stayed long enough to train Ivy, and everybody, including Ivy, was surprised to discover that she had a knack for producing culinary delights. Well, to tell the truth, that's an exaggeration. Let's just say she hasn't given anybody food poisoning ... yet.

Stormy and I had called a truce and were getting along okay. That's really saying something, since Ivy, Stormy, and I are sharing an apartment that is only slightly larger than a postage stamp, so we were constantly invading each other's personal space.

Mutt has been coming around fairly often, and lately, he's been hinting that his interest in me isn't totally based on police business. I'm still dealing with my trust issue, but we talked about my childhood or lack thereof, and he seems to understand my problem. He's very patient and rather sweet. And I'll admit he's kind of cute too ... okay, he's more than *kind of* cute.

We remained on edge about Rodney Butler, who we still thought of as Willie Nelson. Ivy's scarred face is a daily reminder of what he was capable of, and that makes us grateful for Snake's protection, especially in those early-morning hours when we are walking home from the diner. But because no one has seen hide nor hair of "Willie" since the night of the card game, we hoped it meant he has left the area. Even so, we won't let our guard down when it comes to watching out for him.

So, with my world steadily spinning on its axis without so much as a wobble, and the constellations correctly positioned within the cosmos, it was pretty easy to forget about Stanley the Swindler and his memory stick. We hadn't heard from him since our kidnapping and apartment break-in, so I guess it was a matter of "out of sight, out of mind." My mistake.

We still hadn't been able to get a dead bolt for our door although the two-by-fours worked well at night, once we were inside the apartment. But whenever we left, all we had for security was that sorry old lock that didn't stop felons like Stanley's boys or even Snake from breaking in. And let's be real here, it barely even slowed them down.

We should have been more on top of our game, but after you've been on your feet for a ten-hour shift, you are not exactly functioning on all cylinders. Tonight, our regular escort, Jose, a big barrel-chested Latino who looked capable of protecting us from an army of Willie Nelsons, was waiting to walk us home. We said goodbye to him at the top of our stairs, and after he started to trudge down the steps, I pulled out my key and began to fiddle with it, trying to get that totally aggravating door unlocked. So, by the time we let ourselves into the apartment, flipped on the light, and discovered that we had company, Jose was already long gone, and it was too late to yell for help. Now we were staring at two very large Smith & Wesson handguns the size of small cannons held by our old buddies, Boris and Razor.

Boris smiled, flashing his gold tooth at us, and said, "Hello, girls. Welcome home."

They marched us back down the stairs with their guns at our backs and forced us into the van. It was déjà vu all over again except now Ivy was with us, too. They tied us up and blindfolded us, and then we were on our way. I had the sneaking suspicion that we'd end up in the same cellar, lying on the same dirt floor in that familiar old house. It probably wouldn't end well for us since we still had no idea where Shirley or the memory stick were. After all, as Stanley the Swindler had told us before, if we didn't find the missing memory stick, he wouldn't like it. And, he said, if he didn't like it, we wouldn't like it. Oh boy.

After traveling for at least forever, we started bouncing up that familiar dirt road. Yep, we were headed toward a situation that was probably going to turn out very bad for us, for sure.

The van stopped, and then the thugs pulled us out and untied the ropes from around our ankles so we could walk. They guided us into the house and down those familiar rickety stairs into the basement, which was no easy task for us to navigate since we were still blindfolded.

One of them gave me a push, and I stumbled across the floor, lost my balance, spun around, landed on my tail, and then fell back, banging the back of my head in the process. While I was still seeing stars, Stormy and Ivy were dumped down beside me. Our blindfolds were taken off, leaving us squinting in the bright light.

Boris pointed a hairy finger at us and snarled, "Don't move."

After a while, we heard a car pull up. The front door groaned open on its rusty hinges, and heavy footsteps sounded across the floor over our heads and then paused at the top the cellar stairs. Dollars to doughnuts, it was Stanley's bodyguard. Then we heard shuffling, and after a moment, we could hear his labored breathing as Stanley Barron painfully made his way down the steps and hobbled toward us.

His lackey followed close behind. He was the same massive mountain of a man we saw the last time we were held captive here. To tell the truth, of all the ones who made up this motley gang, this guy scared me the most.

The old man stopped when he saw us, and then he glared at Boris and Razor. "Three of them? How come three?"

Boris shrugged his humongous shoulders and answered in a surprisingly high-pitched, whiny voice. "She was with them, and we didn't think you'd want us to leave no witnesses." He glanced warily over at the old man. "Right, boss?"

Stanley shook his head and muttered, "This is what happens when you have nitwits working for you." He jerked his thumb at us. "Stand 'em up."

Boris grabbed Stormy and me and easily lifted both of us up as if we were little rag dolls and set us back on our feet.

Razor stood Ivy up, keeping a meaty hand on her shoulder.

We all looked at Stanley and waited.

He narrowed his eyes and stared at Ivy. "What in blue blazes happened to your face?"

Ivy straightened her spine and glared back at him. "Rodney Butler happened to my face, if it's any of your business."

"Rodney Butler, uh-huh. The Slasher did that? How come?"

"Because I was a fool, that's how come."

"So, what else is new? What happened?"

I kind of expected Ivy to tell him to kiss her foot, but instead, she launched into the story. It was the first time I'd heard about that terrible day.

"Well, I was working my corner, when he pulled up and asked my price. I told him, and he said, 'Okay, get in the truck.' So, I did."

"And?" Stanley was getting irritated.

"And so, we were taking care of business, if you know what I mean, and then all the sudden, he went ballistic. He started hitting me, and then he pulled out a big old knife with a curvy blade and sliced me up. I remember screaming, and then I woke up in the hospital."

The old man stared at Ivy. "Did he say anything before that? Did he ask you about the stick?"

"The stick? Well, that was the weird part. First, he asked me something, like, was I friends with Delilah, and I said, 'Yeah.' Then he asked me where the stick was. I told him I didn't know what he was talking about. Then he got this wild look in his eyes, and all of the sudden, he wasn't making any sense. I mean, he said something like, 'Heard you've been asking around about it, so where is it?' So, I asked, 'What do you mean, where is it? And what's the '*it*' you're talking about?' That's when he wigged out."

Stanley rubbed his face and grunted. "So, somebody has hired the Slasher to find my stick. That ain't good." He stood quietly for a long moment deep in thought and then growled, "Take 'em back."

"Take them back? Back to their apartment?" Boris asked.

"No! Back to the White House! Of course, back to their apartment, you blockhead. Somebody thinks these babes know where the stick is, and I want to know who that somebody is. So, we're gonna use these broads as bait."

By the time we were deposited on the sidewalk in front of our building, it was near dawn. As we started to plod up the stairs to the fifth floor, I growled, "I hope they left our apartment unlocked 'cause I don't have the key."

Stormy pulled up short. "Suppose somebody else is in there, waiting for us."

"I don't care," I muttered. "They'll just have to wait their turn until I get some sleep."

We cautiously swung the door open and stuck in our heads, but the apartment seemed deserted. After checking the bathroom, since that's the only place in our tiny apartment that someone could possibly hide, we confirmed that it was all clear. So, we locked the door and jammed our two-by-four security system in place.

I slung myself onto the mattress, still wearing my dirty clothes. This business of getting kidnapped was getting old, and I was bone-tired and heart weary. Before Stormy and Ivy even had a chance to get into bed, I was out like a light, and I didn't wake up for hours.

Chapter 15

Mutt was having supper at the diner, and we were doing the usual bantering back and forth when he suddenly grabbed my arm as I was putting his plate on the table. "What happened to your wrist?"

I glanced down and noticed the red mark the ropes had left last night. "Nothing."

He snared my other arm and examined the marks on that one too. He looked up with angry eyes. "This is *not* 'nothing.' Who hurt you?"

I did a quick scan of the customers, but thankfully, they were all engrossed in eating their meals. We still were pretty busy, and this was definitely not the time or the place for a private discussion. "I'll explain later."

When I met his gaze, I was shocked by the cold fury in his eyes. "If one of Snake's boys did this ..."

"No, Mutt! They've been perfect gentlemen. To tell the truth, I think Snake laid down the law to them, and they couldn't be treating us any better."

His voice was flat. "So, then ... what happened?"

I leaned down and whispered, "I can't talk to you about this right now. Can you come back after I get off from work?"

"I'll be back and wait until you finish cleaning up. Then we'll talk."

My stomach was churning the rest of the night, and I didn't feel any better after seeing the expression on Mutt's face when he appeared at the door just at closing time. He sat down at a corner table, with arms crossed, and watched as we swept the floors, cleaned the tables, and refilled the napkin holders, saltshakers, and the like.

When we moved into the kitchen, he came and leaned against the doorframe. "Need any help?"

"No thanks, Mutt. We have our own routine."

He was obviously trying to keep his temper under control, but the air fairly vibrated with tension.

Ivy and Stormy could sense that something was going on, and they frowned while glancing back and forth between Mutt and me.

Once, when I tried to brush past him on my way to the dining room, he snared my arm and growled into my ear, "I left my car in front of the apartment building so we can walk home. I figured that would be the only way we could grab a little privacy while we talked."

I thought we would never finish, but finally our chores were done, and we locked up. But when we walked out the diner's front door, Jose was waiting. *Oh, crud. With all my worrying about talking to Mutt, I forgot that Jose would be expecting to walk us home. One more complication.*

He and Mutt immediately began sizing each other up as they circled each other like a couple of alpha dogs. I grabbed Mutt's arm and attempted to defuse the situation. "Mutt," I said a little too brightly, "this is Jose. He's been so kind, walking us home every night to make sure we're safe." I flashed him a brilliant smile.

Mutt nodded stiffly toward Jose. "Thanks for watching out for them, but I'm walking them home tonight."

Jose shook his head stubbornly. "It's my job to walk 'em home."

This was not going well. We were surrounded by a cloud of testosterone that was nearing its flash point. Just before a mass explosion, Stormy stepped in. "We appreciate you so much, Jose. Thank you! How about you walk Ivy and me, and then Mutt and Delilah can follow. Is that all right?"

Before he could object, I took it from there. "We'll be right behind you guys. Mutt and I just need to talk about something first." I clung to Mutt's arm like it was a life preserver and I was drowning. "So, let's get going, okay? We're tired and need to get off our feet."

Unfortunately, our attempts to defuse the situation didn't work. Jose clenched his jaw and set his feet like a stubborn mule, and Mutt started going into full cop mode. Things were going from bad to worse. But, just in time, Ivy snatched one of Jose's elbows, and Stormy hooked her arm around the other, spun him around, and propelled him down the sidewalk before he knew what was happening.

I smiled sweetly at Mutt. "Well, we better get going."

He pulled me up short. "We need to talk."

"Yes, we do," I said. "But I'm thinking that maybe we should include Jose because he needs to know what happened too." Mutt got all tense and bent out of shape, but before he exploded, I touched his lips to quiet him. "Okay, I'll tell you everything, and then I'll give Jose the short version. He'll want to report to Snake."

Mutt glowered at me. "Do you think that's wise?"

"Probably not, but it's inevitable." I glanced up at him. "Look, I'll give you a quick rundown first, but you've got to promise you won't get mad."

"Delilah, I'm already mad. I'll just try not to go ballistic. That's the best I can promise right now."

"Okay, but just don't blame Jose. It wasn't his fault." When he started breathing hard, I stopped walking, let go of his arm and put my hands on my hips. "And don't go snorting like a bull before I even start to explain!"

He clenched his fists, but stood still, glaring at me.

"So, are you going to behave?" I asked. "Or are you going to act like a rabid gorilla?"

It must have taken all his willpower to force his lips into a semblance of a smile. "Okay, I'm behaving. So, what happened?"

We started toward home as we talked. "Well, last night, Jose walked us home from the diner as usual. He went up to our floor and left us in front of the apartment door, like he always does, and then he went back down the stairs and left."

"But?"

"But we didn't realize we had company. When we opened the door, Stanley Barron's hired thugs were waiting for us."

Mutt groaned.

"Then they took us back to that abandoned house, but after Stanley saw Ivy's face, he asked her who had done it to her. When he heard it was Butler, he changed his mind and let us go."

"Why? It wasn't out of pity. He wouldn't be sympathetic, even if it had been his own mother."

"No, he seemed to think that someone hired Willie ... I mean Rodney Butler ... to attack Ivy and make her tell him who had the memory stick. I guess that's why he decided to use us as bait."

I thought the top of Mutt's head was going to blow off. Strange noises were coming from his throat as he tried to gain control. Then, of course, at the worst possible moment, Jose turned around at the apartment building's entrance and yelled, "Are you coming or not? I'm supposed to keep an eye on all three of these girls." He took a step toward us.

"Come on, Mutt," I pleaded. "Don't make things worse."

He grabbed my arm and almost dragged me toward the door. Then we all tromped double-time, up the front steps plus the four more flights of stairs.

By the time we reached our apartment, everyone was breathing hard, but at least the men had burned off *some* of their aggression. Thank goodness.

"Jose," Mutt said steadily enough, although I knew it was taking every bit of his self-control to remain calm, "we need to go in and have a talk."

Our big, strong bodyguard took a step backward and blushed crimson. "I'm not supposed to go into the ladies' home. My wife wouldn't like it ... Snake neither."

Mutt looked grim. "Don't worry. I'll chaperone."

We all filed in, and since we only had one chair, we stood facing each other. I started to explain about last night, and Stormy and Ivy helped fill in the details.

When we finished our tale, Mutt looked like he was going to explode. I think he calmed down a bit when he glanced over at Jose and realized the man had turned so pale that it looked like he was going to faint.

"I'm so sorry!" Jose started pacing as best he could amongst the clutter. "It just wasn't right for me to go into your apartment, but I never thought somebody would be waiting for you inside. Forgive me." He began to sweat. "Snake's not going to be happy with me. He trusted me to keep you safe."

Ivy patted his arm. "Don't you worry about Snake. I'll handle him. I'll just explain that we didn't want to invite you in because … uh … because the neighbors might start to talk since it didn't look proper, and we didn't want to hurt Stormy's reputation."

Jose didn't look convinced, but he nodded anyway.

"Look, Jose," Mutt said, "from now on, you need to check the apartment before you leave, and I don't care if your wife likes it or not. The next time won't end up so good if Barron's goons come back."

I patted Jose's arm. "The girls and I will just wait in the hall while you check out the apartment. That should be acceptable to everyone."

He nodded. "Yes, I will do that. You have my word."

After Jose left, Mutt grabbed our only chair and headed toward the door, but Ivy blocked his way. "Hey, what do you think you're doing?"

"I'm making myself comfortable." He stepped into the hallway and set the chair down.

I followed him out. "You don't have to spend the night here. We'll lock the door and use our security system."

"Security system?"

I grinned and motioned for him to come back into our room. "See, once we are inside, we jam these two-by-fours against the door. They're better than a dead bolt."

Mutt examined our setup. "It seems adequate, but obviously it doesn't work when you leave the apartment. Tomorrow, I'm coming back and installing a dead bolt with a security chain." He pulled me into a hug. "Are you sure you feel okay staying here by yourselves?"

"We'll be fine. I promise."

He gave me a chaste kiss on the cheek and grinned at Ivy and Stormy. "See you in the morning." He chuckled. "Yeah, I know, I know. You guys work the night shift, so don't come too early."

He returned the chair, and we noticed that he waited until he could hear the boards were in place before we heard his footsteps retreating down the stairs. We heard him trying to start the rust-mobile, but its engine just kept turning over.

"He needs to buy his self a decent car," Ivy growled.

Finally, Mutt got it started and pulled away from the curb. The sound of his car sputtering and backfiring followed him all the way down the street.

Chapter 16

SOMEBODY WAS POUNDING ON OUR DOOR. I PRIED AN EYE OPEN AND glared at the clock. 6:30 a.m.! I leaped out of bed with the full intent of murdering Mutt. Kicking the two-by-fours out of the way, I yanked the door open and hollered, "I thought we told you not to come so early!"

It wasn't Mutt.

Ebony was standing in the hallway with several black garbage bags stuffed nearly to the bursting point and a rolled-up sleeping bag. Tottering on a pair of ridiculously high ruby red platform shoes, she was wearing a skintight, V-neck knitted top that left nothing to the imagination and a short gold-colored spandex skirt that barely covered her backside. She was also sporting a black eye and a busted lip.

My jaw dropped. "What are you doing here?"

She pushed past me, dragging in the bulging black plastic bags. Then she went back for the sleeping bag and tossed it in a corner. "I'm movin' in."

"But ..."

"Look, I know you're kinda crowded in here, but I ain't got no other place to go. I done decided to quit turning tricks, so Dutch kicked my butt out. 'Course he went an' give me a beatdown first. Would you believe he wanted me to go turn a trick with Willie Nelson? I done told him this dude is the one whut carved up Ivy. And Dutch says, 'Well, just be on your guard.' And I told him that maybe I ain't too smart, but I sure ain't *that* dumb. And he say, 'He's a customer, so, go!' So I say ..." She glanced over at Stormy. "An' ... uh ... I say a couple of things, and then I quit an' hauled my tail over here." She kicked a few piles of clothes out of her way and headed for the kitchen. "Whut'cha got to eat? I'm hungry."

By this time, Stormy and Ivy were both awake and sitting up. They both gave me 'the look,' clearly meaning, "Do something!"

I shrugged, closed the door, locked it, and replaced the boards.

When I turned around, Ebony had our small apartment-sized refrigerator open. She was bending over and surveying its contents with her behind sticking up in the air, giving me an unimpeded view of her bright red thong. "Ain't hardly nothing to eat!" She grabbed the bread and a package of lunch meat to make herself a sandwich. "Where's the plates—and ain't you got no mayo?"

I sighed. By this time, nothing surprised me. I snared one of our few remaining plates out of the cabinet and located the mayo in the back of the fridge, hidden behind a couple of plastic storage containers.

"Thanks," she muttered as I put the stuff on the table. "Got mustard?"

I handed over the mustard and glanced at Ivy. She just shook her head, laid back down, and pulled the blanket over her head.

Stormy, grumbling to herself, got up and stumbled to bathroom.

As I stood watching our new houseguest eat, I cleared my throat. "Uh, Ebony? How long do you think you'll be staying here?"

"Don't know. Like I said, I ain't got no other place to go, so could be a while. Rent ain't cheap, yah know, and I got to find me a new line of work. Don't you worry none, though. My sleeping bag ain't gonna take up much room, and I'll roll it up every morning anyway, so it won't be no problem."

Sure. Of course it won't be a problem to have another person move in with us. And maybe we could take in an entire traveling circus while we're at it. Why not?

"I'm going back to bed, Ebony. Make yourself at home." I flopped down on my mattress. Ivy had the right idea, so I pulled the blanket over my head and tried to go back to sleep.

"Hey! Where's the TV? Ain't you even got a radio?"

"Go to bed, Ebony! It's only six thirty in the morning!" I wasn't being too pleasant, but then again, I am not a morning person.

She slapped her empty plate back on the table. "Sheesh. Don't have to get so snippy about it."

I rolled over and put the pillow over my head. If she didn't shut up, I was going to take this very pillow and smother her with it. Thankfully, before I was driven to carry out my homicidal thoughts, she stomped over, kicked enough stuff aside to clear a small area, threw down her sleeping bag, and climbed in. After Stormy came back from the bathroom and got back in bed, things got quiet, and I drifted to sleep.

The next time I opened my eyes, the sun was shining through the window. Ugh. The clock said nine fifteen, and I figured that Mutt would be coming soon. Deciding to be the first to stake out a claim for the bathroom, I quietly rummaged around, found some clean clothes, and tiptoed across the room. I slipped into the bathroom and jumped into the shower. While I was washing up, I decided to shampoo my hair and then hurried to finish getting dressed. Just as I was emerging from the bathroom, there was a knock at the door. This time, I remembered to check the peephole and saw it was Mutt.

By the time I managed to get the barriers down and the door unlocked, the rest of the gang was stirring. I was greeted with a chorus of groans when I cheerfully announced, "Mutt's here!" Then I stepped out into the hall.

He had a tool belt around his waist and triumphantly waved a paper bag with the local hardware store's logo printed on the front. "Hey, Delilah. I'm here, I'm ready, and I'm raring to go." He gave me a hug and a kiss on the cheek. "Did you sleep well?"

"Yeah, until six thirty this morning."

Mutt tensed. "What happened? Did Stanley's boys come back?"

"No, but it was almost as bad. Ebony moved in with us."

"You're kidding."

"I don't kid about stuff like that." I stuck my head back into the apartment. "Everybody, get dressed! Mutt is coming in to install the dead bolt. You all have five minutes to get decent." I closed the door again and grinned up at him. "Let's give them a few minutes to fight over bathroom rights."

In less than an hour, the dead bolt was installed. When Mutt finished putting up the security chain, he said, "This will make you safer, but you know anybody who knows what they're doing still can get in. It's not foolproof Delilah; nothing is."

"I realize that Mutt, but this is a whole lot better than that old lock. Thank you."

"I've got a couple of things for you that I left in the car. I'll go get them." He went out and reappeared a few minutes later with four wooden folding chairs. "Thought you could use these. They can be folded up and stored in a corner until you need them." He leaned them against the wall in the kitchen. "Be right back." He soon returned lugging an empty bookcase and shoved it under the window.

"Hey!" Stormy was grinning as she examined the long squat cabinet that had several shelves. "This will be perfect to store our clothes." She gave Mutt a big hug. "This is great! Thanks!"

He seemed a little taken aback, but I could see he was pleased to have made her so happy. "I've got another one that's smaller. If you can find the room and want it, I'll bring it the next time I come."

"That would be great! Especially since there are four of us now. If we can get some of the clothes off the floor, we'll have more space to walk." She looked like she might hug him again, but Mutt ducked out the door.

I followed him out. "I can't tell you how much I appreciate all this."

"Don't mention it. I just wanted to help my ... uh ... friend." He stared at his feet for a moment before meeting my gaze. "May I call you sometime, Delilah?" Somehow, judging from the tone of his voice and his body language, I didn't think he meant he wanted to talk over police business.

"Well, I'd love that, but I don't have a phone, Mutt."

He looked shocked. "Well, I guess we'll have to do something about that."

After he left, I couldn't help grinning like *Alice in Wonderland's* Cheshire cat for the rest of the day. My roommates kept exchanging knowing looks, and they seemed to be enjoying themselves whispering to each other. But so what? I didn't care. Yeah, things between Mutt and me were finally starting to look up.

Chapter 17

I was walking down the sidewalk, sniveling. My nose was running, but I couldn't do anything about it since I had two heavy bags of groceries in my arms. Couldn't even raise my shoulder high enough to wipe the snot off, but I didn't care. It was over, and I didn't even know why.

For the past couple of months, things had been going great ... slow, but great. Mutt had kissed me on the lips a few times, but he had kept it sort of low-key. I think he must have sensed I would have been spooked if he tried to push me into romance too quickly. He also bought me one of those cheap, plain flip phones along with a prepaid card that he would renew every month so we could talk every day. I was falling in love. Let's face it. I was already in love.

Lately, Mutt seemed bothered by something. And he kept trying to preach religion to me, except he said it wasn't about religion at all, but it was about Jesus. *Yeah, sure.* He would talk about this Jesus Guy and I would immediately change the subject. He kept telling me it was important that we talk about it, but I refused to listen. This had gone on for the entire time we were dating. One thing you can say about Mutt: he is persistent.

Then, last night, while we were eating supper in Connie's after closing time, he started in on me again. I told him I wanted to make a bargain: If he would stop talking about this Jesus guy, I wouldn't throw it up to him when he went to church.

"Won't you even listen to what I have to say, Delilah?"

"Why can't you just leave it alone!"

"Because the Bible tells me that I cannot be unequally yoked."

I blinked. "What in the world does eggs have to do with it?"

He looked confused for a moment, and then he gave me a sad smile. "Not egg yolks, Delilah. Yoked, like oxen yoked together so they can pull a cart, side-by-side, working together, helping each other." He spoke so softly that he almost whispered. "We have to believe in the same thing, in the same God, in the same Jesus, in order to be able to live in harmony."

"That's silly, Mutt! You know what they say, opposites attract."

He sat back for a minute, just studying my face, and then he closed his eyes like he was in pain. His shoulders sagged, and he hung his head. When he looked back up at me, I was shocked to see tears streaming down his cheeks. He reached over and gently slipped a lock of my hair behind my ear. "I wish things could be different. I wish I could find the right words so you would listen to me and hear what I'm trying to tell you ... to really *hear* me. But this is just too important to me. It's too important to God. And it's something that can't be fixed." He stood up, leaned down, and kissed my forehead. "Goodbye, Delilah."

"Goodbye? But Mutt ... wait!"

But he was gone. It was over. My heart was broken. I didn't even have a clue what I had done.

So, this morning, I was coming home from the grocery store, sniffling, while my mind was running around in circles like a dog chasing its tail. I wasn't paying attention to my surroundings, and I didn't notice the truck until I heard the roar of an engine and then felt a bone-jarring thunk.

The next thing I knew, I was flying through the air with my groceries going every which way. The last thought that went through my mind was, *Oh, crud, my eggs are going to get busted.* And then the ground came up and clobbered me.

Somewhere in the darkness, far, far away, I heard a voice. "Come on, girl! Stay with us!"

It felt like an enormous buffalo was stomping on my chest, and it hurt like the devil.

The voice became more insistent. "Come on!"

"I'm starting to get a response, doctor."

What were they talking about? And who were these people? What was strapped on my face?

"Pulse weak, but steady."

"Good. Can you hear me, ma'am? Can you look at me?"

I managed to open my eyes for a brief moment and glimpsed the outline of a man leaning over me, but then I squeezed them closed again to shut out the blinding light.

"Ma'am, open your eyes."

I figured this clown wouldn't leave me alone until I looked at him, so I made the supreme effort to raise my eyelids just enough to peek at my tormentor. "What happened?" My voice squeaked like a rusty hinge, and when I tried to move my arm, it felt as though I was struck by lightning. "Ow!" My head was bursting. I closed my eyes and started to drift into the darkness again.

"Ma'am!" It was a different voice this time. "What is your name? Can you tell me your name?"

"Delilah," I murmured. "Delilah Sampson."

"She must be hallucinating," the voice said just before I was swallowed up by the darkness.

I floated around in a shadow world filled with strange smells, odd noises, and pain. I could hear voices, some of which seemed familiar. One time, I thought I heard Stormy crying and a woman quietly comforting her, before I drifted away on my own personal cloud nine. Sometimes the pain tried to overwhelm me, but then I'd be aware of someone murmuring about giving me something to help with the pain. Then they would fiddle with the annoying beeping thing that was located somewhere next to me, and I would sail back into la-la land.

I wanted to stay on Planet Oblivion. It was a nice place, and I liked it, so I did my best to remain there. But now the pain wouldn't let me be. It was intense, it was incessant, and it refused to take no for an answer. I heard voices talking about withdrawing "the patient" from the "medically induced coma." Since I decided that couldn't be me that they were discussing, I continued to resist. I didn't want to come back.

It was remarkably quiet except for a muted, rhythmic beeping. I cautiously opened my eyes and attempted to get my bearings. My left arm and leg were immobile. My head hurt. Honestly, everything I owned hurt. I had a raging thirst, and it felt like my mouth was full of sand. I tried to call for help, but all that came out was a low moan.

Mutt's face immediately appeared above me. At first, I thought I must be in heaven, but then again, I wouldn't be hurting like this if it was heaven. And since Mutt wouldn't be here if I was in hades, I figured I must still be alive.

"Delilah?"

"Water." The word came out in a barely audible croak, and then my eyelids became so heavy that they just slammed shut.

Someone touched my shoulder. "Here, babe."

A straw slipped between my lips, and I sucked wonderful, divine water into my mouth. Swallowing it was another matter, and most of it leaked out and slid down my neck. I felt a towel gently blotting it up.

A deep voice said, "Take it slow."

The straw appeared again, and I managed to drink a bit.

I opened my eyes, and Mutt's face was just inches from mine. He had at least a day's worth of five o'clock shadow, his hair was sticking up in a wild 'doo,' and he had dark circles under his eyes. He was beautiful. "What are you doing here?" I creaked.

"When you didn't come home, Ebony came looking for you. She heard about the accident, so she came here and found you. Then she called me."

"Accident? What accident?"

"You got hit by a truck, honey."

"Oh." I looked up at him. "But you left."

"Yeah, babe. But I'm back. I'm back to stay."

I tried to smile, but my cracked lips hurt too much. That was no surprise; my entire body was one big ball of hurt. I wanted to tell him I was glad he came back, and I wanted to tell him I was glad he was here, but Planet Oblivion was calling me. So, I mounted my cloud and flew off to my own personal nirvana.

Chapter 18

MUTT STOOD BESIDE ME WITH HIS HAND ON MY SHOULDER. AN ENORMOUS, muscular dark-skinned cop sat in a chair next to my bed with a small recorder in his hand. Mutt's partner and best friend, Detective Gaylord Peter Tanner, a.k.a. Pete, had arrived.

We had met before, and Mutt talked about him a lot, yet we still didn't know each other all that well. We were barely on a first-name basis, and to tell you the truth, I felt a little intimidated by the big man. In any case, this was official police business so we were sitting in my hospital room, all formal like.

"How are you doing, Ms. Sampson? I'm here to take your statement about the hit-and-run, okay?"

My brain was still fuzzy from all the painkillers being pumped into my veins. "I ... I really can't remember what happened, but I'll do my best, Detective Tanner." I tried to concentrate and grab ahold of some memory of the accident, but it was like trying to nail Jell-O to the wall. I started to shake my head ... not a good idea. Apparently, my brain was busy using a sledgehammer in its attempt to escape my skull. The rest of my body was in revolt, too.

I tried to organize my thoughts. "I was walking down the sidewalk, coming home from the grocery store. I think I had my back to the street and didn't see the truck coming. But I don't know. I just can't remember."

The pain behind my eyes was getting worse, and my stomach felt like it was being stirred with a stick. I rested my head back on the pillow.

"Look, Pete, can't this wait until another day?"

"Sorry, Mutt, but I need to interview the victim while the memories are still fresh. You know that as well as I do." He sat the recorder on the table next to my bed.

I considered begging off since my head was pounding, but the determined expression on the detective's face changed my mind.

He pushed the record button and spoke his name, the date, and our location. Then he asked me to state my name and address and began to question me. "Miss Sampson, can you give me a description of the truck that hit you or its driver?"

"Is that what hit me? I thought it must have been a train."

Detective Tanner didn't even crack a smile. "Do you know anyone who owns a pickup truck?"

"Well, there's Willie Nelson ... I mean the guy that looks like Willie.'"

"Rodney Butler a.k.a. The Slasher," Mutt explained.

"Same piece of slime who cut up the prostitute?"

"One and the same. Delilah and her sister witnessed the victim entering the suspect's truck and driving away on the day of the attack." Mutt glanced over at me. "They also had another encounter with him a few weeks after that."

Detective Tanner turned his attention back to me. "Want to tell me about it?"

I shook my head again. Dumb move. Still hadn't learned how much it hurt from the last time I tried that move. Like a wise man once said, "Once is an accident, twice is stupidity." Shaking my head was definitely a foolish thing to do.

"Delilah," Mutt said softly, "you need to tell Pete about the incident. He's a good guy. Trust him."

Mutt began to gently massage my shoulders when I started to tremble. Tears leaked out of my eyes and trickled down my cheeks. "Come on, honey, you can do it," he whispered.

I took a deep breath to steady myself. There were two big cops in the room, yet I was panic-stricken. Only Mutt's strong presence gave me the courage to begin.

After I had finished my statement, the detective asked me some more questions: "What color was the truck? Have any idea the make and model?"

"I only know the color of the truck that Ivy got into. It was dark when he tried to run us down in the alley, and I never even saw him this time, but I guess it's the same pickup."

"Okay, so, what's the color."

"I think it probably used to be gold when it was new, but it was faded down to kind of a murky brown."

"Model?"

I shrugged. "Don't know. I didn't notice, but Ebony may have. She was there with Ivy that day."

Tanner reached over and clicked off the recorder. "Why were you and your sister standing on a corner with two prostitutes?"

"They are friends of ours." I felt a little defensive. "They're good people. They're just down on their luck, and they had to make a living somehow. And the four of us were just talking. Besides, they have quit prostitution now and moved in with my sister and me."

He nodded. "Do you think this Ebony would talk to me?"

Mutt intervened. "Not a snowball's chance, Pete. But I'll talk to her. She knows me."

His fellow cop raised an eyebrow.

"No way, man, not like that." He glanced over at me. "Now that Ebony and Ivy both live with Delilah and her sister, I see them when I visit Delilah."

Soon after that, Detective Tanner finished the interview and left, much to my relief.

That night, Ebony came to the hospital to see me. Luckily, Mutt was still visiting so he was spared having to go to our apartment in order to interview her.

She was quite willing to answer all his questions and said, "I'll do anythin' I can to stop this maniac. What you wanna know?"

Mutt got out his notebook and said, "Did you notice the make, model, and color of the truck that Ivy got in the day she was attacked?"

"Sure. It was a funky brownish color, kind'a old, and it had one of them sheep on the hood."

Mutt seemed baffled for a moment. He paused with his pencil hovering over his notebook and glanced up at Ebony. "Sheep?"

"You know … with the curvy horns."

"Ram." He started scribbling again. "It was a Dodge Ram, older model, faded brown or gold." He looked up. "That fits the description our witness gave of the truck involved in the hit-and-run."

"Witness? I didn't know there was a witness." I was a bit surprised.

"Yeah, it was an old man. Couldn't give us many details, but his statement corresponds with what you just told me. He's the one who called 911 and waited until the police and the ambulance arrived. Poor old guy was so shook up that the EMTs ended up treating him at the scene. Apparently, watching a woman getting run down by a pickup truck isn't good for your blood pressure."

"Is he going to be okay?"

"He's fine. Pete checked on him a couple of days ago."

There was a pause in the conversation.

Ebony grinned at me. "Sorry to change the subject, but I've got some good news, girl. Since you can't waitress no more, Connie gave me your job. 'Course it's just 'til you can come back. I start tomorrow night. With me, Ivy, and Stormy working, we'll be able to pay the rent for sure and have some cash left over."

"That's uh …" I paused and looked at Ebony's smiling face. "Have you ever done any waitressing before?"

"Nope. But how hard can it be? Just take their order and then deliver the goods. It's just like turning tricks."

I groaned and leaned back on my pillow.

Mutt stood up and kissed my forehead. I could see he was struggling to keep from laughing. If I had had enough strength, and my arm wasn't broken, I would have strangled him. "We better go. Can I get you anything before I leave?"

"No, in a couple of minutes, the nurse will be coming in to get me settled for the night. So, I'm good."

He kissed me again. "Now get some sleep. You look like you could use some." He held the door open and beckoned to Ebony. "Come on. I'll drive you home."

The door shut behind them, and I closed my eyes, wallowing in self-pity. *Great! Ebony has taken my job ... And just when I thought things couldn't get any worse. Ha!*

So, Connie hired her to take over for me. But would there be a job left for me by the time I got strong enough to work again? And even more important than that, would the diner be able to survive both Ivy *and* Ebony?

The door burst open, and my way-too-cheerful night nurse blew in. "Good evening!" she said in her syrupy sweet, singsong voice. "Time to use the bedpan."

Oh, swell.

Chapter 19

THE NEXT DAY, I WOKE UP FROM A NAP AND SAW THE TOP OF MUTT'S HEAD next to my bed. "What are you doing? You lose something?"

Mutt smiled at me as he stood up, obviously feeling stiff, since he began bending and stretching to work out the kinks. "No, Delilah, I wasn't searching under your bed." He studied my face for a moment and smiled. "I was praying for you, babe." His smile grew wider. "Praying to my 'Jesus guy.'"

I bit back a smart answer. That hadn't worked so well the last time. "Oh, you were?" I asked sweetly. I figured two could play this game.

His smiled widened even more. "I was praying for your healing, and I was also praying for us, Delilah."

"Uh … that's nice. Thanks."

His smile faded just a bit, and uncertainty flickered in his eyes for a moment before he said, "You're welcome, babe. I need to go to work, but I'll be back tonight if I can get here before visiting hours are over." He leaned over and kissed my forehead. "Be good. Hopefully, I'll see you again tonight."

After the door closed behind him, the room seemed terribly empty. I pushed the remote button to click on the TV and surfed the channels for a bit, but nothing caught my interest.

After a while, the door opened and an older nurse came bustling in. I recognized her from the time when Ivy was in the hospital. "I didn't know you were my nurse." I checked her name tag. "That's a nice surprise, Abigail."

She gave me a warm smile. "Why don't you just call me Abby?" She read my chart before she turned her attention back to me. "It seems like every time I come in here, you're sound asleep. We have a big caseload, so that's why I haven't been able to spend as much time with you as I'd like." She took my temperature, and then she checked my pulse and my blood pressure. "Well, you're looking a lot better since the last time I saw you. Much better." She smiled at me. "You've made a lot of progress in the past couple of days." She fluffed my pillow, straightened up my bedding, and refilled my water. "Need anything else?"

"No, thanks."

I must have sounded down, because she paused and studied my face. "Honey, I know you're in a hard place right now, but it's gonna get better. In a couple few weeks, you'll be gettin' those casts off, and then after some PT, you'll be as good as new." She stared out the window, seemingly fascinated by the brick wall that it faced. Sighing, she turned back to me. "You've got a good man there, you know that?"

"Who, Mutt?"

She grinned. "You got a bunch of men stashed away somewhere, besides him?"

I snorted. "No."

She poured some ice water, stuck a straw into the glass, and held it for me. She patiently waited as I took a sip, and our eyes met. "You know, he comes here every day and spends a long time on his knees while you're sleeping. Never saw a man so faithful in prayer. You must be very special to him."

I attempted a shrug, but because of the cast on my arm, it was sort of lopsided one. And besides, moving like that hurt, so I guess that explained the tears threatening to overflow my eyes.

"Oh, honey. It's gonna be okay." She busied herself straightening my covers again and then asked, "How's your friend?"

"Ivy?"

She nodded. "I've been praying for the poor child."

"Well, she's scarred up really bad, but she's doing better, emotionally. She even has a job as a cook at Connie's Home Diner now."

"Well, praise God! That's wonderful! Tell her I'll keep praying for her." She smiled. "I'll be praying for all of you."

A patient buzzed their nurse's call. "Well, I best see what they're needing." Her laugh was musical as she shook her head and then paused in the doorway. "I'll be back later when things calm down a bit." She grinned. "Not that they ever do around here." Smiling, she turned toward the door. "God bless, honey"

Oh boy! I'm surrounded by religious fanatics.

The doctor stood at the foot of my bed as he read the folder holding my chart.

Stormy stood beside my bed, while Ivy and Ebony leaned against the wall, all of them listening intently. I guess it was good to have such an attentive audience since my brain was still pretty much scrambled by all the pain medications. It was so frustrating. My arm was in a cast, and to make matters even worse, my leg was in a cast that went from my foot, nearly all the way to my behind. Every little thing I tried to do took monumental effort. It hurt to move, and my head still hurt. I was miserable and needed to use every bit of my energy to concentrate on what Dr. Keller was saying.

He looked over the top of his glasses and studied my face. "Do you realize just how badly you were injured in this accident, young lady?"

"It weren't no accident, doc. He done run her down on purpose."

Dr. Keller glowered at Ebony. "I am well aware of the circumstances of the incident."

She crossed her arms across her chest and glared back. "Just sayin'," she muttered.

The doctor cleared his throat and continued, "I don't believe you understand just how serious your injuries are, Miss Sampson, not to mention that you have also undergone surgery. A truck struck you! It threw you ten feet, and the resulting impact of your head hitting the sidewalk resulted in a closed-head injury." He paused for a moment, slid his glasses down his nose, and peered at us. "You might refer to it as a 'bruised brain,' which was accompanied by swelling so serious that we had to place you in a drug-induced coma for three days." He studied my chart for a moment. "You also suffered a fracture of the upper left arm that is called the humerus, the upper left leg, which is called the femur, and a fractured, or you might refer to it as, a 'cracked' pelvis."

Even through my drug-hazed fog, I could tell he was talking down to us, and it burned me up. But I figured it wouldn't be a good idea to get on his bad side, so I kept my big mouth shut. I looked over at Ebony and saw that she was ready to blow. I caught her gaze and shook my head.

She glowered and folded her arms over her chest again. That was her way to keep from hitting somebody.

I turned my attention back to Dr. Keller.

"Then there are your fractured ribs and various contusions and lacerations." He paused again to glance up at us. "Commonly called cuts and bruises. The humerus fracture required surgery and it was necessary to cast both your arm and leg."

He adjusted his glasses and glared down at me. "You have only been under our care for six days, young lady, and I will tell you unequivocally that it is much too soon to leave." He scanned the room, and I could see his skepticism about the quality of care I would receive from two former prostitutes and a teenage girl.

He gave a slight shake of his head and zeroed in on me. "Despite the fact that you will have such *excellent* care when you go home, I cannot recommend that you be discharged. In fact, if you do leave, it would be against doctor's orders." He tapped his chest with his finger for emphasis. "*This* doctor's orders." His silky, placating tone grated on my soul, but then his voice hardened. "If you leave without my approval, I can no longer be held responsible for your recovery." He slapped the folder shut. "And I am convinced that every one of my colleagues would agree."

Ebony said, "Yeah. And just how are we supposed to get you up those front steps and then four more flights of stairs up to the apartment?"

Dr. Keller looked back at me. "You live in a five-story walk-up?"

I nodded.

"Then how did you plan on navigating those stairs with your leg and your arm in casts and in your weakened condition?"

I shrugged. "I guess we'll figure it out when I get there. I only have to go up once and then I can stay in the apartment.

The doctor gave me a grim smile. "What are your plans regarding your follow-up doctor appointments? If you somehow manage to descend all those flights of stairs without breaking your neck, do you at least have access to transportation to the hospital and doctor offices? And how did you plan to have your cast removed? With a hammer?"

I was fighting tears. "I've got to go home, doctor. The bills are piling up. I'll be paying off this hospital bill for the rest of my life!" I was also scared to death that somebody would find out my pathetic ID was phony. Of course, I wasn't about to tell him that.

He sighed. "Don't worry about the hospital bill for now, Miss Sampson. Your health is much more important. I'll have someone contact the Office of Financial Assistance and have them come talk to you tomorrow, all right? In the meantime, you just concentrate on getting better." He stuck my chart under his arm, turned, and abruptly walked out of the room.

Well, I guess that was pretty decent of him to let me know that financial assistance is available. He doesn't have the best bedside manner, but at least he didn't try to shove religion down my throat.

Chapter 20

Stormy barged through the door, flounced across my hospital room, and flung herself onto a chair. She hunched over, with arms crossed tightly across her chest, head hanging, and sighed, and then she sighed again. Her lips formed a perfect pout. Miss Drama Queen had just made her entrance. It was teenage angst at its finest.

Her eyes were hooded when she snuck a glimpse at me. I knew she wanted me to ask what was wrong, but I chose to remain quiet. The silence stretched to the breaking point until she sat up straight and glared at me.

"It's not fair!" she declared with her voice fairly vibrating.

"What's not?" I suppressed a smile and tried to remind myself that whatever the "it" was that wasn't fair, it was important to my little sister.

"It's bad enough having you for a mother." I guess she realized how that sounded and had the grace to look a little embarrassed. "I didn't mean it the way it sounded. It's just you're so strict and everything." Stormy flashed me an indignant look. "But now I've got two *more* mothers." She gave her best imitation of Ivy, but in a singsong voice. "'Where yah goin'? When yah comin' back? Where's this here place located?'" She made a face. "And then Ebony has to chime in, like, 'Who y'all goin' with? What's his name?' and all that kind of crud."

Now *that* grabbed my attention. "What's whose name?"

From her expression, I knew she had said more than she had meant to.

I put on my "mother face" and narrowed my eyes. "Okay, Stormy. Who is he?"

She huffed her "nobody understands me" sigh. "Just a boy I met."

"You met a boy? Where?"

"At the diner, where else? That's the only place I ever get to go besides the apartment."

That was the sad truth, and I felt a twinge of guilt. But then I pushed those thoughts aside and returned to the business at hand. "Who is this guy and what do you know about him?"

She stuck out her jaw. "James is a nice boy."

"How do you know?"

She gave a sullen shrug. "I just know, that's all. Okay?"

Our discussion was interrupted by my cell phone ringing. I answered it, "Hello."

"She there?"

I didn't have to ask Ebony who the "she" of the conversation was. "Yep," I said.

"Call me when she leaves."

"Okay." End of the conversation.

Stormy scowled at me. "Ivy?"

"Nope. Ebony."

She sat back, crossed her arms, and snorted. "They won't even let me out of their sight! It's not fair!"

I managed not to grin. "I think I heard that somewhere before."

"How am I ever supposed to get a boyfriend if I'm not allowed to even move without somebody telling me don't do this or don't do that. They're just mean! They don't want me to have any fun."

"They love you, and they don't want you to get hurt or to get into trouble, Stormy. And think about it. I've been practicing this mother thing for the past sixteen years, but this is all new to them. They don't want anything to happen to you, especially since you're their responsibility while I'm in the hospital, so they're being extra careful."

She growled something under her breath and then said, "I just want to go out with a boy like a normal person. All I want is to have a little fun."

It was my turn to sigh. I wanted to protect my baby sister from the big, bad world, but in the back of my mind, I also knew I had to let her try her wings ... but not just yet. "Look, Stormy, this is not the time to start arguing. Wait until I get out of the hospital, and then we'll sit down and have a talk.

I rubbed my temple with my right hand, since if I had tried to do it with my left, I would have knocked my brains out with the cast. My throat began to tighten, and despite fighting for all I was worth, the tears escaped and started to stream down my face.

It was Stormy's turn to be upset. She stood up, came over, and stopped beside my bed. She hesitated for a moment and then wrapped her arms around me. "I'm sorry, Delilah. I didn't mean to make you cry."

"That's okay, honey," I said through my sobs. "It's the drugs the doctors are giving me that make me so weepy." *Yeah, right. It's the drugs, the pain, and most especially, the bills that are piling up, and the fact I don't have a job anymore, and I can't go home, and ... oh, brother. I am really turning into a wimp.*

And wouldn't you know it? That's when Mutt walked in. "What's wrong?" he asked.

"I can't go home," I wailed. "I want to go home, but they said I can't 'cause I can't go up the stairs to my apartment!"

Then Stormy joined in on the pity party. "I'm sorry, Delilah. I didn't mean to get you all upset." It was her turn to sob.

Mutt stood in opened-mouthed amazement, staring at us while we boo-hooed on each other's shoulders, and then he just shook his head and backed out of the room.

Stormy and I looked at each other with tear-streaked faces and laughed. "Men!" we said in perfect harmony.

After a while, Mutt cautiously opened the door and stuck his head back into the room. He must have decided it was safe, so he asked, "Is it all clear now?"

I blew my nose. "Come on in. That is, if you're brave enough."

"Want to tell me what that was all about?"

I sighed. "It's just what I said before. I want to go home, but I can't."

He laughed. "Well, then, this is your lucky day. I came over to talk to you about that very thing. I had a long talk with my grandmother last night, and she offered to let you stay with her until the cast comes off and you are finished physical therapy."

I stared at him, speechless.

"Delilah? Did you hear what I said?"

"Your grandmother? Who's your grandmother? Why would she offer to take me in?"

He grinned. "My grandmother is Hannah Dale, and you'll love her. She is the sweetest person you will ever meet. She lives alone just outside of town in a ranch house." He grinned even wider. "No steps either. She says she'll enjoy the company because it sometimes gets a little lonely living all by herself."

I wanted to dismiss all this as ridiculous, especially since I had never even met the woman. Why would I want to live with a complete stranger? But then again, I didn't see any other way to get out of the hospital in the foreseeable future. I glanced over at Stormy. "But what about …"

She brightened. "I can stay with Ivy and Ebony. After all, I need to go to work. They won't care, and Jose will still walk us home at night." She looked a little too eager about all this to suit me.

"I don't know, Stormy. I'll have to talk to them first, to see if Ivy and Ebony agree to it. Then we'll have to set up some rules."

"Well," Mutt added, "if you can't work things out, Granny already said that Stormy is welcome to come, too."

I nodded and thought, *What other options do I have? And, besides, the sooner I get out of this place, the better.* I looked up at Mutt. "Okay, just let me talk to Ivy and Ebony and see what they have to say."

"Sounds good. And if Stormy does stay at the apartment, I'll keep an eye on all three of them."

He reached over and tucked my hair behind my ear again. I hoped I wasn't reading more into his tender gesture than I should. But his touch made my heart race, and to tell the truth, I wanted to grab him and kiss him silly. *What was wrong with me?*

Chapter 21

I woke up when the door opened. I'd been trapped in this hospital room for ten days and was about ready to climb out the window and scale down the wall like Spiderman, casts and all.

A little old lady, bent and frail, leaning on a cane, slowly made her way into the room, her face pinched with pain. She was tiny, and she kind of resembled a little bluebird with her blue pants and matching sweatshirt. She came toward me, her white sneakers squeaking across the floor, and she stopped by the side of my bed. Now that she was up close, I could see that she wasn't quite as old as I originally thought.

"Hello, dear. I'm Hannah Dale, Clyde's grandmother." Her voice was soft and calming as though she was talking to a frightened animal. And maybe she wasn't too far off the mark. Whether I wanted to admit it or not, I was scared to death about moving in with Mutt's grandma. But Ivy, Ebony, Stormy, and I had a big powwow, and it was decided that this would be the best option. Let's be real. The cold, hard fact was it was our only option.

Stormy would stay at the apartment with our two friends so she could keep her job. She accepted our list of rules and promised to listen to Ivy and Ebony. Yeah, sure she would. It would be interesting how long that particular arrangement would last.

I glanced over at the old woman and cleared my throat. "I sure appreciate this."

She smiled. "So, are you ready to blow this taco stand and get out of here?"

I stared at her in astonishment before I finally found my voice. "Yeah, sure. I've been ready to leave ever since I came out of that coma."

She chuckled. "I'll bet you have." She sat down in a chair. "I was told that the doctor was coming in a bit. Hopefully, he'll discharge you, and we can head home."

I guess my expression must have shown I was wondering just how she and I could manage to get me in and out of her car and into her house by ourselves. She grinned at me. "Don't worry, honey. Once the doctor gives his okay, I'll call Clyde. He promised to take some time off from chasing the bad guys and deliver us back home. He'll make sure we're all settled in before he leaves us to our own devices."

Studying the humongous cast on my leg, she paused and seemed to contemplate the enormous degree of difficulty that would be involved. "We'll have to consider the maneuvers we'll need to carry out when it comes to your bathroom visits." She met my gaze and smiled brightly. "But we'll figure something out, and with the Lord's help, we'll make out just fine."

Oh boy, another religious fanatic. I swallowed a few times before finally managing to squeak out, "Thanks, Mrs. Dale."

"Oh, just call me Granny, dear. Everybody else does." She whipped out some brightly colored yarn from the large bag she had set next to her chair. Needles flying, she concentrated on her knitting as she settled in and then started to chat.

Thirty minutes later, the doctor breezed in and asked a few curt questions. Then he left and a nurse appeared, handed Mutt's grandmother a mess of papers with instructions printed on both sides, and then gave me my walking papers to sign. I was officially discharged. *Huzzah!*

Granny made the phone call to Mutt and then began gathering up my things. The nurse's aide came in and helped me get dressed in the clothes that Stormy had brought from home. When all was said and done, I ended up wearing a tank top and some baggy shorts. Not exactly cool weather appropriate, but it was either that or cut my warmer clothes to accommodate my casts, and that sure wasn't an option, considering my limited wardrobe.

I was raring to go by the time Mutt arrived. Thank goodness Granny had the foresight to insist that we use her roomy sedan, so I could fit in the back seat. I just couldn't imagine how they would have managed to stuff me into the rear seat of his hatchback—and, apparently, neither could Granny. Mutt had brought along a couple of blankets, and after he got me all tucked in, we were on our way.

Granny's ranch house was about a fifteen-minute drive from the hospital, but we had to stop at the drugstore to get my medications. Waiting in the car while the pharmacist filled my prescriptions seemed like it took hours instead of the actual twenty minutes. Then, once we arrived at Granny's, getting out of the car, even with Mutt's help, and getting into the house was just short of a nightmare.

After watching me struggle, he finally just ended up scooping me up and carrying me. By then, I was completely drained. When we got through the door, there, sitting in the middle of the living room, was a wheelchair. Granny was all smiles. "Thank goodness I still kept this thing from when I broke my hip. It certainly will make things easier."

Mutt gingerly set me into the seat and adjusted the doodads on the chair that allowed my broken leg to stick straight out. After he got me positioned and as comfortable as possible, he started for the door. "Well, I've to go. I'll check in on you guys tonight."

"Hold it right there, buddy." Granny's stern voice stopped him in his tracks. "You aren't going anywhere until we make sure that Delilah is able to use the bathroom by herself. It's obvious that I can't lift her, so I need to know whether I need to call your cousin Bella or not."

"You can't call Bella!"

"We might have to." She stared him down. "She has a good heart, Clyde."

"Rumors are that Godzilla does too," he muttered under his breath.

"Don't be silly. And, besides, who else could we call?" Granny clapped her hands. "All right, time's a'wasting. Let's get Delilah into the bathroom and see what she can do."

Mutt turned fifty shades of purple. "Granny, I ... I can't ..."

"Oh put your eyeballs back in your head, Clyde. She'll leave her britches on. I just want to make sure she can get on and off the pot by herself."

I don't know who was more embarrassed. Mutt and I couldn't even look at each other as he slunk back into the living room and turned the wheelchair toward the bathroom door. "Come on, boy! Delilah looks like she's gonna dissolve any minute. She needs to take her pain pills and get to bed. Let's get this over with."

When he rolled me into the bathroom, I was grateful to see safety bars mounted beside the toilet. I suppose they were installed after Granny broke her hip. After positioning the chair and raising the armrest, I managed to grasp one of the bars with my good arm and maneuver myself onto the seat. By the time we got my left leg propped up on a stool, I was totally exhausted.

Granny assessed the situation and then kicked Mutt out. "You wait until I give you a holler, and then we'll get this girl to bed." She helped me pull my shorts down so I could take care of business, and then after I got that accomplished, I was somehow able to plop myself back into the chair. I was completely spent as she washed my hands and face with a washcloth. Then she called Mutt back in.

"We're gonna need some help. Later on, I think she'll be able to get in and out of bed with my help, but right now, she's too exhausted."

Mutt lovingly picked me up and put me into the bed while Granny helped maneuver the cast that encased my leg. After Mutt gave me my pain pills and a drink, he pulled the blankets up to my shoulders and kissed my forehead. "Sleep tight, babe."

I was asleep before the door closed.

Chapter 22

I LAY THERE, HELPLESS, CRYING, SWEATING, AND CUSSING UNDER MY breath. Hopefully, Granny didn't hear what I was saying.

Granny stood next to the bed as sweat beaded up on her forehead, looking grim. "I'm sorry, honey, I'm just not strong enough to get you up. I'm going to have to call Bella."

"Bella? But Mutt said ..."

"Clyde's not here, and we have got to get you up. You'll end up peeing yourself, and this is a new mattress." She started out the door. "I am calling Bella, and Clyde will just have to deal with it."

Twenty minutes later, I heard the front door open and heavy footsteps headed toward the bedroom. Granny went out to the living room and came back in smiling brightly. "Bella's here, coming to the rescue!"

A troll entered the bedroom and tromped toward the bed. I swear it was an honest-to-goodness troll! She was barely five foot tall and about as wide. Her complexion was the texture of leather, and her coarse black hair was cut in a blunt Dutch bob. Her bushy unibrow marched across her forehead and hovered over the two glittering black marbles that masqueraded as eyes. She glowered at me and grunted, "Yah want out of bed?"

Sheer paralyzing terror prevented me from making any kind of response. I lay frozen, defenseless, bug-eyed, and completely at her mercy.

"Of course, she wants to get out of bed, Bella. That's why I called. She'll need to use the bathroom, and then I can give Delilah her medicine.

After that, maybe you can help get her settled on the couch. It's too lonely for her to be stuck in this room all by herself."

Bella flung the blankets out of her way, leaving me exposed to the elements. "Get the chair," she growled.

Granny obediently rolled the chair next to the bed.

"Grab her leg."

Once again, Granny did as she was instructed.

Then Bella gave her final command: "On the count of three." With surprising ease, Bella lifted me up and gently set me on the wheelchair while Granny guided my leg. Bella then wheeled me into the bathroom and expertly assisted me in what I needed to do. Soon I was deposited onto the couch and properly drugged up with the TV on and lunch on the way.

"Thank you so much, Bella."

She merely grunted. When Granny came back with my sandwich and a glass of milk, Bella said, "Guess I best move in for a while."

"Why, honey, you don't have to do that! I don't want to put you out any."

Bella jerked her head toward me. "How you gonna get her off the couch?"

"Well, Clyde will help."

"He gonna sleep here? What if she has to go in the middle of the night? You can't get her out of the bed."

Granny and I exchanged glances. Obviously, we hadn't thought this through, and now we belatedly realized that it was more than we could handle by ourselves.

Bella grunted again. "Got to go home, pack a suitcase, and get my laptop. You still got internet?"

Granny nodded.

"Then get the guest room ready." With that, she left.

I took a swallow of milk and muttered, "Mutt's not going to like this."

Granny shrugged. "What else are we going to do?" She grinned. "You finish your lunch, and I'll make up the guest room bed. When Clyde comes back, you can tell him about our new houseguest."

Oh boy.

I was dozing when the phone rang.

Granny came into the living room and handed me the receiver. "It's for you."

It was Stormy. "Delilah! I miss you so much! Are you doing okay?" I blinked back tears. Just hearing my sister's voice made me want to bawl.

"I miss you too, honey. How are things going? Are Ivy and Ebony still at the diner? What's it like working with those two?"

"Ivy is actually turning into a decent cook. We hardly get any complaints anymore. And would you believe that Ebony is a big hit with the customers? You know how she's always fussing and talking smack, but they love it. She keeps everyone in stitches. You wouldn't believe how much we laugh. It's great." She paused and then asked, "So, how's it going with you?"

She sounded so happy. A big, ugly, green blob of pure jealousy lodged in my throat. I tried swallowing it down before I answered, but I didn't have much success. "Pretty good. The pain is a lot less, but I still can't move around like I want to. I got stuck in the bed this afternoon. I couldn't get up, and Granny had to call Mutt's cousin to come over and help."

"Oh no, do you need me to come and take care of you?"

My heart swelled with love for my dear sister. "No, honey. That's okay. Bella is going to stay with us for a few days."

"Okay, if you're sure."

"I'm sure." There was an odd tone in Stormy's voice that made me think she wasn't telling me something. "Okay, little sister, what gives?"

"What do you mean?"

"You're not telling me everything. Come clean. I promise I won't get mad."

"Oh, yes you will."

I practically had to stand on my tongue to keep from doing my mother thing. I took a deep breath and got myself under control. "Stormy," I said in a deadly calm voice, "what happened?"

"Well ... you know that guy Ronny Gilmore who comes to the diner two or three times a week?"

"Yeah, I know who you're talking about." I could feel my blood pressure rising. *If my baby sister is involved with that slimeball ...*

"Well, last night, when I was serving him his dinner, he reached over and grabbed my boob."

I nearly jumped off the couch. The only thing that kept me from hitting the ceiling was the leg cast that was anchoring me down. "He did what!" I yelled so loud that Granny stuck her head in the doorway, shook her head and then retreated into the kitchen.

"I told you that you would get mad."

"You've got that right, girl. I'm not just mad … I'm cross-eyed, spitting-nails furious!"

When Stormy started to laugh, I hollered, "This is not funny!"

"Yes, it is. You just haven't heard the whole story."

I took a deep breath. "Okay, so what's the whole story?"

Between giggles, she explained. "Well, when he grabbed me, I yelled, of course, and Ebony just happened to see the whole thing. She marched over to the table, picked up his plate, and dumped the entire dinner on his head. Then she grabbed him by his ponytail and yanked him right off the chair." She burst into laughter, and it took her a moment before she could continue. "So, picture this: she still had ahold of his ponytail, and she started kicking his tail-end the whole time she's escorting him out of the diner. She kicked his behind right out of the door and told him if he ever showed his face again, she'd kick something other than his tail so hard that he'd be singing soprano for the rest of his miserable life. Then everybody in the diner gave her a standing ovation."

By this time, I was laughing with tears running down my face. My sister's phone call was just what I needed.

After we said our goodbyes, Stormy promised to call back soon. I couldn't believe how much she had lifted my spirits.

When Granny came back from the kitchen, I shared the story with her. We both laughed so hard that she suddenly gasped, "Oh my goodness, I just wet myself." We cracked up all over again. She headed toward the bathroom, still giggling. "Wait until you tell Clyde. After he finds out about Bella staying here, he'll need a good laugh."

Oh, rats, I forgot about having to tell Mutt about his cousin moving in. Swell. Just can't wait to break the news to him.

Chapter 23

GRANNY AND I SAT IN THE LIVING ROOM, DRINKING TEA AND WATCHING the news on TV, as we waited for Bella to return. She turned to me with a pensive expression and asked, "Do you like dogs?"

I shrugged. "Haven't really been around them much. We always lived in apartments." *Or on the streets, or under a bridge, or in a homeless shelter.*

"Bella will be bringing her dogs with her when she comes back here."

"Oh, what kind of dogs are they?"

"Bonnie and Clyde are small dogs, but they are rather ... opinionated."

"Bella named one of her dogs Clyde?" I burst into laughter. "Oh, I bet Mutt is thrilled with that!" I thought about it for a moment. "Bonny and Clyde? That's so cute."

Granny took another sip as she gazed at me over her teacup. "You might say that."

We heard a car drive up, and after a couple of minutes, the door flew open. Bella came in with two shaggy mops on legs trotting behind her. They immediately sat down in front of the couch and started to snarl.

"Why are they growling at me for?" I asked.

Bella scowled and answered in her deep, coarse voice, "Because they don't like you." With that, she lugged her suitcase and laptop down the hall and disappeared into the guest room, leaving the dogs sitting in the living room and guarding us.

I turned my attention back to Bonnie and Clyde. I decided to make the best of it and try to make friends. When I reached my hand out to pet them, they displayed their prominent underbites as they bared their teeth and growled. That's when I noticed that peeking out from under their thick tangle of fur were the same beady black eyes as their master's. *Yikes.*

They continued to snarl as we sized each other up, but apparently, I failed to measure up to their standards. Since we had just met, I was baffled by their obnoxious attitude. I glanced over at Granny, but she just shrugged.

They continued to stare me down until, suddenly, they perked up their ears and turned their heads in unison at the sound of an engine spluttering up the driveway.

"Mutt's here," I announced.

As soon as he walked through the door, the furry duo met him with a cacophony of snarling and barking. He stopped dead in his tracks, glared down at the dogs, and then frowned at Granny. "So, you ended up calling her anyway."

Granny stood up. "We discovered that Delilah and I just couldn't handle getting her up and down by ourselves, so Bella was kind enough to offer to come and help. After all, you couldn't be here all the time, and you certainly would be worthless when she needed assistance in the bathroom." She crossed her arms and stared him down.

He dropped his gaze and then turned to me. "How are you feeling, babe?"

"Better."

When Mutt took a step toward me, the dogs cranked up the volume and expressed their displeasure.

Bella appeared in the doorway, hands on hips. "What are you doing to my dogs?"

"Nothing yet," Mutt growled while glowering at Bella. "But they better not bite me again or ..."

She snorted. "Never heard so much whining about just a tiny nip. Didn't even need a Band-Aid." She picked up both dogs and buried her face into their fur, nuzzling and cuddling them while crooning baby talk. Bella glanced up. "I swear, cousin," she sneered, "You are such a big wimp." She spun on her heel and left the room, a dog under each arm.

Mutt spluttered as he pointed toward the hall and then back at Granny. "She, she …" He was so aggravated and tongue-tied that he finally just stopped and shook his head.

Granny attempted to hide her smile by ducking her head.

"It's not funny," he said.

She snickered and said, "Actually, it is. You two have been at each other's throats since you were a little kid."

"But those dogs …"

"I really don't want to hear about it, Clyde. We need her help, and Bella and her dogs are a package deal. So, unless you have a better idea, *you* are going to have to find a way to get along with her." She started toward the kitchen and then stopped and turned to face Mutt with her hands on her hips. "As a matter of fact, you'll have to figure out how to get along with all *three* of them." She raised her chin. "Now, if you will excuse me, I have to tend to supper."

Mutt glared after Granny as she stomped into the kitchen, and then he flopped down on the edge of the couch with a thunderous expression on his face.

"I'm sorry to cause so much trouble," I said softly.

He looked up, surprised. "Delilah, you aren't causing any trouble." He gave me a grim smile. "Bella and I have shared diverse opinions on just about everything ever since I was old enough to talk." He glanced over at the doorway and sighed. "But you know the old saying, 'Their bark is worse than their bite'?"

"Yeah …"

"Well, that doesn't apply to Bonnie and Clyde."

After only a few days, I concluded that Bonnie and Clyde were aptly named. They were two criminals disguised in dog suits. They stole things and chewed their plunder to shreds. They growled, snapped, and generally made themselves as objectionable as possible. Yet their adoring master fervently believed that her "babies" were incapable of doing anything wrong. If you so much as frowned at the two, Bella leaped to their defense, and always put the entire blame for any disagreement on your head. To make matters even worse, the whole time all this was going on, Granny kept warning me that we needed Bella's help, so it was imperative that I didn't insult her dogs. *Sheesh.*

One afternoon, I was finishing my lunch at the dining room table while Granny busied herself in the kitchen and Bella rested in her room. As usual, Bonnie and Clyde sat a few feet away, growling. Just as I was taking a bite of my sandwich, Clyde got up and started sniffing around my feet. Before I could react, he lifted his leg and relieved himself right on my cast.

I bellowed, "Clyde, no!"

He spun around and scooted under the couch, with Bonnie right behind him.

Granny and Bella immediately appeared, both wide-eyed.

"What have you done to my dogs?" Bella demanded.

"What have I done? I didn't do a thing to them!"

"Then why are they hiding under the couch?"

"Clyde peed on my cast so I hollered!"

They peered at the yellow puddle under the table and then turned their attention to the wet spot on the side of my cast.

"A little dog wee never hurt anything."

"But I'm not supposed to get it wet. And now it's going to stink!" I wailed.

Bella strode into the living room and extracted her "babies" from under the couch, cradling them in her arms. "You scared them," she snarled as she stormed out of the room.

I was nearly in tears, although I'm not sure whether it was from frustration or rage. "Now I'm going to smell like dog pee!"

"Now, now, Delilah, we can fix you right up." Granny disappeared and then came back with an armload of cleaning supplies and a roll of paper towels. She mopped up the puddle and then turned her attention to my cast. First, she washed it down with Lysol, and then she sprayed it with a can of air freshener. By the time she was done, the aroma of cheap gardenia hung around me like a cloud. But at least its heavy fragrance was better than the essence of dog urine.

We both stared at the large damp spot on my cast. "It wasn't supposed to get wet." I must have whimpered that same phrase at least a dozen times during the cleanup operation.

Granny looked thoughtful and then brightened. "I know! I'll get the hair dryer." She paused on her way to the bathroom. "Remember, Delilah, don't fuss at Bella about what happened and get her upset. We don't want her to leave."

Yeah, sure. Of course we don't.

Chapter 24

COMING HOME FROM MY FIRST DOCTOR'S APPOINTMENT, THE TEARS wouldn't stop. I was splayed out on the back seat of Mutt's car with my leg propped up as best we could manage in such a tight space, but even so, I was suffering from a whole lot of "uncomfortable."

Mutt kept glancing up at the rearview mirror as he drove. "Babe, it's going to be all right. It's just going to take time, that's all. And considering you got hit by a speeding truck, it was by the grace of God that you weren't hurt even worse."

The last thing I wanted to hear was another sermon. "If your God is so great, why did He let me get hit by that truck in the first place?" I snapped. *Oh boy!* As soon as the words left my mouth, I knew I had stepped in it. Mutt stiffened, and I could sense that he was struggling to keep his anger under control.

I leaned my head back and closed my eyes. "I'm sorry, Mutt. I'm just upset. Four to six more weeks in this cursed cast, and *then* it's physical therapy after that. I can't possibly impose on your grandmother for that long, and I don't know what I'm going to do."

By the time we pulled into Granny's driveway, I was a basket case, and I was sobbing uncontrollably.

Mutt got the wheelchair out of the trunk and then opened the car's back door to help me scoot out. After getting situated in the chair, I got ahold of myself, blew my nose, and then nodded to Mutt that I was ready. He was quiet as he pushed me through the front door where his grandmother was waiting. "I'll get the crutches," he said as he darted out the door and headed back to the car.

Granny watched the entire process with a concerned expression. "Didn't you get good news from the doctor?"

I shrugged and began to tear up again.

Mutt came in with crutches in hand. "Be careful with these until you learn how to navigate with them. They can be tricky." He helped me to the couch and then gave each of us a peck on the cheek. "Gotta run. Is it okay if I come for supper tonight, Granny?"

"Of course. You know my grandson is always welcome at my table."

He smiled. "Okay, see you tonight." He scooted out the door. We heard his car's engine groaning and complaining before it finally started up, and he chugged down the road.

"Well, I see you've graduated to crutches, so that must be a good sign," Granny said as she tucked a blanket around me.

"Yeah, I guess so."

"Delilah, what's wrong?"

Tears filled my eyes. "The doctor said I'll need to stay in this cast for another four to six weeks! And *then* I'll need physical therapy. I can't possibly ask you to put me up for that long."

She sat down in the chair beside me, so we were face to face and took my hand. "Honey, we all knew it was going to take some time before you healed, and surely you know you are welcome to stay here for as long as it takes." She paused and studied me for a moment. "But there's something else, isn't there?"

Now the tears really started. "I said something terrible and made Mutt mad."

"What in the world did you say, honey?"

"Well, Mutt started preaching at me, saying God kept me from getting hurt worse, so I opened my big mouth and asked if his God was really that great, then why did his Jesus guy let me get hit by that truck in the first place?"

She gave my hand a squeeze and then sat back in her chair with her eyes closed. I guessed that she was praying; or maybe she was trying to figure out how she could pick me up, casts and all, and pitch me out the door.

But when she opened her eyes and gazed at me, her eyes were shining with nothing but kindness. "In other words, why do bad things happen to good people?" She smiled. "Honey, you just asked a question that is as old as time. And the answer is, nobody knows. It's one of the mysteries of life. You just need enough faith to know in your heart that God loves you and learn to trust Him." She sighed. "Mutt isn't mad with you; he's frustrated. He wants you to understand how much God loves you, and he wants you to meet ..." She paused and gave me another sweet smile. "He *desperately* wants you to meet his Jesus guy."

As the weeks crawled by, Granny would read bits and pieces from her Bible to Bella and me. I began to realize that I enjoyed listening to her. Bella, not so much, although she'd listen in on our discussions and would occasionally join in.

I really found it interesting when Granny would read the Bible and then explain what it meant. She never seemed to get irritated when I asked tons of questions, and thoughtfully answered every one of them. When it seemed like my mind was tied up in knots, she would patiently help me untangle my thoughts. If I just couldn't quite grasp a concept, she'd come at it from different angles until I finally understood.

One time, Granny read from what she called the book of Isaiah: "Fear not; for I have redeemed you, I have called you by your name and you are mine" (Isaiah 43:1 NKJV). She continued to read about walking through rivers and flames. It puzzled me, but she explained that the water and fire symbolized the troubles we all will walk through at some point in our lives. She said it was a promise that God will be at our side no matter how bad life's struggles get. Granny explained that the Bible guarantees that God will help us through it all and assures us that He will never leave us—ever. It was something to think about.

She would also share her faith occasionally, yet somehow, she never pushed it onto Bella or me. I was beginning to get curious about this Jesus, so she would carefully answer my questions and then allow the subject to drop.

Sometimes Bella would join in the conversation. At first, it just helped her pass the time, I think, but she eventually developed a real interest in what Granny was saying about God too.

Mutt also talked to me about God and Jesus, but he was always pushing too hard. After a while, I would try to change the subject as soon as he'd get on his Jesus kick. I knew I was hurting his feelings, but I just couldn't stomach getting religion shoved down my throat.

What amazed me about Granny was how she never seemed to lose faith, no matter what went wrong or how much she was hurting. I know she was in a lot of pain with the arthritis in her hip, yet she always had a smile.

When I asked her what her secret was, she sat down and took my hand. "Delilah, I'm human, and I don't always trust in God like I should. For instance, when my husband died, it was incredibly hard for me, and there was a time when I was so very angry at God. I felt that I had prayed all the right prayers, faithfully attended church, read my Bible every day, done all the right things, and lived my life as a good Christian. So, when Jonathan continued to become sicker and weaker, I even tried to bargain with God, yet the love of my life still died. I knew God could have healed him, but He took my husband from me, anyway. It was one of the lowest points in my life. I turned my back on God, but the Lord was patient with me and never left me. Once I finally decided to talk to Him again, He was right there, waiting for me. Next to losing Jonny and his wife Sarah, it was the hardest thing I ever had to go through."

I thought about what she had said. It surprised me that someone could get mad at God without Him just striking them dead. There was nothing in my life that I could compare to Granny's relationship with God. There was nobody who loved me like that. And, let's face it, there wasn't anybody in my life who I didn't expect something back from either. I mean, if I loved them, I figured they should love me back. Then I thought of something else she had said. "Who are Jonny and Sarah?"

Granny looked surprised. "Didn't Mutt ever tell you?"

"Tell me what?"

She sat for a moment, deep in thought, and then she sighed. "Jonny and Sarah were Mutt's parents. Jonny was our son. We also have two daughters, but Jonny was our only boy." She stopped talking and swallowed. The pain of losing her son was etched across her face. "I don't know why Mutt hasn't told you about this yet, but his mother and father disappeared when he was only seven years old. They had gone to a movie, but they never made it back home. The police found their car abandoned on a deserted country road, yet they never found Jonny and Sarah. That's when Mutt moved in with us, and the court eventually appointed Jonathan and me as his legal guardians."

"So, *you* raised Mutt?"

She nodded and grinned at me. "Yes. And he was such a rascal! There were times when he tested my faith, but I wouldn't trade those years for all the tea in China." She laughed that warm laugh of hers. "He certainly kept us young."

A couple days later, when I was feeling down, I told Granny about how our mother had raised Stormy and me, or to be more accurate, how she *didn't* raise us.

Granny said there was a verse in the Bible about that. She flipped through the pages and then read: "When my father and mother forsake me, then the Lord will take me up" (Psalm 27:10 KJV).

Wow, that business about being "forsaken" about sums up my life. I wonder if God really would "take me up."

I soon got my answer in a spectacular way. Or, as Granny would say, in a God way.

Things were a lot better once I was moving around on my crutches. The doctor said that keeping active and carefully putting some weight on my leg was good for me and would help with the bone's healing.

One afternoon, Granny was visiting her friend at a nursing home, and Bella was taking a nap. I took the dogs outside, and we were enjoying the warm, sunny day.

A car pulled into the driveway. It didn't sound like Granny's, and it sure wasn't Mutt's old clunker.

I started around to the front of the house to keep whoever was visiting from ringing the doorbell and waking Bella. "Hello! I'm in the backyard."

As I rounded the corner of the house, I bumped right into Boris. Razor was a few steps behind him.

"Well, well, well, if this ain't our lucky day." His lips curled into a hideous smile. "Thought we couldn't find you? It took us a while, but you ought to know that you can't hide forever. Now come on, sweetheart, we're going for a ride."

I tried to make a run for it. Not a smart move when you're on crutches. I went down, hit the ground hard, and then tried to scuttle away like a crab.

Boris watched me and laughed. "This is going to be more fun than shooting fish in a barrel."

I moaned. "No!"

"You got the stick?"

"I tried, but I can't find it!"

He pulled out his gun and aimed it at me. "Well, then ..."

"Jesus!" I screamed. "Help me!"

Out of the corner of my eye, I saw two streaks of white, and then Clyde grabbed one of Boris' ankles and Bonnie snared the other. He danced around, shouting a string of curses, and bellowed, "Shoot 'em! Shoot 'em!"

Razor attempted to aim at the dogs. "I can't!" he hollered. "I might miss and hit you."

Boris tried to kick his attackers, but with one on each leg, he couldn't do it. He pointed at me and yelled, "Then shoot her!"

Just then, Bella came lumbering around the corner, armed with a shovel. She swung and connected with the back of Boris's head. A metallic clang, which sounded like a gigantic gong, echoed across the yard. He was felled like a giant tree.

Then everything happened in slow motion. We both turned and looked at the Magnum in Razor's hand. He raised it up and aimed directly at Bella's heart. Time stopped for a moment until a furry maniac launched himself into the air and latched onto Razor's crotch. He screamed in agony.

Snarling, Clyde shook his head back and forth in a frenzy and clamped on even harder.

Razor frantically tried to pull the dog off to no avail and then shrieking—and obviously not thinking about the consequences—he turned his gun toward his tormentor.

Dong! The next thing I knew, Razor was stretched out next to his partner. Bella was a regular Barry Bonds with a shovel. She strolled over and picked up the gun. "Nobody shoots my dogs," she growled as she aimed the gun at the two thugs on the ground. For a horrible moment, I thought she was going to shoot them, but then she looked over at me and said, "You okay?"

Trembling, I somehow managed to find my voice and answered, "Yeah, I'm okay."

"Then, call 911."

I retrieved my cell phone from my pants pocket, but my hands were shaking so hard I could barely punch in the numbers. I must confess it was a rather hysterical conversation on my part, but the operator told me to hold on and stay on the line. Help was on its way.

Within minutes, three police cruisers came roaring up the road, with sirens wailing and lights flashing, and swung into the driveway. Car doors flew open, and cops poured out like clowns from a circus car.

Mutt was the first one to reach me. "Babe! Are you okay?" He knelt down, scooped me up in his arms, and clutched me against his chest.

That's when I had a total meltdown.

Mutt held me tight and carried me into the house. He lay me on the couch and knelt beside me, stroking my hair and whispering, "It's okay, babe. It's okay." Then he took me in his arms and rocked me back and forth as if he were comforting a little child. As I clung to him, I felt safe. I felt protected. I felt loved.

Later that afternoon, after I had calmed down enough to think about what had happened, it hit me. I had prayed for the very first time, and God had answered. Big-time. In the form of two furry mops and a troll. Wow.

Chapter 25

THE JUDGE RULED THAT BORIS AND RAZOR WERE PERSISTENT FELONS AND denied bail. So, I figured now that Tweedledee and "Tweedle Dumber" were out of the picture, Stormy and I were off the hook. Boy, was I wrong. Unbeknownst to us, we were being stalked by a professional hit man. Little did we know that if we didn't find the memory stick, we were dead. On the other hand, if we did find it, the killer would take it from us—and *then* we would be dead. At least that was the directive from the Chicago kingpin who had hired the assassin, yet we had no clue. Sometimes, ignorance is bliss.

Bella went home with Bonnie and Clyde now that I had mastered getting around on crutches and was fairly independent. I was surprised to discover that I kind of missed the three of them.

Granny insisted that I still stay at her house because she claimed she really enjoyed my company. I didn't know if that was true, or whether she just felt sorry for me. Anyway, Stormy, Ivy and Ebony seemed to be doing fine without me, and since navigating the four flights of steep stairs to our apartment using crutches was daunting to say the least, I decided to stay put. Granny drove me to my doctor's appointments, and she said she'd take me when I started physical therapy. In the end, living at her house seemed like the best solution for everybody.

A few days after my encounter with Boris and Razor, Granny began my cooking lessons. The crutches slowed me down a bit, so I did a lot of watching and some learning too. Once Granny finally decided I was ready to go solo, several of my few first tries ended up in the garbage, but she never gave up on me. During my learning curve, I only had one kitchen fire, but Mutt managed to put it out rather quickly—and the kitchen wasn't damaged at all. Now I've improved enough to cook meals, under Granny's supervision, of course, and so far, nobody's gotten sick. Mutt is trying to encourage me, but I notice he slips a few bits into his napkin occasionally. Granny told me not to worry about it. She said we all must learn to walk before we can run, and in the meantime, we'll end up falling once or twice. I told her that, in my case, falling kept happening a whole bunch of times.

One day, Mutt brought me my very own brand-new Bible. He seemed nervous about giving it to me, but I told him I really appreciated it, and I meant it. Now I read my Bible every day, well, almost every day, and since it is one of those Bibles that's written in plain English, it's a lot easier to understand.

Granny gave me suggestions for what I should read, and she also encouraged me to explore scripture on my own. I loved reading the Psalms and Isaiah, but what drew me in the most was reading about Mutt's Jesus guy. I asked Granny a whole bunch of questions, but I was especially curious about how she could be so cheerful and happy when she was always in so much pain. Even when she was hurting so bad that she could hardly walk, she still had a smile on her face. She said, "The joy of the Lord is my strength" (Psalm 28:7 NIV). It sounded a little weird to me, but the more I got to know her, the more I wanted to have whatever she had. I mean, she was so peaceful, even when everything around her was spinning out of control. So, one day, I finally took the plunge, and with Granny guiding me, I prayed the Sinner's prayer.

That evening, Mutt came over for supper, and I made roast beef, mashed potatoes, and corn. I boiled the potatoes over on the stove, but other than that, things went fairly well. I even made chocolate chip cookies for dessert.

I was excited to tell him the news, but Granny and I decided it would be best to wait until after we ate. All through supper, Mutt kept studying me and would occasionally glance over at Granny. I guess the silly grins plastered across our faces during the entire meal made him suspicious. After we finished eating, Mutt carried the dishes into the kitchen.

Granny shooed us into the living room, insisting that she wanted to do the dishes all by herself.

I settled on the couch, and Mutt's expression was wary as he grabbed a chair and sat down, facing me. "Okay, Delilah, what are you and Granny cooking up? And I don't mean supper."

"What do you mean, Mutt?" I asked, my voice dripping with innocence.

"Delilah ..." he growled.

I laughed. I couldn't help it. Joy just kept bubbling up, and I couldn't contain it. I took his hand and said softly, "Mutt, you know how you keep talking to me about your Jesus guy?" He tensed and nodded, his eyes never leaving my face. "Well, now He's *my* Jesus guy too."

Mutt lifted me off the couch, crushed me into a bear hug, and gave me a big kiss right on my lips. When we sat back down, I was amazed to see tears flowing down his cheeks. He raised his hands toward heaven and said, "Praise God! Thank you, Jesus!" He looked toward the kitchen and yelled, "Granny! Come in here!"

The next thing I knew, we were all in a group hug, laughing and crying. It was great.

Now I finally understand why Mutt kept pressing me about Jesus. Ever since I became a believer, I have wanted to share the good news, but Stormy reacted as if I had lost my mind, and when I tried to talk to Ivy and Ebony, they flat-out told me I was a fanatic. They even accused me of being a religious zealot.

I guess it was like when Mutt had tried to talk to me, and I would get mad if he even so much as mentioned Jesus. But Granny is a wise woman. She told me to share by example, not by words. So, I decided to do what she said and back off the preaching bit and just bide my time for a while.

Looking back, it sure was a good thing I couldn't see the future and know how my faith would be tested because I probably would have hidden under a rock somewhere. Later, when I shared what I had been thinking with Mutt, he said, "Well, Delilah, that's exactly what you did. You hid under the Rock, who is Jesus our Savior."

Chapter 26

Now that my cast was off, I was regularly participating in sessions that involved a sadistic maniac inflicting various types of torture on me, particularly concentrating on my left leg. Would you believe that this process was referred to as "physical therapy"? The she-devil who presided over these pain-fests kept insisting that enduring all this agony was for my own good. *Yeah sure.*

After one particularly brutal workout, I was attempting to recover on Granny's couch, wrapped in ice packs, broken and defeated. Granny tried to encourage me, but after a few snarling replies, she handed me my pain pills, flipped on the TV, and retreated into the kitchen, leaving me alone to lick my wounds as I stared at the boob tube.

A little while later, Granny answered a knock at the door. I heard her say, "She is in the living room. Come right in."

I groaned and contemplated just how difficult it would be to crawl under the coach and hide. The absolute last thing on earth I wanted to do right then was entertain company.

The murmur of voices drifted into the living and droned on for several minutes.

I waited—as tense as a couch spring ready to let loose and go "boing." Finally, I heard Granny say, "Why, that's wonderful!"

I could hear footsteps heading my way.

I was in no mood for visitors until I saw Stormy peek around the corner, closely followed by Ivy and Ebony. They all had big smiles, and from the giddy expressions on their faces, I knew something was up, for sure.

Ebony strode over to me and scowled. "Get your lazy tail feathers off this couch, girl. We're taking you home."

I stared at her. "You know it is nearly impossible for me to manage all those flights of stairs on these crutches in order to get to our fifth-floor apartment. And I won't even mention how much harder my broken arm would make it."

"You can manage to get to the second floor, can't you?"

I narrowed my eyes and glared at her. "What do you mean?"

Apparently, Stormy couldn't stand keeping quiet any longer. "We've moved, Delilah!"

"What are you talking about?"

"You know how we always helped Mrs. Blakely, going grocery shopping for her and stuff?"

I nodded.

"Well, she can't manage to walk upstairs anymore, so she decided to move into a nursing home and we got her second-floor apartment. The landlord allowed us to ditch the lease on our old place and let us take over hers." Stormy grinned. "I think Mrs. Blakely must have pulled some strings to get the old grouch to agree and let us switch. And it gets even better! She said that since we'd been so nice to her and she didn't need her furniture anymore, she was giving everything to us! We've got a real bed in the bedroom and a sofa bed in the living room where Ivy and Ebony sleep. She even gave us her dishes and pots and pans. Everything!"

I glared at my sister, dumbfounded. Her smile faltered, and then she asked in a quavering voice, "Isn't that great, Delilah?"

"How are we going to pay for a bigger apartment that's on the second floor?" I snapped. "We could barely afford our old fifth-story studio walk-up."

Stormy's lips began to quiver, and Ebony put her hands on her hips and scowled at me. "What is your problem, girl? This child has been so excited to move 'cause it meant her big sister could come home. And now yah had to go an' get yourself an attitude and make her cry."

"Well, somebody has to face the facts." I glowered at Ebony and Ivy. "You should know that we can't manage to pay the extra rent for that apartment."

"There's three paychecks coming in now, so, yes, we *can* afford it." Ebony studied my face. "If I didn't know any better, I'd think you didn't want to come home."

I felt all defensive and mixed up at the same time. I enjoyed staying with Granny. Well, if you want the truth, I loved Mutt's grandmother, and the icing on the cake was that I got to see Mutt just about every night. If I moved back in with three roommates, everything would change.

I tried to keep my voice calm as I answered through clenched teeth. "Of course I want to come home. It's just that Granny takes me to PT three times a week so, how would I get there?" I crossed my arms over my chest. "And besides, she said she would be lonely if I left."

That's when Granny came in and sat on the edge of the couch. She took my hand and said softly, "Delilah, you know how much I enjoy your company, but I think your place is with your sister and your friends." She smiled. "As for taking you for physical therapy, your apartment is practically on the way. It will be easy to pick you up and drive you over to the hospital and back, just like we've been doing. All we have to do is to make sure someone can help you up and down the stairs."

The next thing I knew, all my things were packed up and I was on my way home. "Who's car is this?" I asked as we backed out of the driveway and started down the road.

"Mine. Snake gave it to me."

I stared at Ivy in disbelief. "Snake gave it to you? Why?"

She glared at me. "Why not? He knew I needed one, and he didn't need this one, so he gave it to me."

Oh, swell. Snake gave it to her? I can almost guarantee that it was stolen. And even if it wasn't, I'm pretty sure it isn't covered by insurance. Ooh boy! Come to think of it, Ivy probably doesn't even have a driver's license. Wait 'til Mutt finds out. I leaned back in the seat and closed my eyes. I could feel a headache coming on.

When I got home, I somehow managed to navigate the stairs. When I walked into our new apartment, I realized just how much I had missed

Stormy and the rest of the gang. My little sister seemed to have grown up a lot during the weeks that I was gone, and we had a lot of catching up to do. For one thing, I was shocked to find out that she had a steady boyfriend. Ivy and Ebony assured me he was a nice kid and that the two of them were well chaperoned.

I had to admit that this apartment was a lot nicer than our old one. Having a separate bedroom for Stormy and me was a big bonus, and the rest of the place was a decent size too. There was a galley kitchen and a table in the corner of the living room that we proudly called "the dining room," where we ate our meals. The sofa bed folded up into a couch during the day, and there was also a recliner, so there was plenty of room for us to lounge around. We even had a TV now, complete with rabbit ears. The three channels came in a bit snowy, but it sure was better than nothing, which was exactly what we had before.

I felt like a lazy bum since I still couldn't work, but I did keep the apartment picked up, I cleaned the bathroom when it got nasty, and on the rare occasion when we had supper at home, I made the meal. Granny's cooking lessons sure proved to come in handy.

I missed Granny something awful because I guess she was the mother I'd never had. At least we got to see each other three times a week when she drove me to PT, and we talked on the phone every day.

Unfortunately, spending time with Mutt was another matter altogether. The only time we had any privacy was when the "girls" were working. But for some reason, Mutt wasn't comfortable being alone with me in the apartment. He said, "It just doesn't look right."

I said, "Oh, for pity's sake, we're both adults," but he still insisted that we meet at the diner, or at the park, or at Granny's, or someplace like that.

Overall, though, things were going pretty good. The PT was getting easier as I grew stronger, and my leg healed. I had mastered the art of using crutches and could even navigate the stairs without assistance.

The four of us girls were getting along fairly well once we worked out a bathroom schedule. Most nights, I would join them at the diner for supper and then visit with my friends and the customers until Jose walked us home. After the diner closed for the night, I could do piddly things like refill the salt and pepper shakers, replenish the napkin holders, wipe down the tables, and little things like that while the girls did the heavy cleaning. Of course, I wasn't doing enough to get paid, but Connie said I did enough to earn my supper, so that was good.

Then, one afternoon, when I had just gotten home from PT and was icing down my back and leg, there was a knock at the door. After checking the peephole, I opened the door to a beautiful woman with long black hair and violet eyes. I stared at her for a moment in utter shock before I gasped. "Shirley? Where have you been?"

Chapter 27

I stood frozen with a white-knuckled hold on the doorframe with one hand and the other wrapped around the doorknob in a death grip. I hung on, determined not to do a face-plant in front of my wayward mother. She looked amazing. Gone was the pinched, emaciated appearance that's the classic signature of a druggie. Now she was gorgeous! We stared each other down until Shirley glanced over my shoulder into the room. She spoke in the same low, sexy voice that drove men up the wall. "May I come in, Delilah?"

Somehow, I managed to release the doorframe and step aside as Shirley swept past me, and then I followed her into the room after closing the door.

She turned and watched me make my way back to the couch on my crutches. "What happened?"

"I got hit by a pickup truck."

She clutched her throat. "Oh my, when was that? I hadn't heard about your accident, or I would have come back sooner."

A thousand questions came to mind, but I merely said, "It was no accident. He did it on purpose."

Shirley looked shocked. Either my mother was a good actor, or she really didn't know anything about it. "Do you know who was driving the truck?" she asked as she sank down on the recliner.

"Willie Nelson."

It took a second for her to digest what I had said. "What?"

"It was a guy who looks just like a young Willie Nelson. His real name is Rodney Butler."

"The Slasher? Why in the world would he run you down?"

"You know him?"

"I know of him. But why would …"

"He was trying to find out where the stick was."

She stared at me like I had three heads. "The stick?"

"Stanley Barron's stick."

Shirley continued to stare. "I'm confused. Just what is Stanley's stick—and why was Butler looking for it?"

Anger surged up my spine and exploded into my brain. "It's the stick that you stole from Stanley Barron." By this time, I was nearly screaming at her. "It's the stick that nearly got Stormy and me killed!"

She sat back in her chair as the color drained from her face. Then she leaned forward and grasped my hand. "Delilah, I have no idea what you are talking about. Why in the world would a little stick be so important?" Her eyes sparkled with unshed tears. "And why would anyone want to kill you and Stormy?"

I couldn't figure out if she was sincere, or if she was scamming me. "You tell me." I pulled my hand away.

"Delilah, please! I honestly have no idea what you are talking about. I don't understand why a stick could possibly be so important. And I certainly can't imagine why anyone would try to kill you for it."

I hugged myself and studied the woman who sat across from me. She certainly seemed clueless, but I knew from years of experience that when it came to my mother, looks were almost always deceiving.

"Delilah?"

I just stared at her and kept silent.

"Why is this … stick … so valuable that people would kill for it?"

"You really don't know?"

"I don't have the slightest idea."

"It's the memory stick that you used to download all of Stanley Barron's records from his computer. You stole it, and now Stanley wants it back."

Her hand went to her mouth, and she shook her head. "No, no! I never did that! I don't know the first thing about computers, and don't have a clue how to download things. And I certainly didn't steal the memory stick. I don't even have any idea what one would even look like."

Now we were getting somewhere. I just caught her in a bald-faced lie. "I happen to know that you worked for Stanley for three months as a secretary."

"No, that's not right. I never worked as a secretary. How could I? I don't even type."

"So, you never worked for Barron?"

She blushed scarlet. "I was with Stanley, but I never worked for him. I'm a bookkeeper, not a secretary, but he already had an accountant who took care of everything, so he didn't need to hire me for that."

I sneered and shook my head. "Yeah, sure. So, since he's such a good guy, he took you in out of the goodness of his heart."

"I ... I was his ... companion."

My head jerked up. "Well, that explains a lot."

"But I never stole anything from Stanley. I swear!"

"Someone downloaded all Barron's data onto a memory stick and then wiped his computer clean. Both you and the stick disappeared at the same time. Stanley's not happy, and he wants that memory stick back."

"And he's willing to kill for it?" she whispered.

"Right. So where is it, Shirley?"

"I don't know! I have no idea! You've got to believe me, Delilah."

I couldn't read her. I honestly wasn't savvy enough to know whether she was telling the truth or not, but history proved that she didn't have a good track record in that particular department. "Okay. Let's suppose you are telling the truth. So, clue me in. Why does Stanley think you took the memory stick?"

"I don't know." Her eyes met mine. "I really don't."

I just shook my head in disbelief. "So, where have you been for the past five months? We've been looking all over for you. So have Barron's goons and Willie Nelson and the police and who knows who else. Why did you disappear like that if you weren't hiding from Stanley? Where were you?"

She closed her eyes and sighed. When she looked at me again, I felt a shock wave go through me. It was as if God Himself had spoken to me. I knew without a doubt that she was going to tell me the truth.

"I was upstate at a drug rehabilitation center run by a man called Preacher John ... John Robinson. I've kicked the habit, Delilah. I've been clean for almost four months now." She paused and seemed to weigh her words. "I know this will sound strange to you, but God delivered me. He took away all my desire to do drugs and set me free."

I think she was shocked when I replied, "Thank You, Jesus."

Tears started trickling down both of our faces as we exchanged smiles. "Are you a believer too?"

I nodded, and her smile broadened. "Thank You, Jesus," she whispered.

We embraced each other as we laughed and cried before we pulled apart to look at each other. I grabbed a box of tissues and offered them to her. We laughed again and started to wipe our eyes and blow our noses.

Just then, the door swung open, and Stormy stood in the doorway with an armload of library books. There was a protracted pause as mother and daughter stared at each other.

Shirley stood and took a few wobbly steps toward her. "Stormy ..."

The books crashed to the floor as Stormy spun around and ran out the door and back down the stairs. A moment later, we heard the entrance door of the apartment building slam shut.

Shirley slowly turned to face me. "She left. She left me."

"No, Shirley," I said. "*You* left. You're the one who left *us*."

Chapter 28

MY MOTHER SLOWLY SANK TO THE FLOOR AND PUT HER HANDS OVER HER face. I knew I should go to her, but I couldn't do it. Every emotion in the book swirled around my brain and then slid down and kicked me in the heart just for good measure. So many years of neglect. So many years of a hand-to-mouth existence. So many years of desperate longing to hear my mother say she loved us, or even to just acknowledge that we existed. Fury, despair, regret, loss, and overwhelming weariness nearly crushed me.

I got up, crutched across the room to close our front door, and then sat back down on the couch and studied my mother. She was hunched over, sobbing. It should have been heart-wrenching to witness, yet somehow, I merely felt self-righteous satisfaction. I knew my attitude was despicable, especially after sharing such a special moment with her just a few minutes before, but I didn't care. In the back of my mind, I knew I had to forgive her, especially now that I was a Christian, but I didn't want to. So, I hardened my heart and just sat and watched.

As her sobs subsided, she began to murmur. After a while, I realized she was praying, "Forgive me, Lord. I'm so sorry, Jesus. Forgive me. Please, please forgive me."

The next thing I knew, I was on the floor beside her, crying my eyes out. My mother reached out, and we clung to each other, weeping and mourning over what might have been. When we finally quieted, reality hit—and I realized that my leg was killing me. "I've got to get up. My leg!"

Shirley helped me up and over to the couch. I was crying again, but this time, it was because of the ferocious pain. She got some ice packs out of the freezer and handed me my pain pills and a glass of water. Once I settled down and the pain subsided, she sat on the edge of the couch and held my hand. "Delilah, can you ever forgive me? I have no excuse whatsoever. I was a horrible, completely self-centered person who didn't deserve to have the two beautiful daughters God gave me. I am so sorry. Please forgive me."

I just stared at her. I knew what I had to do, but I fought it every inch of the way. Then I heard God whisper to my heart. Of course, it wasn't an actual whisper, but it was just as real to me as a shout would have been: "Forgive, as the Lord forgave you." (Colossians 3:13 NIV)

I thought about what Granny said when she was explaining the Lord's Prayer to me. She said it every time we prayed, "Forgive us our sins as we forgive those who sin against us," (Matthew 6:12 NLT) we were asking God to pardon our sins, but only if we also forgave others. I sighed and said, "Okay, God."

I closed my eyes. It was just too hard. I couldn't do it, yet I knew I had to. It felt like a war was going on inside of me, so I prayed, "God, help me to *want* to forgive her." Peace came over me, and I opened my eyes.

"I forgive you, Shirley." I said it, but it wasn't quite right. I tried again. "I forgive you, *Mother*."

It was as though a wall came crashing down … or maybe it was more like a dam bursting … and joy came flooding in. I suddenly understood the "joy unspeakable" that Granny sang about.

I didn't think we had any more tears to shed, but sure enough, my mother and I hung onto each other and bawled our eyes out again. We emptied the entire box of tissues, and then my mother had to go get toilet paper out of the closet—and we used half a roll of that.

We had just finished gathering up all the wads of tissues when the door opened, and Ebony and Ivy walked in.

"What happened to Stormy?" Ivy fumed. "She's crying and all upset, but she won't tell us what's wrong." She stopped in her tracks when she noticed my mother and glared.

Ebony stood in front of her, hands on hips, and looked her up and down. "I take it that you're back, Shirley. So, wha'cha say to my girl to get her all tore up like that?"

"I … I didn't say anything to her. I didn't get the chance. As soon as she saw me, she turned around and left."

"Uh-huh. So, that's why she's crying her guts out and sayin' she ain't never gonna go home again."

"She really didn't say anything, Ebony," I said. "As soon as Stormy saw her, she slung her books on the floor and took off."

Ebony was still furious. "Nobody hurts my girl, or they answer to me. Got it?"

My mother hung her head. "I've been hurting Stormy ever since she was born, and I'm so sorry." Tears filled her eyes again as she turned to me. "I hurt her, and I hurt you even worse … and then I expected you to clean up my messes." Her voice broke. "And you were just a child!"

"It's okay."

"No, no … it's not okay."

"But I've forgiven you," I said gently.

Ivy stepped closer, and a soft gasp escaped from my mother's lips. Ivy leaned forward until she was just inches away. "You wondering what happened to my face?" she demanded. "I'll tell you what happened to it. You did."

"I … I don't understand."

Ivy barely managed to keep her rage under control. "Well, let me clear that up for you." She began to pace. "Somebody hired Rodney Butler to get me to talk. They wanted to find that memory stick you stole from Barron."

"But …"

Ivy held up her hand to silence her. "If it hadn't been for you, they wouldn't have been looking for that stick, and I wouldn't never have been sliced up." She clenched her fists and took a step toward my mother. "I ought to do you like he did me!"

I sat up straight. "She didn't do it, Ivy! She never took the stick. She doesn't know anything about it."

"And you actually believe her?"

"Yes, I do. She's innocent. I'm sure of it."

Ebony stepped in. "Okay, cool it. Best we talk some."

We all sat down and had a soul-searching discussion. My mother answered all our questions and kept apologizing over and over again.

Finally, Ebony slapped her legs and stood up. Okay, I'm gonna go see if I can talk some sense into that girl. She's upset, but she's smart." She smiled. "Don't worry, Shirley. It's gonna be okay."

As soon as the two of them left, my mother grabbed my hand. "Let's pray."

We continued our prayers to the Lord for what seemed like an eternity, although it must have only been a few minutes. Then we heard footsteps on the stairs, and the door opened.

Stormy stood in the doorway like a statue.

Ebony put an arm around her. Come on, girl. Go on and talk to your mama." When she didn't move, Ebony gave her a little shove. "Now go on, girl."

Shirley stood up as Stormy trudged across the room and stopped in front of her. They stared at each other for a moment, and then our mother held out her arms. My heart seemed to stop beating when Stormy didn't even move. The tension in the room grew until you could have cut it with a knife. Finally, a little sob escaped from Stormy's lips, and Shirley pulled her into an embrace.

The two melted into each other's arms. As they stood in the middle of the living room, rocking back and forth, I hoped and prayed that the years of hurt had finally started to fade—and perhaps the healing had begun.

Chapter 29

THIS WAS TURNING OUT TO BE ONE DOOZY OF A FIGHT. I STOOD IN THE middle of the living room, hands on hips, and Mutt was halfway out the door with his hand on the knob. We glared at each other. Round one had ended in a draw.

I had thought Mutt would be happy when my mother came back and moved in with us girls. We bought a cot at the Salvation Army store for a couple of bucks, and now she shared the bedroom with Stormy and me. And, yeah, it's five women and one bathroom. It will be a miracle if we don't eventually kill each other. Anyway, Mutt shocked me when he nearly hit the ceiling after finding out where Mother was staying. We'd been arguing ever since, though this little discussion topped them all.

He closed the door and turned to me with a sigh. "Look, Delilah, I only have what's best for you in mind."

Oh, boy! Here comes round two. "Oh, I suppose you and your superior mind know exactly what is best for me."

He bristled. "Having Shirley live here is just asking for trouble. She is the reason Stanley's thugs, and that weirdo Rodney Butler are after you. They'll stop at nothing. And do you really think they're going to believe that she doesn't know where that memory stick is? Honestly, Delilah, I can hardly believe it myself."

"Oh? Are you calling my mother a liar?"

He closed his eyes for a moment and then looked at me. "What I meant was it just doesn't sound believable."

"That's not what you said."

"Delilah, you are putting words in my mouth. And don't try to change the subject. I'm telling you, with your mother living here, it's not only unsafe for you, but it's putting your sister in danger too."

Okay, round three: the guilt card. "I've been protecting my sister ever since she was born, so don't tell me how to keep her safe."

He ran his hand through his hair. He was so sexy when he did that, but I was determined not to let it distract me.

"Stormy and I are just beginning to get acquainted with our mother," I said. "Besides, she's learning about us too since she never really paid any attention to us before." I saw a flash of pity in his eyes, and resentment washed over me. "And don't feel sorry for me. Besides, how come you are always preaching about forgiveness, but you don't want me to forgive my own mother?"

"The Bible says we are to forgive, Delilah, not that we are to be foolish."

Oh, boy. Round four was coming up, and Mutt was on the ropes. I could see by his expression he realized he had gone too far with that remark.

He reached out and took my hand. "Babe, I'm just worried about you. When Butler ran you down and hurt you like he did, it scared me so bad. I don't know what I would have done if you hadn't made it, and now I just can't stand the thought of anything happening to you." His gorgeous brown eyes turned into melted chocolate as he whispered, "I love you, Delilah." Then he pulled me into an embrace and hungrily kissed me.

Bong! End of round four. Mutt Dale declared the winner by knockout!

Mother and I hit it off right away and did a lot of catching up. It seemed like we had so much to talk about; not the least of which was our faith and what we believed in. But, Stormy was a different matter altogether. She still called our mother "Shirley" and really hadn't warmed up to her all that much. I had high hopes that things would be different after that emotional moment they had shared a few days ago, but for some reason, Stormy seemed to back off. Oh, she was polite and all, yet she remained standoffish. And she sure didn't want to hear anything that even remotely concerned our belief in Jesus. Mother and I discussed it and decided it would be best to tread easy on that subject for a while.

We both shed a lot of tears when my mother talked about the years of neglect Stormy and I suffered through as kids. She had so many regrets about what she had done, or to be more specific, what she *hadn't* done. I wish Stormy had heard the overwhelming sorrow in Mother's voice when she asked my forgiveness for not being there when we needed her.

When I asked her about the circumstances that led to her leave town, enter rehab, and eventually turn to Jesus, she explained that she had gone to the revival meeting on a bet. She and a friend challenged each other to see who would be the first one to seduce one of the ministers, or better yet, win the grand prize of Preacher John himself. As it turned out, after arriving at the revival, she heard his message, and God moved. Mother said that she was listening to the preacher, and the next thing she knew, she walked down the aisle and accepted Jesus as her Lord and Savior.

Afterward, when she talked to one of the counselors, she confessed to being a drug addict. They told her about their drug rehabilitation program, and she enrolled right on the spot. Amazingly enough, there was an opening available, and she got on the ministry's bus and headed upstate. She completed the program and promised me that she's been drug free ever since.

I was worried about Granny meeting my mother, but when I asked if it was all right for her to come with us the next time I had a physical therapy session, Granny said it was fine with her. Even so, I was still nervous. Granny had become like a mother to me, and I was concerned that there might be hard feelings between them. But when they met for the first time, Granny opened her arms to Mother. After they hugged and shared a few tears together, I knew it was going to be okay.

Mutt was still uneasy about Mother staying in our apartment. First thing off the bat, he came and mounted a dead bolt and security chain on our door like the one he had installed at our old apartment. He lectured us about how we needed to remain vigilant and that we were never to walk by ourselves after dark. I appreciated his concern, but it annoyed me, nonetheless.

I should have listened to him.

Chapter 30

Mother and I were in a deep discussion about scripture and our beliefs when I happened to glance out the window and noticed it was getting quite dark. We should have left for the diner an hour ago.

We were chattering as we made our way down the sidewalk and didn't so much as glance at the darkened alleyway we passed. Our mistake.

Someone stepped out of the shadows, grabbed me from behind, and pressed a gun to my temple.

My mother spun around, wide-eyed, as he growled, "Make a sound, and I blow her head off." He nodded toward the alley. "Please step into my office, ladies."

My bum leg kept me from moving fast enough to please him, so he half dragged me toward his pickup truck. That's when it hit me. Willie Nelson! If we got into that truck, we were dead. It would be an ugly kind of death too, sliced up like pieces of salami and then dumped into a ditch somewhere. I had nothing to lose, so I twisted around, sank my teeth into his hand, and stomped on his foot in a desperate move.

He cursed and flung me to the ground. When I looked up, his contemptuous smile and wild eyes chilled my blood as he took aim with a handgun the size of a small cannon. I knew I was going to die.

Suddenly, my mother screamed like a banshee and launched herself at him, scratching and biting. They struggled while I staggered to my feet.

"Run, Delilah! Run!"

He backhanded her and slammed her against a dumpster. Mother slid down its metal side and crumpled onto the ground. Then he slowly turned and pointed his gun at me.

"Freeze! Police!" Mutt's voice echoed around the buildings that lined the alley. My would-be assassin spun and began to shoot wildly. Gunshots filled the air as I threw myself down and covered my ears.

Suddenly, a ghostly silence filled the alley. I waited an eternity or so before cautiously getting to my knees and then standing up.

Willie Nelson just lay there, eyes wide-open, with a bloody hole in the center of his chest. Dead.

I looked toward the street. "Mutt?" No answer. I glanced over at my mother. She was still out cold. My legs were shaking so hard I barely remained upright, yet I somehow managed to totter down to the end of the alley. Mutt was lying on the sidewalk, facedown, a dark stain on the sidewalk forming under his head. I heard someone screaming and screaming. I think it was me.

Beep. Beep. Beep. The sound was driving me up the wall. Stormy was sitting next to me, with her arm around my shoulder. She pulled me closer. "It's going to be all right," she whispered.

Anger surged through me. "How do you know that it's going to be all right? He was shot in the head. In the head, Stormy!"

A nurse popped her head in the doorway. "Time to leave. Sorry."

"I can't leave him!"

Her voice was hard as steel. "You can come back in an hour for ten minutes … but only if you can control yourself. You don't do him any good when you act like this."

Stormy pulled me to my feet and maneuvered me toward the door. "She's right, Delilah. Let's get you calmed down so you can visit him again in an hour."

Mother, Granny, Ivy, and Ebony were all waiting for us in the hall.

Mother opened her arms, and I fell into them. "You saved my life," I said through my sobs. "If you hadn't jumped him, I would have been dead.

And then Mutt took down Willie Nelson, but he got shot in the head! And it's all my fault!"

She rocked me back and forth, as I clung to her. "Shh. It's okay, Delilah. It's not your fault. It's okay. God has Mutt safe in His hands."

Ivy turned to me and said, "Come on, let's get Shirley off her feet." She guided us toward the waiting room. "She needs to sit down. As a matter of fact, what she really needs is to lie down, but she's just too stubborn to leave you."

Once we got settled in our chairs, Granny leaned forward so she could see my mother's face. "Shirley, you need to go home. You suffered a concussion, not to mention all the rest of the trauma that you've been through tonight." Granny patted my leg. "Stormy and I will stay with Delilah. We won't leave her alone."

My mother pinched the bridge of her nose. "Thank you. My head is killing me, but we need to stay here until the police finish questioning us."

Right on cue, a big, dark-skinned police officer walked through the door. It was Pete Tanner, Mutt's friend and fellow detective who had interviewed me after I got hit by the truck. He nodded toward us and then scoped out the room. There were several people waiting to visit their family members, and they were all wide-eyed and staring.

"Would you come with me please?" he said to us, and we all stood up. He held up his hand. "Just the two witnesses please. The rest of you can wait here." He flashed a smile before motioning Mother and me toward the door. "I'll bring them back to you shortly."

We followed him down the hall to the consultation room. "Please have a seat." He shut the door, sat down, and pulled out his notebook from one pocket and his recorder from another. He pushed the record button, spoke the date, location, and his name, and asked us to state our names. He cleared his throat and said, "I know you both have had a difficult time, but I need to ask you a few more questions. Please tell me exactly what happened tonight."

"We've been through this a dozen times!" I started to sniffle.

Mother handed me a box of tissues.

"I know." His voice was gentle. "But let's go through it one more time. The last time tonight ... I promise."

"The last time *tonight*?" I squeaked.

He smiled at me. "You caught that, huh. Well, I can't guarantee that my superiors won't want to talk to you later, but if I file a complete report, maybe they will leave you alone."

"You don't believe that, do you, Detective?" my mother asked.

He grinned. "Nope. But it sounded good." He became serious. "Ms. Sampson, Miss Sampson," he nodded first to Mother and then to me, "Look, I take it real personal when somebody shoots a fellow officer, much less when they shoot my best friend. I want to make sure we look in every corner and under every rock. I want to know if Rodney Butler acted alone or if somebody hired him. I want to know why he was waiting for you in that alley, and I want to know why he, or whoever hired him, wanted you dead."

I looked over at my mother, and she nodded. I took a deep breath and told Pete everything, starting with Stormy and my kidnapping when all our troubles began. He listened intently, interrupting when he needed me to clear up some details, and occasionally scribbling something down in his notebook. Then he turned to my mother and interrogated her.

When he finished questioning the two of us, he asked, "Is there anything else either of you would like to add?"

We both shook our heads.

"Please respond verbally," he said.

We both said no.

He leaned forward, clicked off the recorder, looked at his watch, and smiled at me. "I think it's almost time for another visit with Mutt. Have you got it together, Miss Sampson?"

"I … I think so." I looked into his kind eyes. "Delilah. Please call me Delilah."

"Okay, Delilah. When we're not discussing official police business, I'd be glad to be on a first-name basis." He smiled warmly. "And I'm Pete."

Granny and I watched Mutt's chest going up and down. His breathing was regular, which I took as a good sign, but he still wasn't waking up, and that scared me.

Earlier, Mother had joined Granny and me in prayer before she agreed to let Ivy and Ebony take her back to the apartment. Jose, ever faithful, was waiting to escort them home, but he gave me a stern warning before he left. "You ain't to leave without nobody walking with youse. Snake's orders."

Granny faced him and said, "I'll drive her home."

Jose looked her up and down and crossed his arms. "How you gonna protect her? You gotta gun?"

Granny pulled herself up as straight as she could and waved her cane at him. "I don't need a gun, young man. I've got the Lord."

He shook his head. "Yeah but sometimes the Lord uses people to help Him. You wait for somebody." He glared at me. "You hear?"

I nodded.

He looked at my mother and jerked his head toward the door. "Okay, let's go."

"You want us to stay?" Ebony asked.

"No, we'll be okay. Thanks anyway."

Granny spoke up. "Why don't you take Stormy home with you too? I think I just may take Delilah back to my house tonight."

"That probably would be best," Ivy said.

They all gave me a hug and then followed Jose out the door.

Granny and I kept watch and continued to pray quietly. I noticed the nurses were allowing us to stay past the ten-minute limit now that I had my emotions under control. They told me to page them if anything changed, but Mutt was motionless with all kinds of wires and tubes attached to him. The machine next to his bed continued its incessant beep, beep, beep.

Granny grasped her cane and heaved herself out of the hard plastic chair. "I've got to move around. And I think I'll visit the ladies' room while I'm at it."

After she left, I shifted on my chair. My leg was throbbing, but my head hurt so bad I hardly noticed the leg. Then I thought I saw Mutt's finger move and I stood up. *Yes!* His hand twitched a bit, and then he opened his eyes.

I reached for the nurse's call button and pushed it.

"Babe?" he whispered. "What are you doing here?"

I burst into tears. "Oh, Mutt! Are you okay?"

"What happened? My head is killing me." His eyes started to close, but he struggled to keep them open.

"You got shot when you saved Mother and me."

A smile flickered across his face. "That's good." I guess the drugs were making him loopy. His eyelids started to droop, but then they popped open again. "You okay?"

"I'm fine, Mutt. Mother and I are both fine."

His eyes slowly closed.

A nurse came in and grasped his wrist. "His pulse is strong. He's sleeping now. Why don't you let him rest?"

"Is he going to be okay?"

She smiled at me. "He's going to be just fine, honey. That bullet just bounced off that hard head of his. It didn't penetrate his skull, so although he does have a severe concussion and a hideous headache, there's no permanent damage. Now, go home and come back in the morning."

I limped into the hall and saw Granny walking toward me. "He woke up, and he knew me!"

"Praise the Lord!"

"Yes," I said. "Praise the Lord." And then I dissolved into a big ol' puddle of boo-hoo.

After I got ahold of myself, I noticed Jose leaning in a corner, watching.

When he saw me look at him, he pushed off the wall and strolled toward us.

Granny smiled at him. "This dear young man has agreed to walk us to my car. I'm going to check on Clyde one more time, and then I'm taking you home."

I was just too tired to argue.

Once we got to her house, Granny gave me a flannel nightgown and settled me into the same bedroom I had used before.

As I stared into the darkness, it struck me just how amazing the past few hours had been: I was still alive, and so was my mother. My mother loved me enough to die for me, and Mutt was going to be okay. God had been very busy tonight. "Thank you Jesus," I murmured as I drifted off into a dreamless sleep.

Chapter 31

Pete Tanner gingerly perched his large frame on the small wooden folding chair Granny had placed next to Mutt's bed. He looked as ridiculous as one of those big ol' circus bears attempting to ride its tiny bicycle, and if his expression hadn't been so grim, I would have heckled him about it. Instead, for once in my life, I kept my mouth shut, leaned up against the wall, and watched as he squinted in the dim light and tried to read his notes.

Since Mutt still had a bad headache, Granny kept the curtains in his room closed and just a dim light on because any kind of glare bothered him. His head was swathed in bandages, and he sat in bed, propped up by with bunch of pillows, and listened intently as Pete filled him in on the investigation.

"It's a good bet that Butler was hired to kidnap Delilah and her mother, or maybe he was supposed to grab one of them, and the other one was just collateral damage." He paused and glanced up at Mutt. "Haven't figured that one out yet." He went back to his notes. "But we found a cool grand in his pocket, and he wasn't the kind of dude to just be carryin' around that kind of money. I'm guessin' that was a down payment."

They both turned their attention to me. "Are you sure that your mother doesn't know where that memory stick is?" Pete asked. "She's not foolish enough to think she could hold it for ransom or something dumb like that, is she?"

141

It irritated me that neither man completely believed Mother when she said she didn't know anything about the missing flash drive. I was positive that she was telling the truth now that she was a Christian, especially since the theft was putting both of her daughters in danger.

When I looked over at Mutt and saw him grinning, my mood went from irritation to full-out, foot-stomping, door-slamming, bug-eyed, pedal-to-the-metal fury.

Mutt noticed how mad I was and smothered a laugh as he and Pete exchanged glances.

I crossed my arms so I wouldn't be tempted to throw any punches and snarled through clenched teeth, "Look, you two, Mother swore to me that she doesn't have that cursed stick, that she never took it, and that she doesn't know who has it or where it is." My voice kept increasing in volume. "I know she's telling the truth, and I don't appreciate you questioning her honesty." I managed to restrain myself enough that I didn't stomp my foot, although I did consider exiting the room and closing the door hard enough to knock it right off its hinges.

Granny stuck her head in the doorway. "What's all the fussing about?"

I nailed Mutt with a look that dared him to make a comment. "I was discussing the fact that Mutt and Pete don't believe Mother is telling the truth about the stolen memory stick."

Granny turned her attention to the two men. "And why is that?"

Pete cleared his throat. "Well, you see, Granny, it's like this here. Shirley … uh … worked for Stanley Barron for about three months and then suddenly disappeared. That's precisely the time when Barron started searchin' for her and his missing memory stick. Strange coincidence, don't you think?"

Granny snorted. "Sounds to me like the perfect opportunity to set her up, Peter." Granny steadfastly refused to call him Pete, but since he begged her not to use his given name, Gaylord, she always referred to him by his middle name: "Peter."

He turned his full attention toward her. "What do you mean by 'the perfect opportunity'?"

"Don't tell me that you two smart, seasoned officers with all your experience in law enforcement and police investigations never considered the possibility that someone used her disappearance as an opportunity to steal this memory stick, or flash drive, or whatever it's called. Think about it. From the very beginning, you both speculated that it probably was an inside job, isn't that right? Barron would never suspect the real thief if they could convince him that Shirley had taken it."

"That's an intriguing theory." Mutt frowned, deep in thought, and glanced over at his friend. "You know, that is a real possibility. Maybe they're laying low and waiting until Shirley is eliminated. Then Stanley will think it will just blow over ..."

"But it ain't over," Pete said, continuing the train of thought. "They covered their tracks, so all they have to do is wait for the right moment and then, bam, drop the other shoe. Then, they either blackmail Stanley or sell the flash drive to the highest bidder. Rumor has it that not only does it have information about Barron, but it also contains some interesting information about a crime syndicate in Chicago. Stuff like names, dates, account numbers, contracts that were put out, and even where the bodies were buried. Specific info that could not only put Stanley away for good, but that bunch in Chicago too."

The chair creaked ominously as the big man shifted his weight. "You know, Granny, you'd make a mighty fine detective. 'Course your theory may not play out, but it sure does make me look at it from a different angle."

Mutt grinned. "I would have thought of it a too, if I hadn't been shot in the head."

Pete snorted. "Just because that bullet rearranged the few brain cells you got left in that hard skull of yours, it don't mean it's gonna make you any smarter."

The doorbell rang, and Granny went to answer it. Soon, she and Mother appeared in the bedroom doorway. I stood up, gave her a warm hug, and led her to a chair.

"Miss Sampson, how are you doin'?" Pete's huge mitt of a hand engulfed hers. "I heard you are quite the hero."

"Nonsense, Pete. I only did what any mother would have done." She grinned at him. "And it's Shirley to you."

Granny appeared, lugging a chair, and Pete rushed to take it from her. "Let me get that for you," he said. "How many more we gonna need?"

"Well, it depends just how big this party is going to get."

I nestled in the bedspread beside Mutt as he reached for my hand. "We'll only need that one for you, Granny, if you're going to stay."

She glanced over at Mutt, and he nodded. "Wouldn't miss it for the world," she answered.

"You take my chair, Granny. I'm gonna stand for a while."

She smiled up at him as she sat down. "Thank you, Peter. You are a true gentleman."

Actually, I think Pete was afraid to tempt fate by parking his thick frame on that petite chair again. He paused a minute before he started to speak. "Okay, here's the plan, people. We are going to brainstorm and see what we come up with. Granny already posed an interesting theory." He grinned at her. "You want to fill Shirley in on that?"

"Well …" she paused and settled herself on the chair and met my mother's gaze before she continued. "I was wondering if it was possible that after you left for the drug rehabilitation center, someone took advantage of your absence and took the flash drive. Then they made sure that Stanley thought you had stolen it."

Both men were studying Mother's reaction. She sat back and hung her head and seemed to be considering what Granny had said. When she looked up, there was a new awareness in her eyes. "That makes a lot of sense. But why is this particular flash drive so important?"

After Pete explained what information it might contain, she nodded. "That would make it extremely valuable to whoever stole it, wouldn't it?"

"Yep. Do you have a possible suspect in mind, Shirley?"

She leveled her gaze at Pete. "As a matter of fact, I do. There's only one member of that Gang Who Couldn't Shoot Straight who would have enough smarts to pull it off. The rest of them are dumber than a box of rocks and wouldn't even think of planning it, much less how to get away with it."

"And who might that be, Shirley?"

"Clarence. Clarence Murphy, better known as Bull. He's Stanley's private bodyguard, and in his mind, he's big-time. The way he throws his weight around, you'd think he was a member of the Secret Service or something. He's the only one who had access to Stanley 24-7." She stared into space for a moment and then said softly, "Yeah. If anybody close to Stanley stole that stick, it would have had to have been Bull."

Chapter 32

LATER THAT EVENING, I LAY ON TOP OF THE BEDCOVERS, SNUGGLED UP against Mutt. As we talked, we could hear Granny rattling pots and pans and getting ready to cook supper. She had chased me out of the kitchen a few minutes before, saying that Mutt needed company. I don't know whether she was really worried about Mutt being lonely or if she just needed a polite excuse to get me out of her way.

"You know," Mutt said softly, "since I came back to this house to recover from the gunshot, sometimes I can close my eyes—and I'm seven years old again, lying on the bed and waiting for Granny to call me for supper."

"Why don't you ever talk about your childhood? I didn't even know that Granny and your grandfather raised you until she mentioned it to me."

He sighed. "Yeah, well, it's kind of difficult for me to talk about it. It was hard, you know? I was a little kid, leading a normal life, living at home with my mom and dad, going to school, hanging out with my friends, playing Little League baseball, and enjoying a great childhood. But then, one day, my parents just up and disappeared. One minute, they were there, and the next minute, they were gone … forever. No goodbyes, no closure, no answers."

He stared into space for a while, and as he turned his face toward me, it about broke my heart to see the pain in his eyes. "Don't get me wrong. Granny and Papa did a great job of raising me. They took me into their home, and I never felt unwanted. But it must have been hard on them to start all over with a young child. Especially one who was hurting and lost." He shrugged. "Not to mention that their hearts were broken too."

"And they never found out what happened to your parents?"

"No. The police never found so much as a trace of them, other than their car. Of course, this was more than twenty years ago, and they didn't have a lot of the investigating technology they have today. Back then, they didn't have the ability to detect the tiny traces of DNA from a suspect that may have been in the interior of the car. And my folks, like a lot of people in those days, didn't own a cell phone, which eliminated the chance of tracking it. My mother's purse was left on the front seat, and there was never any activity on either of their credit cards.

"So, Mom and Dad's car was the only thing connected to the case that the police ever turned up. It had been abandoned on a dirt road, way out in the country, where my parents normally would have never gone. There were no fingerprints, no witnesses, and no clues. They just disappeared without a trace."

"And left behind a little boy who couldn't understand why his parents had gone away and never came back," I said softly.

"Yeah." Mutt was quiet for a moment and then grinned. "But, as you can imagine, being raised by Granny was a riot. She used to say that she wasn't entering her second childhood because she never outgrew her first. She always had time for me, and she was my best friend when I needed her the most. Then, after a while, she helped me come out of my shell so I could make friends at school with kids my own age.

"She kind of pushed me to join Little League, but I eventually loved it—and she was my loudest cheerleader at every one of my ball games. Papa would always clap and whistle when I came up to bat." He chuckled. "But Granny would yell all kinds of smack at the umpire ... all in good fun, of course ... like, 'Open your eyes, ump! That was no strike! It was a mile high!'" He smiled at the memory. "And if I happened to connect my bat with the ball, she would scream, 'Run, Clyde! Run!' It didn't matter even if it was a foul ball or a pop-up that had already been caught. Granny didn't care; she just would holler for me to run."

Since he seemed to be lost in his thoughts, I waited a while before I picked the conversation back up. "Do you remember much about your parents?"

He shrugged. "Not too much because, after all, I was only seven when they disappeared. I do remember my dad playing ball with me in our front yard though." He closed his eyes for a moment before he continued in a soft, almost dreamy voice. "My strongest memories of my mom were when she worked in the kitchen. I used to do my homework at the kitchen table while she cooked dinner. And she always hummed while she cooked."

There was a long pause. Finally, I asked, "What did your mom and your dad do for a living?"

"Mom was an elementary school teacher, and Dad was a CPA for Dickens & Sons, a small accounting company. They didn't make a lot of money, but it was enough. We had a good life." He paused for a moment and then turned back to me. "Soon after I moved in, Bella came to live with Granny and Papa too, so not only did they have a rambunctious little boy to raise; they also had to deal with a troubled young woman too."

"Your grandparents also raised Bella?"

"No. She was already in her late teens when she moved in."

"But why?"

"Bella was … uh … always different. Always unhappy, couldn't make friends, and not very attractive. She just couldn't fit in, and she didn't get along with her mom very well either. But Granny just accepted her the way she was and didn't try to change her into something she wasn't. She would argue with my Aunt Lydia that Bella was exactly the way God wanted her to be, so people should stop trying to make her into someone different. She used to say that the only thing accomplished by jamming a square peg into a round hole is that you damage the peg." He grinned. "It's a wonder Bella and I didn't drive Granny and Papa completely over the edge, especially the way we would fuss and argue all the time."

"And you still argue and fuss at each other."

"Yep, we still do." He chuckled. "Anyway, after a few years, Bella found her life's calling, went back to school, got a degree, and began a life of her own."

"What *is* her life's calling?"

"Research. She specializes in canine diseases."

"Oh. And she's happy now?"

"I think so, in her own way. It's just her, her dogs, and her computer. She doesn't have to interact with people, and her work benefits dogs, so she seems content. As Granny always says, 'Bella is Bella, and there's no use in trying to change her.'"

I thought about my next question, but since it didn't seem like there was any diplomatic way to put it, I just said, "So, why did your parents name you Clyde?"

He laughed. "It's one of the mysteries of life. I'm named after mother's father. From what I'm told, she was adamant about naming her firstborn son after her dad. I often wonder if she really thought the whole thing through. If she had, maybe Clyde would have been my middle name."

"So, what is your middle name?"

He grimaced. "I was named after mother's grandfather ... Simon."

Clyde S. Dale? Oh, brother. I guess the name "Delilah Sampson" pales in comparison.

Chapter 33

THE FIVE OF US WOMEN WERE STARING AT THE PILE OF PAPERS ON OUR
kitchen table.

When Ivy cleared her throat, four sets of eyes locked onto her. "Okay,
Delilah, we all know you can't go back to waitressing with that leg of
yours ... at least not for a long time."

Everyone looked at me and nodded.

"And you always whine about not being able to get a decent job because
you don't have a convincing-looking ID." She waved a hand toward the
stack in the middle of the table. "So, Snake decided to help you out and
provide you and Stormy with all the documents you need." She reached over
and began sorting through them. "Here are your birth certificates, Social
Security cards, driver's licenses, school records, high school diplomas, work
histories, and referrals. Everything you could possibly need."

I sat back, still reeling from the shock of it all. "But ... but are these
legal?"

Everyone stared at me in disbelief."

You're kidding, right?" Ivy asked.

"But what will Mutt say?"

"Look, Delilah, Snake decided you needed some help, so he put himself
out to get you all of this. He even gave you and Stormy middle names.
You are now Delilah Marie, and your sister is Stormy Rose." She paused.
"Snake's mother's name was Rosemarie."

Our gazes locked as she waited for this bit of information to sink in.

"He went through a lot of trouble for you, and you'd better appreciate it." She stared me down until I dropped my eyes. "And you best leave Mutt out of this," she growled.

I was torn about what to do, but Stormy apparently felt no such compunction. In fact, she seemed delighted. "Stormy Rose? I like it! And to think he used his own mother's name." She shuffled through the papers. "Oh look, I graduated high school with honors."

"You're only sixteen. You haven't graduated yet," I grumbled.

She studied the documents as she twirled her midnight-black hair around her finger and grinned. "Accelerated classes. I graduated early."

Swell.

Stormy gave a little squeal. "I even have a driver's license!"

"You don't know how to drive."

"I'll teach her," Ivy said. She sat up straight in her chair, and her expression seemed to dare me to object.

I glared at her. "Then I guess you better teach me too."

She shrugged and settled back in her seat. "Sure."

"I'll teach them to drive." This was the first comment Mother made since Ivy had us gather in the kitchen. "It's the least I can do." She traced her finger over the scratches that spider-webbed across the top of the table. "But I'll need to borrow your car."

"Sure, Shirley. We can figure out a schedule so you can use it."

"Just until I teach the girls how to drive."

Ivy nodded.

I tried to corral my racing thoughts. *I can look for a decent job now. Granny already mentioned a friend of hers who wants to hire a clerk for her bookstore. Now, there's a job I would really love. But what about Mutt? He'll be furious when he finds out that Snake got us all these documents.* I searched my brain. *Did I ever tell him that I never had a real birth certificate or a Social Security card? I must have mentioned it, but I can't remember. And even if I didn't, do I want to keep these papers a secret from him? Well, yeah, actually, if I am truthful with myself, I guess I do.*

I pulled out the birth certificate. It had my name, Delilah Marie Sampson, and the date of birth, September 28. For the first time in my life, I had an actual birthday. I glanced over at my sister. "When is your birthday, Stormy?"

She sorted through the papers until she found the certificate. "June 14. Isn't that great? June is the perfect month for me with all the beautiful flowers, the gardens starting to grow, and the trees so pretty with their green leaves. I love it!"

Mother watched her youngest daughter quietly, and tears filled her eyes. "I never realized …"

"You never realized that your daughters needed actual birthdays?" Ebony snapped. "You never realized they needed an identity of their own? Come on, Shirley. Give me a break."

The tears overflowed and trickled down our mother's cheeks. "Yeah, you're right, Ebony. I'm a totally self-centered person who never thought of anyone but myself." She turned and faced Stormy and me. "I'm so sorry, girls. Believe it or not, I always loved you." She hung her head and spoke so quietly that we almost didn't hear what she said next. "I loved you, but I guess I loved my drugs even more. I would feel guilty and swear to myself that I would be a better mother, but somehow, the drugs always got in the way."

"A *better* mother?" Stormy's laugh was laced with bitterness. "Let's face it, Shirley, you were never any kind of a mother at all. Delilah is my mother. She always *was* my mother, and she *will always* be my mother." She slid her chair back and stood up. "Shirley, you were nothing but a stoned-out druggie who drifted in and out of our lives. And that's all you'll ever be." She walked out and slammed the door.

We sat in stunned silence and just stared at each other.

After a long pause, my mother began to cry.

Ivy gave her a few awkward pats on her shoulder and then pushed back from the table and left.

Ebony shrugged and got up. "Guess we best go see if we can find Stormy."

That left just Mother and me. I knew I should comfort her, but I just couldn't make myself do it. I guess all the hurt accumulated over the years had managed to burrow into my heart like a tick. It was stuck tight, and Shirley couldn't remove it with a few nice remarks and a couple of driving lessons. I was surprised at the intense anger I felt. I thought I'd forgiven her. I had *said* I'd forgiven her, but I guess I really hadn't, at least not completely. In fact, if I were to be brutally honest with myself, I'd admit that I hadn't truly forgiven her from my heart. I suppose I needed to talk to Granny about it, and to God too.

"I'm going to take a shower," I said. I went into the bedroom to gather my clothes and then escaped to the bathroom, leaving her sitting at the table, alone.

Chapter 34

IT WOULD BE A MIRACLE IF GOD DIDN'T STRIKE ME DEAD RIGHT IN THE middle of Mrs. Anna Marple's office. As a matter of fact, it probably was a given that it *would* happen, and it was only a matter of how. Would I be hit with a bolt of lightning, would the earth open up under my feet, or would I just swallow my tongue and strangle myself to death? I stuffed my hands into my pockets so the gray-headed lady behind the desk wouldn't see how badly they were shaking as I watched her examine my bogus paperwork.

Then, just when I thought I would hyperventilate until I passed out, she looked up and smiled. "Well, it looks like everything is in order. Shall we begin your training?"

Somehow, I managed not to collapse from relief and followed her out to the huge main room of the bookstore. I slowly turned 360 degrees, trying to take it all in. When I turned back to Mrs. Marple, I noticed a twinkle in her eyes. "How many books do you have in here?" I whispered.

She laughed. "Honey, this isn't a library, so you can talk in a normal voice."

When I blushed at her words, she immediately patted my arm. "I'm not fussing at you, sweetie. I'm sure this is a bit overwhelming when you see it for the first time."

I just nodded.

"Hannah mentioned that you are a voracious reader, is that right?"

"Yes, ma'am." She seemed to expect a longer answer, so I added,

"I practically live at the library. I've had a library card ever since I can remember."

She smiled. "That's wonderful. What types of books interest you? Do you have any favorite authors?"

As we began to discuss my passion for reading, my shyness magically disappeared. We wandered around the store, and she would ask me what I knew about certain authors and genres. When I finally glanced up at the clock, I was shocked to see that more than an hour had gone by.

Mrs. Marple grinned broadly. "You certainly have eclectic tastes and are quite knowledgeable about a wide spectrum of books and their authors. I am sure you will fit into the Reading Nook's family perfectly." She strode across the room. "Now, let me show you how to run the cash register."

I was in seventh heaven working at the bookstore. I never realized how much someone could love their job. Every morning, I woke up full of anticipation for what the day would bring, and on the days when I wasn't working, I felt out of sorts and kind of lost. Mrs. Marple was a wonderful boss and thank goodness I was a fast learner, so it wasn't long before I was able to "go solo." I've had gotten the routine down pat and could tend to the store by myself.

Mrs. Marple would often come into the store, pull up a rocking chair, and chat with me. As I waited on customers or puttered around, dusting, restocking, and straightening up the books, she talked about how she and her husband had started the business thirty years ago. She described how they gradually began to add different amenities, such as quiet reading corners complete with rocking chairs. At first, they set up a coffee machine and provided a few complimentary snacks for their customers. Over time, that grew in popularity, and they eventually added a small coffee shop.

Recently, their daughter had developed a website for the Reading Nook that reached potential customers all over the country. Their efforts, plus a lot of hard work, helped the business expand until it became the largest bookstore in the state, and it was fast becoming one of the largest in the country.

But now, even though they weren't even close to retirement age, they wanted to slow down a bit. Mrs. Marple said that their daughter would take over the business someday, but for the moment, she just wanted to stay home and raise her young children.

One day, Mrs. Marple mentioned that they were looking for an experienced bookkeeper, and that caught my attention. "My mother is a bookkeeper," I said.

"Oh, really? Then why don't you have her come by for an interview?"

Mother was hired immediately, and although I knew Mother was a certified CPA, I never realized she was such a wiz with numbers. As soon as Mrs. Marple hired her, she jumped right in.

"Who in the world did your books?" she grumbled.

"Ah ... that would be Charlie, my husband. He has his own system."

"How in heaven did he ever do your taxes? This is a disaster!" Mother looked like she wanted to pull her hair out. "It's a wonder that the IRS didn't break down your door and haul him off to jail! Thank goodness they never did an audit of your business."

"Charlie always made sure we paid all the taxes we owed." Mrs. Marple sniffed. She looked like she was starting to regret hiring this rather outspoken bookkeeper. "He is a very honest person," she added.

Mother sighed. "I'm sure he *is* honest, Mrs. Marple. It's just there are many different business deductions allowed, and I doubt if he took advantage of them. And there is supposed to be a set way for a business to record their transactions and not this ... weird modus operandi." She stood up and then flopped back down in the chair and held up her hands in a hopeless gesture. "It's going to take me a while to figure out this mess and get it to conform to all the government regulations."

"Will you be able to do it?"

Mother grinned at her. "Of course. I love a challenge."

Eventually, we fell into a nice routine. Mother and I would catch the bus and ride to work together. At lunchtime, we would sit in the back of the store and eat our brown-bag lunches in between waiting on customers. We had some great talks, and I felt the years of resentment slowly melting away. It was too bad that Stormy still held her at arm's length, but we both were hopeful that she would come around, someday.

Once, the subject of Mutt and his family came up. We talked about his parents and their mysterious disappearance. We also chatted about his mother being a schoolteacher. When I mentioned that his father was also a CPA, Mother asked, "Oh? What company did his dad work for?"

"It was Dickens & Sons. I remember the name because it reminded me of Charles Dickens." I glanced up and was surprised to see that Mother's hand, still clutching her sandwich, was frozen halfway to her mouth.

"What did you say?" she asked.

Her reaction left me confused. "Dickens & Sons. Why?"

"It's just … well, Stanley Barron mentioned that firm to me once. He … he didn't like them. He said that they tried to gather evidence in order to put him in jail, so he had to 'take care of the situation.'"

"What did he mean by that?"

"I don't know. I never paid much attention to his ramblings." She stared at me for a moment. "How long ago did Mutt's parents disappear?"

"It's been over twenty years now." I frowned at the disturbed expression on her face. "What are you thinking?"

She shrugged. "Nothing. I guess it's just a strange coincidence."

Chapter 35

I CAN LOOK BACK ON IT NOW AND LAUGH, BUT I REMEMBER HOW I NEARLY wigged out the first time Granny and Mutt took me to their church, Open Door to Grace. Keep in mind that I had never even been inside of a church building in my entire life, so this was really jumping off into the deep end for me.

First of all, it wasn't just a big church; it was humongous! It was bigger than any theater you can imagine with acres and acres of seats set in this big ol' auditorium that sloped down to a stage the size of a football field ... or so it seemed to me. Mutt told me that the funny kind of stand in the middle of the stage was called the pulpit, and it was where the preacher would speak. On the left, there was an area with a piano, drums, guitars, and other instruments where the band would be playing. Behind all that, there were chairs on two tiers, but I couldn't guess what they were for.

Just before the service started, the stage started filling up with musicians, and then people dressed in long robes marched in and sat on the chairs in the back.

Mutt pointed to a screen mounted up on the wall and told me that it would display the lyrics to the songs so I could sing along.

Yeah, sure I would.

A guy came out and welcomed everybody and then yammered on and on about this and that, but I really wasn't paying much attention. I was still looking around when a dark-skinned man in jeans and a turtleneck sweater took his place behind the pulpit.

Granny whispered to me that he was Pastor Tim Alexander.

The band started playing, and the entire crowd stood up, and all people began singing and clapping. It sounded pretty good, and I was surprised to hear Mutt's amazing baritone. I had never realized what a beautiful singing voice he had or that Granny's soft soprano would sound so sweet.

I was kind of enjoying the music as they sang a bunch of songs, and then everything broke loose. The next thing I knew, people started dancing! No kidding! They were dancing in church! People started shouting, "Praise God!" and "Hallelujah!" and raising their arms up toward the ceiling.

When I turned to Mutt, he had his arms raised, and tears were streaming down his cheeks. That really spooked me, and I was just about to bolt for the door when Granny pulled me into a big hug and whispered, "It's okay honey. We're just telling the Lord how much we love Him."

That calmed me down some, so by the time the preacher started talking, I was able to settle in and listen. Wow! It felt like he was talking directly to me. He talked about the prodigal son. I had already read about that in my Bible, but the story came alive for me when he told it. Then he did what he called an altar call, and the next thing I knew, I was bawling like a baby and walking down the aisle with Mutt and Granny at my side. We all knelt, and the preacher put his hand on my head and began to pray. It felt like … I don't know … I guess it felt like somebody had dumped a big ol' bucket of love on my head. I felt warm all over, and I felt loved. *Really* loved.

I wish I could say I've done a complete 180-degree turn in my life, but to be honest, I still struggle at times. I still get ugly and snap at people. I still cuss on occasion when I'm aggravated. I forget to read my Bible every day, and I don't pray as much as I should. But, overall, my life is different, and I'm a better person now, for sure.

After a few weeks, I felt more comfortable about going to church. Everyone was so friendly, and they made me feel welcomed. I began clapping in time with the music, and I even started singing along. Next thing I knew, I was looking forward to Sundays. I invited Mother to come, and I was tickled when she fit right in. Now, every Sunday, Granny and Mutt pick us up so we can attend services with them.

When I stand between Mutt and Mother, it sounds like angels singing. The preacher always seems to have a good message, and it doesn't even bother me anymore when people in the congregation holler, "Amen!" or "Preach it, brother!" I love when we all go home to discuss the sermon and what it meant. Granny and Mutt always have amazing insights about things I hadn't even thought of.

You know, when you don't have any extra money, you need to find ways to entertain yourself that don't cost anything. We sang together because, as Mother said, "Talk may be cheap, but singing is free." It just seemed natural that Mother and I would start to sing the songs we had learned in church when we were at home.

At first Stormy, Ivy, and Ebony would grumble about our musical selections, but the tunes were so lively and so much fun to sing that they eventually joined in.

After weeks of singing about Jesus, Stormy started to ask questions about the meaning of some of the lyrics. Mother and I answered as best we could, but we were both what the church people called "baby Christians," and many of the things she wanted us to explain were over our heads. That's why Granny and Mutt decided to start a kind of "Sunday school" at our apartment, even though it usually wasn't held on Sundays. They tried to come at least once a week to discuss the Bible and answer all of Stormy's questions. Granny and Mutt did their best to help her understand, and my sister seemed quite interested in what they had to say.

I could see her gradually softening, and the day finally came when Stormy agreed to come to church with us the following Sunday. I sat down with her and warned her about what to expect so she did pretty good the first time she attended. The church warmly welcomed her and after several weeks, Stormy accepted Jesus as her Lord and Savior and soon became involved with a group of other young people. I was so happy that I thought I would burst!

Even Ivy and Ebony have started to ask questions. Sometimes they join in our discussions about the Bible, but I'm taking it nice and slow with those two, so they don't get scared off. I want to make sure they are ready before inviting them to church. Come to think about it, I'm not really sure whether the *church* is ready for *them*.

Pastor Tim assures me that everyone is welcomed at Open Door to Grace, but I wonder what the reaction will be when Ebony walks in dressed in one of her low-cut, skintight, super-revealing outfits. She should cause quite a sensation, and I don't know how people will react to Ivy's poor scarred face. We're used to it, but for someone who is seeing her for the first time ... well, she is very sensitive about how she looks.

Guess I'll just do what Granny suggests and wait for the Lord's leading.

Chapter 36

Now that "Willie Nelson" was dead, and Boris and Razor were out of the picture, I guess I felt invincible. After all, I had survived two attempts on my life, and except for a slight temporary limp, I was none the worse for wear.

The search for the missing memory stick had faded into the background, and I was busy working on my new job and my new life—a life that revolved around Mutt. Little did I know that the light I thought I saw at the end of the tunnel was, in reality, the headlight of an oncoming locomotive.

One night, I was, as Ivy put it, "all gussied up" and waiting for Mutt to arrive. But when he knocked, I could see something was wrong as soon as I opened the door. Majorly wrong. The thunderous expression on his face made my stomach twist.

He took my hand, pulled me out into the hall, and hissed in my ear, "Eddie just told me something, and we need to talk … privately."

I knew about Eddie and recently had met him. Mutt has always talked about a program called Helping Hearts, that helped underprivileged and at-risk teens. Mutt was deeply involved and volunteered countless hours mentoring young people, and those who had turned eighteen and "aged out" of the foster care program. Many of them were former gang members. Graduates of the Helping Hearts program received scholarships, training for job interviews, suitable clothes for work, and sometimes assistance with rent and things like that. Mutt donated every spare penny he had to the program, which probably explained why he still drove that rust-bucket of a car.

Eddie was one of the teens who Mutt met through Helping Hearts, or "Double H" as the kids dubbed it, and he was one of Mutt's favorites. He had survived a horrendous childhood that left him emotionally scarred. Last year, Eddie had taken a gigantic step forward and quit his gang. Now it seemed as though he had finally got it together and was heading in the right direction. I think Mutt felt particularly close to Eddie and spent a lot of time with him. Lately, he has been tutoring him so he can pass his SAT and enter college next fall.

I was thinking about all this and wondering what Eddie had to do with Mutt's foul mood. He had a firm grip on my arm as he propelled me down the steps, across the street, and into a small park. We had the park to ourselves since you didn't go there after dark unless you were looking for trouble. With the way Mutt's jaw was set, and the angry glitter in his eyes when he sat me down on a bench under a streetlight, I figured that somehow or other, I had managed to find all the trouble I could handle.

"What's going on, Mutt?"

"That's what I want to know. Just what are you and your mother mixed up in, Delilah?"

I glared at him for a moment. *How could he possibly have found out about the phony IDs?* I opened my mouth to ask, but he interrupted.

"Eddie told me that there is a contract out on both you and your mother for ten grand apiece." He was quivering with rage.

My jaw nearly hit the ground. "What are you talking about?"

"Delilah, this is no time to play games. Eddie said that a professional gun from Chicago has been hired with the expressed purpose of taking out you and Shirley." Mutt looked madder than I had ever seen him. "You need to come clean and tell me exactly what is going on and what you two are involved in."

Tears started to fill my eyes. "How can you accuse me of being dirty? Don't you know me well enough by now?"

"Oh, no you don't. You're not pulling that trick on me, Delilah."

"Trick? What trick?"

"By trying to twist my question around to make me out to be the bad guy. You didn't forget that I'm a cop who is trained to interrogate people, did you? Now, answer the question. What are you and your mom into?"

My entire world was spinning out of control, yet I still had no idea what Mutt was talking about. "Mother and I are working at the bookstore. We started a few weeks ago, but it's all legit. I swear it is, Mutt." I thought about it for a minute, and then I asked, "How come Eddie knows about this, anyway? He's just a kid."

"You know that Eddie comes from a bad home situation. I already told you about how his mother committed suicide, and then his father was killed in a mob hit. So, the only family he has left is that no-good uncle of his who's mixed up with local drug dealers. I've tried to get Eddie to break ties with him, but you know what they say: 'Blood is thicker than water.'"

Mutt started to pace in front of the bench, and then he paused in front of me. His voice vibrated with tension. "Eddie heard his uncle talking on the phone, complaining about how he wanted to get a piece of the action, but he couldn't because the mob had already hired somebody out of Chicago.

"Since he knows we are dating, Eddie came and told me what he had overheard." He started to pace again. "Delilah, a hired gun doesn't come cheap, and whoever is behind all this isn't playing games. They mean business!" He ran his fingers through his hair. "Listen to me, Delilah, you are in way over your head. You've got to tell me everything, and you can't hold anything back."

He crouched down, took my hand, and gently stroked it. "Delilah, you know I love you, and nothing will ever change that, but you have got to tell me the truth. Whatever you're into, whatever the consequences are, we'll get through it together."

"But, Mutt, I really don't know what you're talking about. Honest! I don't have a clue!"

He hung his head for a moment, and then he looked up and met my gaze. He studied my face in the streetlamp's harsh light for a while and then nodded. "Okay, babe, I believe you. But something's going down, and we've got to figure out why it's happening." He flopped down on the bench beside me. "This is serious, Delilah. Not only is your life in danger, but so is your mother's and the lives of everyone else around you. You all are at risk of being killed. And that includes your sister, your friends, and even my own grandmother."

"And you too," I added with a shaky voice.

He nodded. "Yep. These hired guns are notorious for overkill. Now, I want you to tell me everything. I don't care how unimportant it seems."

I took a deep breath and told him about the phony IDs that Snake had supplied. He just shook his head. "But why, Delilah? Why would you need a different identity?"

"It's not a *different* identity, Mutt. Stormy and I never had an official identity in the first place. We weren't born in a hospital, and there wasn't a doctor involved, so our births were never recorded. And since Mother didn't register us for school or anything, there was never a record of us."

He stared at me in disbelief. "So, it's like you never existed?"

I nodded. "I couldn't get a good job because I needed a Social Security number, and I didn't know how to get a Social Security card. Besides, I was afraid that I'd get into trouble for not paying taxes and stuff. And then there's the fact that I've never been to school. That lack of an education alone keeps me from even being considered for a decent job. I eventually got a phony ID, but it's so obviously fake that I'm amazed that anyone was fooled by it. Anyway, Ivy told Snake about our situation, and that's when he decided to help Stormy and me. He got us all the documents we needed."

Mutt rubbed his face with both hands and sighed. "Oh, boy. Well, I guess we'll have to deal with all of that later. For now, we need to figure out why somebody wants you dead."

His words brought me up short, and I felt a chill run up and down my spine. "I don't know, Mutt. I guess it must have something to do with Stanley Barron's memory stick. I mean, what else could it possibly be?"

Chapter 37

WELL, THE DAY HAS FINALLY COME. I HONESTLY DIDN'T THINK IT EVER would, but sure enough, this Sunday morning, Granny is driving Mother, Stormy, and "the girls" to church. Mutt and I are following in his car. I had never pictured this scenario in my wildest dreams, but somehow ... well, Granny said it was all God's doing, and she must be right 'cause I can't imagine it happening any other way.

Once we found out that Ivy and Ebony might attend church services with us, Mutt went and had a long talk with the pastor, explaining the situation and warning him what to expect. Pastor Tim promised he would "advise the troops" so that the congregation would be ready to receive their unconventional visitors with "love and grace." And I'll tell you what, considering the circumstances, the old saying, "From his lips to God's ear," is very appropriate.

As Granny would put it, the seeds of this momentous occasion were sown a few weeks ago when Stormy walked down the aisle of our church and accepted Jesus Christ as her Savior. Ever since then, she's been so bubbly and jubilant that it's hard not to be affected. I don't care how dark of a mood you are in, just being around her, listening to her sing, hearing her laugh, and seeing the joy on her face will change your entire outlook.

At first, Ivy and Ebony both tried to avoid her. They called her "Little Miss Sunshine" and said that her "super-cheerfulness" grated on their last nerve. But as time went by and Stormy's volatile temperament didn't resurface, they began asking why she was so happy. Since Stormy has never been shy about sharing her thoughts, she spoke about both her newly found faith and the Gospel with her typical enthusiasm. I just sat back and watched in amazement as my friends were drawn in by the strength of my little sister's passion for the Lord.

I nearly fell over when Ivy and Ebony accepted Stormy's invitation to come to church with us. And today was the big day.

To be honest, I had fully expected that they would back out at the last minute. So, when I came out of the bathroom this morning, I couldn't believe what was going on. Ivy and Ebony were in a serious discussion with Stormy about which clothes in their wardrobe were appropriate "church clothes." It was kind of funny how intense they were, but I guess it was important to them to look nice for their first visit to church.

One of them would hold up a skimpy skirt or a very revealing blouse, and Stormy would shake her head. Eventually, I decided to join in, and after going through my and Stormy's paltry selection of clothes, we found a decent outfit for Ivy.

Ebony was another matter. She put her hand on her hip, jutted out her jaw, and dug in her heels. "I ain't wearing no sorry white-girl clothes. Next thing yah know, you'll be wanting me to straighten my hair and wear them nasty shoes. Uh-uh. Ain't no way! If they can't take me the way I am, then I don't wanna be there."

After sorting through all her clothes, we chose a gold satin blouse that kept her boobs in check, more or less … if the buttons held out. We discovered that agreeing on a skirt was a little more difficult. Finally, we decided on the longest skirt she owned: a ruby red spandex mini that only reached down a couple of inches below her behind. At least she didn't flash her thongs every time she moved, so we figured it wasn't too scandalous. Besides, the bright red color matched Ebony's hair.

As we drove toward the church, I was so nervous that I thought I would puke. I dearly wished I had brought a barf bag, but I gritted my teeth and managed to hold on until we arrived without causing a disaster. I was worried because I knew this was the one and only chance for Ivy and Ebony to attend church. If so much as *one* person was unkind, it would all be over. I was hyperventilating as we walked down the sidewalk, and all I could do was pray, "Please, God. Please, God."

Pastor Tim was waiting at the door. I thought I saw a flash of panic in his eyes when he saw Ebony's outfit, but he smiled warmly and held out his hand. "Welcome, sisters! I'm so glad you were able to come today. Come on in. There are some people I want you to meet."

We followed him into the vestibule where several women were waiting. If they were shocked by their visitors' appearances, they didn't show it. They welcomed them with warm smiles and hugs.

Pastor Tim guided us over to a beautiful, tall, dark-skinned woman. "I want you to meet Naomi Tanner," he said.

She clasped Ivy's hand. "I'm Pete Tanner's wife, and I'm so happy to meet you," she said. We had met before, so she and I just exchanged smiles before she turned her attention back to Ivy.

An elderly woman did something that brought tears to every person in the room. She walked up to Ivy, took her scarred face into her gnarled hands, and said, "Oh, you sweet child." She tenderly kissed both her cheeks and her forehead.

When Ivy began to sob, the woman pulled her into a hug and rocked her back and forth. "Come, dear," she said softly. "Let's find a seat before the service starts. There is so much I want to talk to you about."

A young woman wearing a colorful traditional African dress and a big smile hooked her arm in Ebony's. "Hey, girl, I'm Makena Branson." She looked Ebony up and down. "I see you love bright colors too. That blouse is just perfect for your skin tone."

Ebony grinned. "I don't wear no sorry vanilla colors, that's for sure." Ebony glanced around and gestured for Stormy to join them. The three of them continued to chat as Naomi Tanner corralled everybody together and herded the women through the sanctuary doors.

Pastor Tim gave us a thumbs-up. "Gotta go and prepare to preach the Word. See y'all later."

Mutt, Granny, and I just stood there and stared at each other.

Granny laughed and said, "Well, after all my worrying, I guess the Lord had it all in hand after all. I should have known."

Mutt winked at her. "Oh, ye of little faith."

"Oh, hush up, boy." She gave him a playful slap on the arm. "Let's go in and grab some seats before we end up having to sit in the balcony."

"But there isn't any balcony, Granny," I said.

She gave me a sly smile and started toward the doors. "All the more reason to get a move on."

After the services, Ebony came out arm in arm with her new friend on one side and Stormy on the other. She was grinning from ear to ear. "Hey! How come you didn't tell me that preacher of yours was a brother?"

I shrugged. "It didn't seem important. So, what did you think of his message?"

"He was pretty good. Could really talk, yah know? It was pretty interesting."

"So, will you come back?"

"Yeah. Makena and me hit it off real good. We're gonna sit together again next week." Ebony grinned. "She said she might even let me borrow one of them African dresses of hers to wear."

"I sure will, and you'll look stunning. Now, come on, sisters," Makena said as she led Ebony and Stormy down the hall. "There's coffee and doughnuts waiting, and there's some people I want you to meet."

As Granny, Mutt, and I were waiting for Ivy to come out, a woman came through the sanctuary doors and paused to speak to us. "If you are looking for your friend, she's with Miss Martha and the pastor. I think they'll be a while, so why don't you go down to the fellowship hall and grab yourselves some coffee and doughnuts."

Mutt gave Granny a hug as tears filled her eyes. "Oh my," she said in a shaky voice. "Isn't the Lord amazing?"

"Well, I'll admit I was concerned," Mutt said. "Sometimes I forget that nothing is impossible with God." He looked up toward heaven, and I could hear the joy in his voice as he said, "Thank You, Jesus!"

We gave each other high fives, and then the three of us headed for the fellowship hall. Besides, the coffee and doughnuts were calling our names.

Chapter 38

As I was washing dishes and looking out the small kitchen window, I noticed a strange little red dot dancing across my chest. My brain kicked in, and I suddenly realized what it was. I had seen enough TV shows to know that someone with a rifle was aiming at my heart. I jerked back and spun around just as the window exploded. I fell to the floor in a shower of glass and lay stunned for a moment until I became aware of a big ol' shard of glass sticking out of my arm. I panicked and yanked it out, it but as soon as I did, I realized that was a big mistake.

Oh, crud. I shouldn't have done that, I thought. I reached up, grabbed a dish towel from the counter, and attempted to stem the bleeding, but it didn't help—not even a little bit. I was in big trouble.

Gradually, I became aware of a bunch of shouting, and someone was pounding on the apartment door. I knew that I probably should let them in, but by then, my brain was so full of cobwebs, I couldn't figure out where the door was, much less how to get up and open it. I was kind of drifting away when I heard the lock turn.

Someone ran into the kitchen, and a face appeared through the mist.

"Jose?" I whispered. "What are you doing here?" I felt something tight on my arm, and as someone lifted me off the floor, everything went black.

The smell of antiseptic assailed my nostrils, and I could hear a familiar beep, beep, beep. *Oh, crud, I'm back in the hospital again.*

When I managed to pry my eyes open, Mutt's face was just inches from mine. "Delilah? Are you awake, babe?"

"What … what happened?"

He stroked my hair and then leaned over and kissed my forehead. "Don't worry about it right now. Get some rest, and we'll talk later."

My eyes popped open. "Did I get shot?"

"No, babe. You got shot at. They missed, but a piece of window glass embedded in your arm and severed an artery. Thank goodness Jose got you to the hospital in time. You're going to be fine."

I looked past Mutt and saw Jose wearing a badly stained shirt. He was leaning against the wall, arms crossed, and staring at me.

"Jose!" I croaked. "You're hurt."

He looked confused for a moment, and then he looked down at his clothes and shook his head. "This ain't my blood. It's yours."

I felt even more lightheaded. "Your shirt's ruined! I'm so sorry. I'll buy you another one." I realized how dumb that sounded as soon as I said it, so I tried again. "I mean, thank you for saving my life." I tried to say more, but my brain decided it was time to shut down, and overwhelming sleep washed over me.

That evening I woke up to a big, black thundercloud in the form of a certain Detective G. P. Tanner sitting next to my bed. As usual, he had his notebook out, and the recorder was sitting on the bedside table at the ready. "Okay, Delilah. You know the routine." He sounded weary. "Tell me exactly what happened."

"Why can't I just go home?"

The cloud got darker, and I expected lightning bolts to shoot out of it at any moment. "That's not an option. That hired gun found you so, you can't go home."

"But …"

"You were almost assassinated, Delilah! You are *not* going home!"

The door to my hospital room opened, and Mutt walked in. "Take it easy, Pete. I could hear you all the way down the hall." He came over to my bedside and I welcomed him with a kiss.

Pete rubbed the back of his neck. "Sorry."

I reached over and took hold of his enormous hand. "I know you're upset about what happened, Pete. I'll try to answer your questions, but I don't think I'll be much help because it happened so fast."

He smiled at me and squeezed my fingers before he released my hand and clicked on the recorder. After recording the basic information needed before starting the interview, he turned to me and said, "Okay, Delilah, tell me what you remember."

"Well, I was doing dishes when I noticed the red dot on my chest, and I ducked. The next thing I knew, the window exploded, and there was glass everywhere. Then Jose was leaning over me." I searched my memory for a while, but I couldn't come up with anything else. "Then I woke up in the hospital. That's all I can remember. Sorry."

He and Mutt exchanged glances, and Pete sighed. "High-powered rifle with a tactical scope. It was our hired gun, for sure."

There was a soft knock on the door, and Mutt went over and opened it. "Good timing, Jose. Come on in. Detective Tanner has just finished taking Delilah's statement."

The men all shook hands, and Jose turned his attention to me. "You doing okay?"

"I'm fine, Jose. Thank you. I owe you my life."

He shrugged. "Just took you to the hospital. That's all."

"But if you hadn't done that, I'd be dead."

Mutt pulled him into a bear hug and slapped his back. "Yeah, Jose. I owe you a big one."

As he pulled away, Jose hung his head and muttered, "It weren't nothing."

Pete sat back down and turned the recorder back on. "Okay, break it up. Let's get this over with."

Jose stated his name and address, and then the questioning began.

"Why did you go to Ms. Sampson's apartment on the afternoon of the ninth?"

"I heard a rifle shot. Can't mistake that sound. It sounded like it came from the direction of Delilah's apartment house, so I raced over there. When I saw the busted-out window, I ran up the stairs and started banging on the door. The old man across the hall opened his door and asked me what I was doing. I told him that Delilah might be hurt, and he said he had extra keys to get into the apartment. When we unlocked the door, I found her lying on the kitchen floor with blood all over the place.

"Did you see anyone else … other than the older tenant?"

"No."

"Then what did you do?"

"I used my belt to make a tourniquet on her arm, put her in the old guy's car, and drove her to the hospital. Then I called Mutt … I mean Detective Dale."

"How did you know that it was a rifle shot you heard?"

"I served in Iraq. You never forget the sound of a high-powered rifle. Ivy had already told me about the contract put out on Delilah, so when I heard that shot, she was the first one I thought of. Nobody uses them kind of rifles around here." He thought a minute and then said, "I guess that's all."

Pete turned off the recorder and leaned back in his chair. "So, what are we going to do with this girl?"

"I've got that covered, bro." Mutt cleared his throat and turned to face me. "Uh, Delilah, you know I want to keep both you and your mother safe, and I only want what is for your own good, right?"

I narrowed my eyes at him. "What exactly does 'only for my own good' mean?"

"Well, whoever wants that memory stick is getting desperate, so anyone who gets in their way is in danger."

"Okay. Just what are the plans?"

He took a deep breath. "Granny and I already talked it over."

I glared at him. "And?"

"And you're staying with Bella."

"What?" My voice was so high-pitched that I squeaked.

"You can't stay at the apartment, and you can't stay at Granny's. It's too dangerous for everyone involved. Bella volunteered to let you stay with her until we catch the guy who's trying to kill you. He won't connect Bella to you, so you should be safe."

I crossed my arms and glared at him. "I think I'd rather face the gunman."

Chapter 39

THE FOLLOWING NEXT DAY, WITHOUT FURTHER ADO, THEY BUNDLED ME up and delivered me to Bella. The next thing I knew, I was camping out in Bella's living room on her foldout couch and engaged in serious negotiations with Bonnie and Clyde about just how much space each of us were allotted on the sofa bed.

Mother had wisely decided to forgo the joy of accepting Bella's kind offer of bed and board. She had decided to stay with someone she met at church instead. She had explained the circumstances of why she needed a safe house, but Nellie Ryan seemed unperturbed by the prospect of a hired killer making an appearance at her door. She just quoted from the Bible: "He delivereth me from mine enemies: yea, Thou liftest me up above those that rise up against me; Thou hast delivered me from the violent man" (Psalm 18:48 KJV). With that, she said the subject was closed. *Wow. I sure wish my faith was that strong.*

After taking a few days to recover, I was raring to go back to work. I'm sure Bella was just as eager for me to be gone during the day as I was to leave, since we both needed a break from each other. She just wasn't used to having someone underfoot all the time, although I must admit that she did her best to take care of me. Of course, with Bella being Bella, and me being me, it made for some uncomfortable situations.

For instance, the living room window where I slept was facing east, so every morning at dawn, the sun grabbed me by my eyelids and shook me awake. Early one morning, I was trying to decide whether I should try to squeeze out a few more minutes sleep or just give up and hit the shower. But when I glanced over at the dogs, I gasped. Clyde was dead!

Have you heard the saying about a noise being loud enough to wake the dead? Well, apparently, my shriek was loud enough to prove that axiom because while my scream was still echoing around the room, Clyde jumped up and stared at me. With those beady little eyes, his underbite, and the way his tongue hung out, he looked even goofier than usual, although, at that moment, I failed to see the humor of the situation. Of course, with all the commotion, Bonnie started to whimper.

Bella came lumbering into the room with baseball bat. "What's going on?"

My hand was shaking as I pointed to the dog. "Clyde was dead!"

She looked at the dog, and then at me, and then back at Clyde. "What are you talking about?"

"When I woke up and looked over at him, and he was dead! He was upside down with his legs sticking straight up in the air … like he was major roadkill!"

Bella slowly and deliberately leaned the bat against the wall and crossed her arms over her chest. "Let me get this straight. You saw Clyde lying on his back, and you thought he was dead?"

I nodded. "His legs were stiff and pointing at the ceiling, and his tongue was sticking out. He was dead!"

She sighed. "He was sleeping, just like the rest of us were, until you screamed and woke up the entire neighborhood. That's the way dogs sleep when they're relaxed." Bella shook her head as she gathered up the dogs. Then, without another word, she padded back to her bedroom with a dog under each arm and slammed the door.

Despite that incident, for some unknown reason, Bonnie and Clyde decided that my bed was their territory. They insisted on sleeping with me, and every time I rolled over and opened my eyes, I was either nose to nose with one of them, or I had a dog's tail-end in my face. *Swell.*

At least I had managed to wrangle a compromise out of Mutt before he deposited me at Bella's. On the days I was scheduled to work the bookstore, he would arrange for me to be picked up and then taken home at the end of my shift. After hearing what had happened, Mrs. Marple told Mother and me to use the back door, so we would be less likely to be seen by the hired killer.

The following Monday, I felt strong enough to go to work. When Mutt picked me up and delivered me to the bookstore, I don't know who was happier, me or Bella.

The next few weeks, it was slow at the bookstore for some reason, so I took advantage of my downtime to teach Mother how to use the computer. I had used the computer at the library for years and discovered a talent for ferreting out all the little tricks and the ins and outs of using one, plus I had a knack for surfing the web. So, between my lessons and the instructional videos she watched on the internet, Mother took to it like a duck to water. Soon, she was able to set up a specialized bookkeeping program for the Reading Nook.

We settled down to a comfortable routine. I took care of the customers and kept the store straightened and clean, and Mother plugged away at the computer. Thankfully, she was making great strides in untangling the bookstore's financial records so they would meet the IRS regulations. She told me she was confident that everything would be ready when it was time to file taxes in April. The thing that pleased her the most was finding several qualifying tax breaks that would save the business a boatload of money.

After a couple of uneventful weeks, a man I didn't recognize walked into the store while I was alone. He was tall and carried himself like a soldier, with his back rigid and his steps measured. I could feel the hair on the back of my neck prickle. I couldn't understand my reaction; he hadn't done a thing to make me feel threatened, yet I was afraid.

He walked up to the counter where I was standing, and when I looked into his eyes, absolute terror washed over me. I ducked my head and pretended to read some papers in my hand until I was able to get it together. I took a deep breath and looked up with something that I hoped would pass as a smile plastered on my face. "May I help you, sir?"

His expression reminded me of a snake just before it struck. "Yes, I believe you can," he said and reached into his jacket.

Just at that moment, the door opened, and Pete walked in. "Detective

Tanner! What are you doing here?" My voice must have sounded strained because he paused and studied my face with narrowed eyes. Then he turned his attention to the stranger and nodded before meeting my eyes. "Just was in the neighborhood and decided to drop by. You busy?"

"Well, thank you anyway," the man said softly, and then he spun on his heel and left.

I nearly collapsed with relief and hung onto the counter to keep from falling on the floor.

Pete watched the man leave and then turned to me. "What's going on, Delilah?"

"I don't know, but that guy scared the snot out of me."

"Did he threaten you?"

"No, not at all. It was just … it was his eyes. I've never seen such cold, dead eyes before."

Pete grunted as he glanced toward the ceiling. "Don't suppose you have security cameras."

"No, I don't think so."

"Well, you need them." He sighed and checked his watch. "It's almost time to close the store, isn't it?"

I nodded.

"Well," he said, "Mutt should be coming soon, but I think I'll stick around for a while, okay?"

"I would really appreciate it, Pete."

He looked thoughtful. "You think you could pick him out from some mug shots?"

"Probably."

"Might be best for me and Mutt to take you downtown so you can take a look."

My eyes felt gritty. I'd been flipping through book after book and hadn't recognized anyone. But after I opened up the last book and turned a few pages, I froze. There he was, staring up at me. The men must have noticed a change in my demeanor because they both leaned forward.

"What have you got, Delilah?" Pete asked.

"It's him."

He pulled the book closer and studied the photo. "Yeah. I do believe you're right. He looks like that guy at the bookstore." He read the information beneath the picture. "Huh. It's Harry 'Hawkeye' Wilkerson." He looked up and exchanged a meaningful look with Mutt and said, "We've got trouble, bro."

Chapter 40

I SHED A BUNCH OF TEARS, BUT MUTT WAS ADAMANT AND WOULDN'T budge an inch. He flat-out said that it was just too dangerous for me to work at the bookstore and I had to quit. Period! He wouldn't even discuss it.

When I explained what happened, Mrs. Marple promised that after everything had blown over, I could have my job back. But I knew it could be a long time before this mess was straightened up, and she would eventually be forced to hire someone to replace me. So, let's face it, losing my job is as good as done. After all, Mr. and Mrs. Marple have a business to run, you know? They can't afford to have an extra full-time store clerk and who knows when they'll catch this gunman. I'm brokenhearted, but nobody else is on my side ... not even Granny!

Talk about going from up on the mountaintop to down into the valley. All my dreams had been destroyed. It wasn't long ago when I was on a huge high after Ivy and Ebony had attended church service with us. So, I tried to hold onto those memories, but to tell you the ugly truth, it didn't help much. Yeah, I know, I should be ashamed of myself.

I'm grateful that Ivy had been so moved when Miss Martha and Pastor Tim prayed for her that now she is close to accepting the Lord. Really, I am. And I am thrilled that Ebony enjoyed meeting Makena and now plans to start attending church. Like Granny says, although she may think of church as a social gathering, Ebony will eventually come around. The people around her will be a good influence and help guide her, and God will take care of the rest.

But all that doesn't help when I really enjoyed working at the Reading Nook more than I could have ever imagined. The pay is good, too. It's a lot more than what I was making at the diner, and the hours are much better, too. Now, I'm going to lose it all.

I had been as happy as a fat tick on a hound dog until Mutt walked in and told me that I had to go into hiding. Talk about your world crashing down around you. He tried to reason with me, but come on, get real. How could he expect me to give up my dream job just like that? So, of course, I tried to argue with him, but it was like beating my head against a brick wall. Didn't get me anywhere, and it gave me a headache. Then, when he told me he had already spoken to Mrs. Marple, I threw a royal hissy fit. Didn't help.

Mrs. Marple phoned me and tried to make me feel better. She even said that she wanted me to go online to search for some rare books they wanted to find. Well, whoop-de-do! Nobody understands how much the bookstore means to me. Working there made me finally feel like I was somebody. All my friends and family seem to think, *Oh well, it's just a job.* But it's not! Not to me. It … it proved to me that I'm as good as everybody else. And now it's going to be torn away … and it hurts.

Strangely enough, Bella was the only one who understood even a little bit. "That stinks," she said and handed me a chocolate candy bar. That's the best she had to offer as far as comfort, yet it helped to know she did care … in her way.

Pete and Mutt had a big powwow and decided I needed to go to a "safe house." Believe it or not, even the FBI had their noses stuck in all this now. Mutt said it was because the gunman was from Chicago, so it involved organized crime over state lines.

Swell.

Bella argued that I could stay with her, but Mutt said that it was too dangerous for both of us. The FBI was going to make the arrangements and find a place for me to stay. So, I had no more say in all this than a cow does when it's shipped to a slaughterhouse.

A few days later, I was sitting in a tiny little house in a minuscule living room, smack dab in the middle of nowhere, watching a bunch of nonsense on TV. I was ready to climb the walls, but they wouldn't even let Stormy, or any of my friends, visit. So, I was all by myself, throwing a big ol' pity party for the one and only person in attendance: me.

Mutt had threatened to lock me up if I even so much as stuck my nose out the door of this dratted place. I probably would have done it anyway, just to show him, if it hadn't been for Granny. Before I left, she sat me down and helped me understand that Mutt wasn't deliberately being controlling. He honestly believed this was the only way to keep me safe. She explained that he was doing all this out of love and helped me see what it would do to him if something bad happened. That's why I promised to behave myself and stay put—at least for the time being. So, here I sit. *Great.*

At least I have a brand-new cell phone with a different number than my old one, so I could keep in touch. It was my lifeline, and it was the only thing that kept me somewhat sane.

Tonight, when it rang, I picked up and was surprised that it was Ivy. She wasn't one to talk on the phone much.

"Snake says it's okay for you to come home. That killer ain't gonna bother you no more."

A chill ran up my spine. "What do you mean, Ivy?"

"That hired gun left town, and he ain't coming back, so it's safe for you to come home. You can even go back to the bookstore. I know you've been worried about losing your job."

My stomach lurched, I could hardly get a breath, and my knees turned to rubber. "What did he do, Ivy?"

"Snake didn't do nothing. He just talked to the guy. Snake don't want his kind invading his turf. He keeps his hood nice and quiet, and he don't want no killer running around here with a big ol' assault rifle. And, besides, he's protective over me and my friends, so he's gonna make sure nothin' happens to you."

I wished I believed Ivy, but I didn't—at least not the part about Snake "just talking" to the guy. I felt sick to my stomach, yet, to be honest, I felt relieved too. "Are you saying that the gunman is still alive?"

"I'm telling you that he left town, and he ain't coming back." She paused and then added, "Yah don't sound very happy about it. I thought you'd want to get back home. You sure whined enough about having to leave the bookstore and losing your job and all. You should show a little gratitude."

"I *am* grateful, Ivy. It's just …" *How do you thank someone for murdering another human being—even if that human was trying to kill you?* I chose my words carefully. "How am I going to get Mutt to believe me? He'll probably still insist I stay in this ratty little dump for the next decade or so."

"Well, Snake ain't gonna tell him, so it's up to you. And you best not give Mutt any ideas about arresting Snake for something he didn't do."

"I won't." I figured I wouldn't need to give him the idea because that would be the first thing Mutt would think of. I paused for a moment before I very cautiously said, "You know, Ivy, the more I think about it, the more I think maybe I shouldn't mention it to Mutt right now. He's a cop, after all, so he's going to be suspicious about the circumstances, you know?"

There was silence, and then she sighed. "Yeah. I know it don't look too good for Snake to have any contact with that killer, so maybe it would be for the best if you don't say nothing and just lay low for a while."

My heart was pounding when I clicked off the phone. If Mutt found out what Ivy had just told me, he would be furious that I hadn't clued him in. On the other hand, I kind of owed Snake not to say anything. So, after much soul-searching, I decided to keep my mouth shut … at least for the time being. That was a new concept for me.

A little while later, there was a knock on the door. Three raps, then two, one and two more. It was Mutt. I opened the door, and as soon as I saw his face, I knew something had happened.

He and Pete came in and closed the door.

"What's going on?" I asked … although I was pretty sure that I had it figured out already.

Mutt stood in the middle of the room with his hands jammed in his jean pockets. "I've got some news for you, Delilah."

I waited and didn't say anything.

He glanced over at Pete and then turned his attention to me. "They found the gunman."

"Oh? Were they able to capture him? Anyone hurt?"

"He won't be hurting anyone anymore. He's dead."

I searched his face, and dread overflowed in my gut. "I take it he didn't die from natural causes."

Pete cleared his throat. "No, he didn't, Delilah."

My knees went weak, and I flopped down on the bed. "Where did they find him?" I whispered.

"Stuffed in a barrel and floating in Lake Michigan, right off a Chicago pier."

"Chicago?" I squeaked. My thoughts were all jumbled. *Did that mean Snake didn't have anything to do with the murder? I doubt he would have traveled hundreds of miles just to deliver the gunman's body back home. Could he have ordered the killing? That was kind of stretching it since he was just a two-bit gangster. I doubt he would have had any influence in a city as big and as far away as Chicago.*

My confusion must have shown on my face because Mutt frowned and said, "This still doesn't mean you are safe."

"Why not?"

"Because there is more than one gunman available for hire in Chicago." He kept studying my face. "Delilah, is there something you're not telling me?"

Oh, crud. He can read me like a book. I took a deep breath and avoided looking him in the eye. "I just want to go home." *Well, that much is the truth.*

"Babe, it's not safe. Whoever that kingpin up in Chicago is, he won't give up just because of what they would consider a minor setback. They'll merely hire another gun because these guys play for keeps."

"Well, I can't hide forever. I want to go home, Mutt. I miss my family and my friends, and I just want to sleep in my own bed!" I took a deep breath and gave him my best pitiful hound dog look. "Please?"

Pete put his hand on Mutt's shoulder. "She's right, you know?"

Mutt scowled and then sighed and reluctantly nodded. He shoved his hands back into his pockets and turned to me. "Okay, get your stuff packed, and we'll you get out of here."

Chapter 41

Ivy glared at me from across the kitchen table. "Snake didn't kill that pile of garbage even if he did deserve it. Even back in his wildest days, he didn't kill nobody. Maybe he cracked a few heads and broke a kneecap or two, but he never offed nobody."

I wanted to believe her, but oh, boy! He used to break kneecaps?

"Why are you so worried about that hired gun anyway? He shot at you with a high-powered rifle, and you can bet that he wasn't just trying to wing you."

I hung my head for a moment and then met her eyes. "Look, Ivy. Pete didn't go into details, but he hinted that the gunman was mutilated before he was killed."

Ivy jumped up so fast that her chair fell over with a crash. "Are you saying Snake tortured that guy? What kind of a sick monster do you think he is?" She was huffing like a locomotive. "I thought you were my friend!"

"I am your friend, Ivy." I was trying to keep calm and cool in the situation, but to tell the truth, I was a bit steamed myself. "You just said that he used to bust people's kneecaps, so what am I *supposed* to think? Come on, Ivy. You tell me Snake talked to the guy, then that same guy disappears, and the next thing you know, he's fish food. And now I'm supposed to believe Snake didn't do anything?" By now I had raised my voice to an ear-splitting shriek. "How naive do you think I am?"

"Do you really want me to answer that?" she screamed back.

We glared at each other. Our claws were out, and we were ready to pounce on each other like two alley cats.

Just then, the phone rang.

I grabbed the receiver and snarled, "Hello!"

"Well, hello, dear. How are you and the girls? I bet they are so grateful that you're home."

"Oh, hi, Granny. We, uh … we're doing okay."

"Are you going to be home for a while? Our new study guidebooks just came in. This series has such a beautiful lesson this month. It's called "Loving the Unlovable." I thought you and the girls might like to get together with me and go through the first lesson. Would this be a good time for me to come over? I won't stay too long because I promised Mildred I would visit her. That nursing home is a wonderful facility, but she still gets lonely and looks forward to our little chats."

I must have blushed from my head right down to my toes. Talk about being unlovable. I felt as though God Himself had just reached down and given me a swat on my behind.

Ivy was watching me with a wary expression, and when I turned scarlet, she whispered, "What's wrong?"

"Hello? Delilah?" Granny's voice startled me.

I jumped and just stared at the phone in my hand, unable to move.

Ivy finally yanked the phone out of my hand.

"Hi, Granny." She listened for a moment and then answered, "Oh, she's right here. She must have choked on something, but she's okay now." Ivy narrowed her eyes at me. "Yeah, I'm sure. She looks fine."

I stuck out my tongue and made a goofy face. I guess I wasn't so mad anymore.

Ivy grinned at me and then turned her attention back to the phone conversation. "I don't know if it's a good time to come right now or not, Granny. Stormy and Ebony aren't here. Neither is Shirley." Ivy was interrupted by raucous laughter as the three missing women burst through the front door. "Yeah, that's them you're hearing. They just came in."

Stormy flung her library books on the sofa when she noticed Ivy was on the phone. "Who are you talking to?"

"Granny."

"Oh, let me talk to her." She snatched the phone away as she gave Ivy a good-natured little shove. "Hey, Granny! When are you coming over to visit?" She smiled. "Oh great! We'll be here. See you in a few minutes."

"Granny's coming over," she practically sang as she headed toward the kitchen. "I'll make some sweet tea."

I knew Ivy and I would have to finish our conversation later that night, but for now, we had buried the hatchet. To tell you the truth, it's amazing we hadn't ended up burying it in each other's heads. Good thing Granny called when she did.

When Granny arrived, she was all excited about our new study guide. She handed each of us a copy and started enthusiastically explaining the main focus of the lesson.

Ebony began to cry.

"What is the matter, dear? Did I say something to offend you?"

"No. But it's just that it ain't no use. Just wastin' my time doin' these here studies and goin' to church and all."

Granny looked dumbfounded. "What do you mean?"

Ebony lifted her tear-streaked face and met Granny's sympathetic gaze. "I turned tricks! I can't never change my past. Everybody knows what I am ... a worthless, dirty ol' streetwalker. God don't want nobody like me."

"Oh, sweetheart, you are so wrong!" Granny picked up her Bible and flipped it open. "Let me tell you about Rahab the prostitute." She smiled at us. "Do you remember how God crumbled the walls of Jericho and delivered the city to Joshua and the Israelite army?"

We all nodded since that had been the subject of one of Pastor Tim's recent sermons.

Granny turned a few pages and began to read the story about a prostitute who saved the lives of the Hebrew spies just before the Battle of Jericho took place. When she finished reading about how Rahab was allowed to join the Israelites after the battle and live among them, she turned the pages and ran her finger down through the verses until she found what she was looking for. She placed the opened Bible on the kitchen table and reached over to clasp Ebony and Ivy's hands.

"But that's not the end of the story, girls." Her smile just beamed as she nodded toward the Bible. "The very first book of the New Testament is Matthew, and at the very beginning of Matthew, there is a list of our Lord Jesus's genealogy." Tears of joy ran down her cheeks. "And guess what, girls! Right smack in the middle of His family tree, listed as plain as day, is Rahab—that very same prostitute from Jericho. Jesus is descended directly from her."

Ebony and Ivy stared at her.

"Go ahead, girls. Read it for yourselves." She smiled. "And just for good measure, God tells us that even prostitutes are forgiven. Scripture says, 'And that is what some of you were.'" She paused to explain that Jesus was talking about prostitutes and then she continued reading the verse. "'But you were washed, you were sanctified, you were justified in the name of the Lord Jesus Christ and by the Spirit of our God'" (1 Corinthians 6:11 NIV). Granny looked at us with tears sparkling in her eyes. "And it even says that Jesus told the self-righteous church elders that prostitutes would enter the kingdom of God before they did." She grinned at us. "So, you see, all you have to do is accept Jesus as your Savior and ask Him to cleanse you of your sins, and you will be forgiven."

Ebony shook her head. "It can't be that easy."

Granny leaned toward her. "But it is, sweetheart."

"Well," Ebony said as she stood up, "I'll have to think on it for a while." She headed toward the door, "See yah."

We all sat still for a moment before turning our attention to Ivy.

She pulled the Bible closer and ran her finger down the list of names until she came to Rahab's. She looked up, grinned, and said, "Well, how 'bout that!"

Chapter 42

Ivy and I never got back to our discussion. The atmosphere in our home changed dramatically after Granny's Bible lesson. There was much less fussing over little things, like whose turn it was to clean up or whether one of us was hogging the bathroom. Sure, we still had disagreements and all, but we'd been much more civilized toward each other lately.

Both Ebony and Ivy seemed to be mulling things over in their minds, but I guess they still weren't sure about what Granny told us. I must admit that this grace thing is a hard thing to swallow. I mean, if you've been a rotten person all your life, how can God say with a wink and a nod that it's all good just because you have accepted Jesus as your Savior? That's got to cost you a whole bunch to get all that mess cleaned up, right? I guess it's natural to think that you need to *earn* God's forgiveness somehow or another. To tell you the truth, I still struggle with the idea that God's grace is completely free. I mean, I know it in my heart, but knowing it in my head is another matter. Mother said it had been hard for her to accept that concept too, but she promised understanding would come as my faith grew.

Anyway, things between the five of us were fairly calm, and everything was going along pretty good. I guess that's why it was such a shock when Mother disappeared.

The two of us had finished working that day, and we closed the bookstore just like always. Mrs. Marple had been expanding Mother's responsibilities at the shop; now she did the bookkeeping, counted down the cash registers at night, made the bank deposits, and helped me with ordering new stock, among other things. She usually worked the same hours as I did.

Over time, Mother and Mrs. Marple had become good friends, and they often went shopping together. When Mother told me to go ahead and catch the bus because she had some things to do, I didn't think twice about it.

I began to worry a little when she didn't get home in time for supper and hadn't called, but I really hit the panic button when the last of the buses had run and she still wasn't home. Concerned, I phoned Mrs. Marple, and she told me that they had planned to go shopping, so she was a little surprised when Mother didn't show up. But she thought she had changed her mind or had just forgotten about it. She said she hadn't seen Mother all day. That's when I called Mutt.

He pulled up a little while later in Granny's car, and we drove all around town, looking for her. After searching for a couple of hours and talking to countless people, we hadn't turned up a thing. It was as if Mother had vanished into thin air. We finally had to admit defeat and drove back to the apartment just as Jose was walking the girls home.

Stormy jumped me as soon as I got out of the car. "Where were you? How come you and Shirley didn't come to the diner for your meal tonight?"

"So, you haven't heard from Mother tonight?"

"What you talkin' bout?" Ebony asked.

I was fighting tears, and the tears were winning. "Mother was supposed to go shopping with Mrs. Marple, so she didn't ride the bus home with me. But when it got late and she still hadn't come home, I called Mrs. Marple, and she said Mother never showed up. Mutt and I went looking for her, but nobody has seen her."

Everybody just stared at me for a moment, and then all three started talking at once, bombarding me with questions. As we walked up to the apartment, they kept grilling me. That's when I wilted and just started bawling.

Mutt guided me over to the sofa and sat down with his arms around me.

I leaned into his embrace and sobbed. "What could have happened to her? You don't think one of Barron's goons kidnapped her, do you?"

"I don't know, Delilah, but I'll call Pete. I promise you that we won't stop looking until we find her."

The next morning, I got madder than fire at Pete. When we told him about Mother's disappearance, he had the bald-faced audacity to suggest that the Reader's Nook's books should be examined. He tried to calm me down, but I was too furious at him to even listen. Then, to top it off, Mutt actually defended him! That burnt me to a crisp.

Mutt let me vent for a while, and then he took my hand and waited until I met his gaze. "Babe, I know you don't want to hear what Pete has to say, but he's right." I was about to melt his eardrums, until he gently put a finger on my lips and spoke so tenderly that I stopped and listened to what he had to say.

"Believe me, Delilah, I don't think that your mother skipped town after stealing something, but we must prove without a shadow of a doubt that Shirley didn't take off with the Marple's money or Barron's memory stick or ... whatever. We've got to eliminate any possibility that Shirley is guilty of a crime, and we must prove her innocence. In order to do that, we need to have someone go over the Reading Nook's books. Understand?"

I sighed, and then nodded.

He pulled me into a hug as he spoke to Pete. "Okay, buddy, we better get moving and have Charlie Marple check his books. In the meantime, we'll do another sweep of the neighborhood and see if anyone saw her last night. I'll interview the bus and cab drivers in the area. She's quite a striking woman, so they might remember if they picked her up." He turned his attention back to me. "Babe, you already gave us a description of what she was wearing. Is there anything else you want to add?"

Tears started to flow again. I guess I was exhausted from worry and lack of sleep. "I can't think of anything."

Pete patted my arm. "We're gonna find her, Delilah, even if we have to look under every rock from here to California and back."

I sniffed and gave him a wobbly smile. "Thanks, Pete." But what condition would she be in when they found her? That's what was really scaring me.

Chapter 43

IT JUST DIDN'T SMELL RIGHT TO ME. MOTHER SEEMED SO HAPPY SINCE she had come back, and we had gotten very close. As the old wounds healed over, we developed a strong mother-daughter bond that we had never had before. Even her frosty relationship with Stormy was beginning to thaw. She fit right in with the rest of us at the apartment and seemed to enjoy Ivy and Ebony's odd little quirks. And, besides, she was making other friends too ... good, Christian women like Granny, Mrs. Marple, and Nellie Ryan, not to mention how much she loved her job at the bookstore.

Mutt told me that Charlie Marple had gone over the Reading Nook's books with a fine-toothed comb, and not so much as one thin dime was missing. So, that took care of any suspicion that she had stolen from the bookstore.

There wasn't a single logical explanation for why she would need to sneak out of town and hide. In fact, she had every reason to stay. Besides, I just couldn't believe that Mother would up and leave without telling anyone or saying goodbye. Would the old, druggie/hippie mother do that? Oh yeah, that's exactly what she would have done. But the new, born-again Christian mother? No way!

It had been over a week now. I know Mutt and Pete were doing everything they could to find her, but they had other cases they had to investigate too. They were putting in as much time as they possibly could on Mother's case, but you just can't be in two places at once. In fact, they had five or six places they needed to be. Our small city's budget was stretched to the max and Brenville's police force was understaffed, so every department was stretched thin.

We all never stopped searching for Mother, but none of us had turned up a thing. Even Snake and his men were on the lookout, yet no one had seen hide nor hair of her since last Wednesday.

I was on my knees praying that we would find her, safe and sound. To tell the truth, I normally don't get down on my knees to pray. I usually lay down in bed or sit in a comfy chair when I have heart-to-heart talks with God, but for some reason, I felt compelled to kneel before Him this time.

As I was pouring out my heart to Him, a vivid image flashed before my eyes. I saw that dirt cellar where Stanley Barron had taken Stormy ad me when we were kidnapped by his thugs. The picture in my mind was so clear that I might as well have been standing right in the middle of that horrible old basement. As soon as I experienced that vision, I had the strongest feeling that God was speaking to me. I knew without a doubt that's where Mother was being held. The trouble was, I had no earthly idea where the old farmhouse was located.

I was so sure about my epiphany that I called Mutt to tell him. He was polite and all, and he said he would "check it out," but I could tell from the tone of his voice that he didn't take me seriously. Talk about a letdown! So, since Mutt wasn't going to be much help, I decided to take matters into my own hands. After all, as they always say, God helps those who help themselves.

I talked to Mrs. Marple, and since she was familiar with local real estate, she helped me to do an online search of abandoned property in and around our area. Considering that the house could be within about a half hour's drive in any direction from here, I ended up with a huge search grid drawn on my map. It was a daunting task to say the least.

When I asked to borrow Granny's car and explained why I needed it, she insisted on coming along. We spent the next few days, map in hand, driving up and down isolated country roads, searching. Even though I had only been to that house twice, both times blindfolded and lying in the back of a van, I was sure God would help me recognize the dirt road leading to it. Now, if I only could find the right one! But after spending hours driving around without the slightest idea where I was supposed to go, I was losing hope. Even Granny's enthusiasm was waning, although she still encouraged me to keep at it.

"Honey, if you are sure that God is leading you to do this, then you cannot quit. He will show you the proper path and the right way to go." She gave my hand a pat. "I won't be able to accompany you for the next couple of days because I'm committed to serve on the refreshment committee during our church's revival. Don't worry though, I'll catch a ride with Nellie Ryan, so you can continue to use my car." She gave me a hug. "And you can be sure that we will be praying for you and Shirley."

So, today, I'm on my own. I racked my brain, trying to remember how long Barron's van drove on blacktop roads and what direction we turned, but it was no use. I had been scared simple during the kidnapping, and my memory of what happened was totally messed up in my mind.

The longer I drove, the more discouraged I became. After driving down yet another old country road for a while, I was crying so hard that I couldn't see to drive. I pulled off to the side and sobbed. Eventually, I began to pray, explaining to God that I was completely lost, had no idea where to go from here, and was terribly afraid for my mother. I begged Jesus to guide me and show me the right way to go.

Once I cried myself out and had used every tissue in my pockets, in my purse, and in the partial box I found in the back seat of Granny's car, I felt a calmness come over me and pulled myself together. Starting up the car, I pulled back onto the twisty road and slowly continued until I came around a sharp curve and saw a narrow dirt road that was hardly wide enough for a car. My heart started to hammer as I turned in and followed it, bumping from pothole to pothole. It occurred to me that the car was kicking up a big ol' cloud of dust. I sure wasn't sneaking up on anybody, but it was now or never, and I couldn't stop now.

The sound of bushes scraping against the side of Granny's car made me wince, but it also triggered a forgotten memory. Yeah, I remembered hearing that same kind of noise while I was bouncing around in the back of that van. My heart was racing as the twists and turns on that old dirt road seemed so familiar. *Yes! Thank You, Jesus! I am sure now. This is the road I am looking for.*

It was still early in the afternoon, and the sun was bright when I turned onto that long driveway and pulled up to a seemingly abandoned house. I thought I recognized the sagging porch. True, I had been blindfolded and never saw it with my eyes, yet I remember being led up dilapidated steps, across a sloping porch, and through the front door.

I parked the car and got out. As I retraced my steps, the terror of what I had experienced in that dank cellar came back and nearly smothered me. I beat down the urge to turn around and hightail it out of there and carefully made my way up the steps. When I reached to door, I was amazed to find it unlocked. The door groaned on its hinges as I opened it and stepped into the living room. *Yes! I remember that sound. This is surely the house.*

Walking through the living room, I entered the kitchen and marched over to the door that led to the basement. Taking a deep breath, I grabbed the doorknob, gave it a twist, and cautiously opened the door. I made my way down the steps, located the light switch at the bottom of the stairs, and flipped it on.

It took a moment for my eyes to adjust even though the light wasn't nearly as bright as I remembered when Stormy and I were here. Glancing up at the fixture, I noticed that two bulbs had burned out, and only one remained. Well, that explained why the cellar was so dim.

Peering into the gloom, I saw something in the corner of the basement. I stared for a moment before realizing that it was a person chained to a post, crouching in the corner.

Reality crashed into me and nearly knocked me down. "Mother!" I gasped.

Chapter 44

I SLAPPED MY HAND OVER MY MOUTH TO KEEP FROM SCREAMING. MY STEPS faltered as I made my way toward the prisoner. My brain was having difficulty accepting that this poor creature was really my mother. She was naked, bruised, filthy, and marked with strange little circles all over her body, which I later found out were cigarette burns. Her hair! It had been her crowning glory! Her beautiful raven-black hair that had reached down to her waist was shorn off, and tufts of hair were sticking up every which way. Her lips were cracked and bleeding. Her fingernails were broken. I barely recognized her.

She looked at me with dull eyes. "Delilah, no! Run! Get away before he comes back. Please go!"

I struggled to find my voice and was only able to speak in a trembling whisper. "Who did this to you?"

"Delilah, you must leave right now! He could come back any minute. Go!"

"Who?"

"Bull. He comes every day to bring me food and water. You've got to go before he catches you here."

Suddenly, someone grabbed me from behind. "Too late!" he said and barked a harsh laugh.

"Bull, please! Please let her go."

"Are you kidding me? She'd go right to the police. She's not going anywhere, Shirley."

He dragged me over to the wall and handcuffed my left wrist to an old pipe that came down from the first floor. "There. That hold you for a while."

"Bull," Mother said through her sobs, "please let her go. Don't hurt her, Bull. I'll do anything you want. Just let her go."

That seemed to amuse him, and his maniacal laughter sent chills up my spine because not only was this man evil, but he was insane! "Shirley, you are going to do whatever I want anyway. You have no choice."

"Oh, dear Jesus," I prayed. "Please help us."

That caused his attention to turn back to me. He grinned, and then his brazen smile got even wider. "Honey, you and me are going to have some great fun, and your Jesus ain't gonna help you." He reached over, grabbed the front of my blouse, and ripped it open. The buttons flew everywhere. "And what's even better is your mother gets to watch."

"I swear I don't know where that memory stick is, Bull." My mother sounded frantic.

He threw his head back and roared with laughter. "Of course, you don't know where the stick is, Shirley. I know you don't have it. You *never* had it."

The truth hit me with the force of a sledgehammer. I stared at him. "*You* stole it. You copied all the information from Barron's computer, took the stick, and then framed my mother."

He grinned at me. "Stanley was right. You *are* the smart one." He chuckled. "Yeah. I copied all the dirt about Stanley on a memory stick, and as an extra bonus, I even found some interesting facts about a big kingpin in Chicago. Then it was like taking candy from a baby. I just put the memory stick in my pocket and walked out. That doddering, senile old man didn't suspect a thing.

"When Shirley disappeared, it was a perfect opportunity. All I had to do was to feed poor old Stanley a bunch of baloney about how your mother tricked him and stole his information. That simpleminded old fool believes everything I tell him." He took a few steps toward me and laughed. In a strange singsong voice, he said, "And now the fun begins."

Suddenly, there was such a huge explosion that I slapped my hands over my ears. Then time stood still for a long moment before I gathered enough courage to look over at Bull's body. There was a stunned pause before Mother and I realized that the top of his head was missing and we screamed in horror.

"Shut up!"

We both became mute with shock at the sound of that familiar raspy voice.

"Simpleminded old fool, huh? Doddering, senile old man?" He tottered over closer and stood over Bull's body while he wiped his mouth on his sleeve. "I guess I showed *you*, you meathead."

He glanced over at my mother. "So, you were telling the truth after all. Guess you expect an apology, but you won't be getting one from me, Shirley." He looked back down at his deceased bodyguard. "Just goes to show you can't trust nobody." He thought a moment and then cursed. "I guess I should have made him tell me where the stick was before I shot him."

"Let us go, Stanley. Please!"

"Are you out of your mind? You two just saw me blow somebody away. You think I don't know that you'll go right to the cops if I let you get out of here?"

"I would never turn in my sugar daddy to the police," my mother crooned. "And I guarantee that Delilah wouldn't turn you in either. Why don't you just let us go, Stanley? We didn't see anything. I promise!"

He snorted. "Yeah, sure."

"I *promise* you, Stanley."

As he turned, he looked over at me and squinted. "Hey, ain't you the dame what's dating that cop?" He surveyed the cellar. "Got his folks down here someplace. Dumb blockhead thought he'd expose my financial stuff to the authorities. Didn't mind taking him out, but I did hate to off his wife though. She didn't do nothing, but I couldn't take the chance she might know something and squeal." Shrugging, he headed toward the stairway.

Mother said, "Please, Stanley, I promise you. We won't say a word! Just let us go."

He paused and seemed to think about it for a moment, but then he shook his head. "Nope. Can't take the chance. I guess you girls will just have to stay here and keep each other company." He glanced around the cellar and then snickered. "Sorry about the mess. Back in the day, I used to bury them all here. Later, I got the boys to do it for me. Now I ain't got no boys left, and I'm too old to do it myself. It's disgusting."

"You can't just leave us here, Stanley. We'll die!"

He shrugged. "Well, that's the idea." He scratched his chin. "Of course, I could get me some gas and burn the place down. That would take care of the problem." He contemplated on the idea for a while and then said, "Maybe, maybe not. Might have the fire marshal snooping around here. That wouldn't be good." He shrugged. "Have to think on it for a while."

He reached over and turned off the light. "Now you won't have to look at him. He's not gonna be very pretty in a few days." He chuckled. "Come to think of it, he ain't too pretty now."

We heard him wheezing and struggling to catch his breath as he made his way up the steps. The cellar door closed, and his footsteps sounded over our heads until the front door slammed. We heard his car start up and drive away. Then, silence.

Mother started to sob. "I'm sorry, Delilah. I'm so sorry."

I didn't answer her right away since I was too busy checking out where I was handcuffed to the old pipe. I had noticed before Stanley left that it looked corroded, and now I wished the light was still on so I could see what I was doing. But it wasn't, and I was mostly feeling around in the deep shadows and trying to figure out how to get loose.

Finally, I just wrapped both hands around the pipe, braced my feet against the wall, and heaved with all my might. The pipe kind of groaned, but it held its ground. I tried again, but with the same results. I couldn't give up and do nothing but wait until Stanley decided to come back and barbecue us alive, so I kept pulling and straining until my arms and legs were shaking with fatigue. I rested a bit and tried again, but it wouldn't so much as budge. Then I remembered Granny reading the story of how Sampson pulled the temple down after praying to God, so I prayed and asked Him to give me strength. I tried one more time, and this time, the pipe made a groaning sound and then gave way.

"Delilah? Are you okay? What was that noise?"

"It was the pipe. I managed to pull it from the wall." I worked the handcuffs down and slipped them off the broken end. "I'm free, Mother!"

"Oh, thank You, Lord! Now get out of here, Delilah!"

"I'm not leaving you."

"Stanley could come back any time now and burn this place down."

"That's exactly why I won't leave you here, Mother."

I slowly made my way toward where I hoped the stairs were located, giving Bull's body a wide berth to avoid tripping over it. Somehow, I managed to find the light switch and flip it on. I was almost sorry I did since the full horror of Stanley's handiwork was now in full view.

I sucked it up and walked past Bull with eyes carefully averted to where Mother was chained. The chain was anchored to a post, and there was no way I could break her loose.

"Please, Delilah, get out before Stanley comes back."

"I told you, Mother, I'm not going to leave you. Do you know where Bull kept the key?"

She shook her head.

I pulled the cell phone that Mutt had given me out of my back pocket and checked it. Not even a single bar. *I guess there isn't any service out here in the middle of nowhere.*

I glanced over at my mother. "Okay. I'm going to have a look around" and then began to search for the key. First, I steeled myself to check Bull's pockets, yet I still nearly lost my lunch. They weren't there, so I kept on searching the cellar, but came up empty. "I'm going upstairs to look around. I'm sure he kept the key in this house somewhere."

"Delilah, please ..."

"Don't argue with me, Mother. We are going to leave together or we're not leaving at all. Period."

I did a quick search upstairs, and since there wasn't any furniture, it didn't take me long. I also checked all the kitchen cabinets and the medicine cabinet in the bathroom. Nothing. Nada. I did take the time to peek out the window to check if Granny's car was still there, and I breathed a prayer of thanks when I saw it in the driveway, right where I had left it. Since the car keys were safely tucked in my jeans pocket, the biggest hurdle we faced was getting Mother free and out of the basement.

I decided to return to the cellar and look around again. As I walked down the steps, I noticed a small alcove just above the light switch. I stuck my finger in it and pulled out a key. *Yes!*

Once Mother was released, we discovered that after being chained for two weeks, she couldn't walk. Since I wasn't strong enough to carry her, we had a major problem. She leaned on me, and we managed to make it to the foot of the cellar steps, but that stairway may as well have been Mount Everest.

"Delilah ..."

"No. We are going to figure out a way to get you up these stairs."

After some thought, we ended up sitting down on the steps, with me two risers above Mother. I put my hands under her arms and heaved while she pushed with her legs until she was able to sit on the next step up. We managed to conquer the basement stairs, one step at a time. It took an agonizingly long time and a whole lot of sweat and tears, but we finally made it to the top and into the kitchen.

After resting for a while, we were able to face the challenge of getting to the driveway. Once again, it took a monumental effort, but we finally made it to the car. I wrapped Mother in the blanket that was on the back seat, got the car turned around, and took off.

We prayed that we could safely escape and not meet Stanley on the way out while I navigated down the narrow dirt road. Both of us breathed easier when we reached the paved road, but as I came around a sharp curve, I almost collided with Stanley. I just caught a glimpse of his face, but I knew by his expression that he had recognized us too.

I floored it.

"What's wrong, Delilah?" Mother called from the back seat.

"It's Stanley. He was coming back toward the house, and now I'll have to outrun him." I screeched around another curve. "And you had better pray!" To say that I was an inexperienced driver was an understatement and driving down a twisting back-country road at fifty miles an hour was quite a challenge to say the least. When I caught a glimpse of his big green car careening around the curves right behind us, I begged Jesus to take over the driving and stepped on the gas.

It was by God's grace that we didn't end up in a ditch or crash head-on into a tree, but somehow, we had made it. Somewhere along the way,

Stanley had disappeared from my rearview mirror. So, by the time we pulled onto the highway and were on our way to the hospital, we gave a sigh of relief and began to sing praises of thanksgiving.

I pulled into the emergency room parking lot and ran into the building to get help. It wasn't until the woman at the desk stared at me that I realized I still had the handcuffs dangling from my wrist, my stained blouse was in tatters, and my bra was completely exposed. I didn't care. "Please ... I need help. My mother is in the car ..."

The next few hours were just a blur of doctors, nurses, and police officers. The only thing that I clearly remember about that entire time was Mutt running into the room and pulling me into his arms as tears ran down his face.

Mother was dehydrated, and some of her wounds were infected, so she had to stay in the hospital overnight. Granny insisted that once she got discharged from the hospital, Mother should come and stay at her house. "There's plenty of room, and I want her here so I can fuss over her a bit. Besides, she shouldn't be alone while the rest of you are at work."

The paint on Granny's car was worse for wear, but she said she was so grateful that Mother and I were safe that she couldn't care less about the car's finish.

The other thing I remember about that night was Pete stomping into Mother's hospital room, madder than a hornet. "What is it about you and trouble, Delilah? You attract it like flies to honey." He flopped down on the chair, slapped the recorder onto the bedside table, and yanked his notebook out of his pocket. He scowled at me and shook his head. "If you don't stop getting into one mess after another, I'm gonna have to get me a bigger notebook."

Chapter 45

MUTT WAS FURIOUS! I DON'T KNOW WHICH ONE OF US HE WAS MADDER at: me or Granny.

"Of all the harebrained, mutton headed, foolhardy things to do! And to top it all off, Granny knew all about it and didn't tell me!" He paced back and forth across the room. "Why would you go off by yourself and not tell anybody?"

I guess Granny didn't get around to mentioning that she had accompanied me for the first few days, but I figured this wouldn't be the best time to enlighten him.

"When I think of what that animal did to your mother and what he would have done to you ... and then Barron coming back to the farmhouse with the intention of burning you alive!" He flopped down beside me on the sofa. "Why in the world didn't you ask me to come with you?"

Now that made me see red. I mean, I could handle Mutt being upset, but to blame me for going out on my own? *Uh-uh. No way.* I sat up straight and got right into his face. "Listen here, Mr. Self-Righteous. I tried to tell you that I knew Mother was being held in that old farmhouse, but you brushed me off. Did you expect me to sit back and say, 'Oh well, it would be too much trouble to look for her, so forget it,' when I knew my mother's life was in danger? God told me where she was, and He expected me to go get her. I couldn't help it if you wouldn't listen."

That shut him up right quick. His face turned white, and he got real still. He swallowed a couple of times, and his voice was a bit shaky as he said, "You're right, Delilah, and I'm so sorry. I should have taken you much more seriously when you called. But it seemed as if it would be like hunting for a needle in a haystack, blindfolded. I should have realized that with the Lord's guidance, you would find her." He met my gaze. "I am really sorry, Delilah."

How can you stay mad at a guy whose eyes soften like melted chocolate when he's apologizing? I leaned over and gave him a big ol' kiss right on his lips. "You are forgiven."

I grinned at him, and he grinned back before the worry returned to his eyes. "But you still are in danger, babe. Barron is out there, and he's a lot more dangerous than he seems."

I snorted. "He already seems dangerous to me. Afterall, he shot and killed a man right in front of us!"

"Yeah." Mutt rubbed his face. "Forensics is scheduled to start digging up the cellar floor tomorrow. We'll see if old Stanley was just bragging, or if he really does have bodies stashed down there."

I put my hand in his. "If he does, I hope you find your parents."

He nodded. "It would bring us some kind of closure, especially for Granny."

"Are you going to be there when they dig up the cellar?"

"Yes. I need to be there. Granny wants to be there too. I'm not sure that's a good idea but trying to stop Granny from doing something she has her mind set on is like trying to stop a runaway locomotive." He grinned. "Kind of like it is with you."

"Would it be okay if I came too?"

"Do you really want to be there?"

"I really want to be with you—and with Granny. No matter what, it will be hard on you both, whether they find anything or not. I just want to be there for you."

He gave me a small, sad smile, and then he reached over and gave me a kiss. "Thanks, babe," he whispered.

The next day, a small crowd of mostly law enforcement people gathered at the farmhouse. Bull's body had already been removed, and Mutt told me that the coroner was performing an autopsy. Why in the world they needed to do that, I'll never know. He was missing the top of his skull and most of his brain, courtesy of Stanley Barron, so it had to be fairly obvious as to what killed him, don't you think?

Since they couldn't get any heavy equipment down into the basement, cops were digging up the cellar with picks, shovels, and a whole lot of sweat. Of course, doing it that way will take a lot longer, but it couldn't be helped.

Granny and I stood outside in the warm sunshine and waited. I tried to chat with her, but she was too tense to really talk. She did tell me that Mother was doing fine, but that was about it.

As Granny stood facing the house, she remained perfectly still. When I saw her lips were moving, I realized she was praying. Suddenly, she stood up straighter, tightened her grip on her cane, and turned all her attention to the lone figure who was walking toward us.

Mutt had a strange expression on his face as he tramped across the grass. It seemed to be a mixture of hope, dread, and excitement all jumbled together. As he got closer, we could see that he had something clutched in his hand.

He walked over to where we were standing and stopped.

"What have you got there, Clyde?" Granny asked.

He held out his hand and slowly opened it to show her a broach.

Granny gasped and swayed a bit.

Mutt grabbed one of her arms, and I took the other.

She looked annoyed and kind of shook us off. "I'm perfectly fine. It's just a shock to see it again."

"So, you recognize it?"

"Of course, I do, Clyde. It originally belonged to my grandmother. Grandmama gave it to me, and then I gave it to Jonny's bride to wear on their wedding day. From then on, your mother wore it every time she dressed up. She must have been wearing it that night." She put her hand up to cover her mouth, and tears filled her eyes. "Is Jonny down there with her?"

"We will have to use dental records to confirm it, but, yes, I'm almost positive he is. There were two skeletal remains in the grave." He worked his jaw as he faced the farmhouse, and then he looked down at the broach in his hand. He turned to Granny and said softly, "You can hold it until we're done here, but then we need to turn it in as evidence. You'll get it back eventually, but it will probably take a while."

Granny put out her hand, and Mutt gently placed his mother's piece of jewelry in her palm. Granny closed her fingers over it and brought it to her cheek. "After all these years," she said softly. Tears glittered in her eyes as Mutt pulled her into an embrace. They clung to each other while I stood nearby with tears in my eyes.

Mutt finally released her and wiped his tears away with the back of his hand. "I've got to get back." He gave us each a hug. "Why don't you go home now? You can take the broach with you, and I'll pick it up later." He looked at me. "Pete is going back to the station, and I asked him to follow you to Granny's. Barron is still out there, and I don't want you driving back by yourselves." He gave us a peck on our cheeks, strode across the grass, and went up the steps into the house.

Granny was so quiet on the drive home that I asked if she was okay.

She sighed and answered, "I'm fine, dear. It's just that this broach holds so many memories." She laid the piece of jewelry on her hankie, which she had unfolded and put in her lap, and then she picked it up and cradled it in her hand. She started to stroke it as if it was a living thing, and I guess, to her, it kind of was. Like she said, it held so many memories.

Mother was waiting for us and put her hand to her mouth when we pulled into the driveway. As we got out of the car, she looked at me with questions in her eyes, and I nodded.

Granny stepped onto the porch and said in a shaky voice, "They found them."

Mother closed her eyes for a moment and then reached out and drew Granny into a warm hug. As she gently led Granny toward the living room, Mother asked, "Would you tell me about your son and his wife?"

Granny smiled through her tears. "I would love to."

Chapter 46

It didn't take long to compare dental records and confirm that two of the bodies found were Jonathan and Sarah Dale. Both had been shot in the back of the head, execution style, and they most likely had died instantly. Granny said it was a comfort to know that they hadn't suffered, and she was at peace because she knew she would see them again in heaven someday.

A third body was initially identified by the driver's license that was in his wallet. Fred "The Fink" Finklestein was a two-bit drug dealer who had disappeared about ten years ago. They were still trying to figure out the identities of the other three remains.

The family made the arrangements for Mutt's parents' memorial service. So, on the day of the funeral, when family, friends, Mutt's fellow police officers, former students of Sarah Dale, and the inevitable curiosity seekers showed up, it was a huge turnout. It was standing room only, with an overflow crowd. It seemed like everyone in town came—even Bella.

The service turned out to be a celebration of two people who had touched many lives. People stood up and gave testimonies about how this couple had quietly and unselfishly given their time and money to help others. I think even Granny was surprised to learn of the scope of their good works.

Although the community mourned that this young couple's lives had been cut so short, it was surely a time of healing for both Granny and Mutt.

The police had been searching for Stanley Barron ever since that terrible day he killed Bull, but he had seemingly disappeared from the face of the earth. They had gotten search warrants for both his house and for Clarence "Bull" Murphy's apartment, but the memory stick was nowhere to be found. Neither was Stanley and that had everyone worried. Mutt and Pete were assigned to the case, and I was beginning to wonder if either of them ever slept. They seemed to be working 24-7, but they hadn't been able to turn up a thing. It was so frustrating, and I'm sure they were discouraged.

The strange thing was they hadn't even found his car. I mean, how many people are driving around in a 1960 green Cadillac? Mother said it looked like a giant pickle on wheels, so you would think somebody would have seen the homely old thing. After all, it must stick out like a sore thumb. But with all the fuss and feathers about Stanley "The Swindler" Barron, I was about to find out that he was the least of my worries.

Mother was healing, both physically and emotionally. Her injuries were much improved, and she was at peace about what had happened. I knew it had to be the Lord. No one could have traveled through such a dark tunnel, experiencing what she did, and come out the other side unscathed. Yet, Mother was so strong that when I got upset thinking about it, *she* was the one who did the comforting.

A few days after Mother came to live with her, Granny took her to the hairdresser, and Peggy was able to do wonders. She trimmed and styled Mother's hair into a short pixie cut that really looked cute. That did a lot to help her self-image. It had only been a few days since Mother had gone through that horrible ordeal, yet she was already able to laugh again. Most importantly, her faith had never been stronger.

She stayed with Granny while she recovered, and the two friends became closer than ever. So, after a while, they worked out the details for her to become Granny's live-in companion and housekeeper. It was also decided that Mother would continue to work at the bookstore at least part-time. Both were very happy with the arrangements. It turned out to be the best of both worlds for everyone: we girls had a little more room to move around in the apartment, Granny had someone to keep her company, and Mother had her own bedroom.

A week or so after the funeral, Mutt and Pete sat down with Mother and me to talk about Mother's case. Pete leaned forward and clicked on his recorder. "Shirley, you already have given your statement about all that happened in that cellar with Clarence Murphy, also known as 'Bull.' Now, we need you to tell us everything you know about Barron and Murphy. We need every detail you can think of, even if it seems unimportant to you."

Mother told them everything she knew about both men's routines, habits, friends and acquaintances, and even which restaurants they ate in. She paused to reflect on all she had told them and then said, "That's about all I know ... I really can't think of anything else."

"Any hobbies?" Mutt wanted to know.

"Stanley liked to watch porn movies."

"That figures," Pete muttered under his breath. "What about Bull?"

"He wasn't into that kind of stuff. This might surprise you, but he loved to read. I never was in his apartment, but he used to brag about how he had floor-to-ceiling shelves filled with books."

Pete looked over at Mutt. "That's something we might check out."

"What, the porn movies?"

Pete threw his pencil and hit Mutt in the chest. "Funny, bro. No, I mean the book collection. Might give us an insight into the man's mind and give us a clue as to where he may have hidden the memory stick."

"That's something to consider. Everybody and their hairy hound knows that we have turned over and looked under every rock we could possibly find." Mutt leaned back in his chair and closed his eyes. "And we sure found a whole bunch of rocks, but nothing was under them." He sat up straight, rubbed his face, and looked at us with weary eyes. "His books just might point us in the right direction."

"Mother and I could go with you to look. If he has that many books, it will take a while to go through them. Two extra people would speed the process up quite a bit."

Mutt grinned at me. "We don't intend to read them all, babe."

"Ha ha. But wouldn't it be a good idea to flip through the pages? A lot of people hide notes, lists, and even money in the pages of books. You would be surprised at what Stormy and I have found stuck in some of the library books we've read. We even found a couple of love letters. Bull might have left some important information; like the number to a safe-deposit box or some such thing."

"You know, come to think of it, that may be a good idea." Mutt stood up and stretched. "We still have an active warrant, so why don't we all go over there?" Just then, his phone beeped. He checked the screen and sighed as he showed Pete the message. "We've got to go but I'll call you and we'll make arrangements to check out the apartment another time."

After they left, Mother and I continued to kick around ideas about where the missing memory stick was hidden.

"You know, the more I think about it, the more sense it makes to check out Bull's book collection," she said. "He loved those books, and they represented something very special to him. I know that Stanley paid him good money, but Bull didn't wear jewelry, didn't have an expensive car, and didn't even have a girlfriend to spend his money on. As far as I know, the only luxuries he indulged in were those books. They were the only thing of value that he owned, so I guess they were the most important things in his life." She leaned forward and put her chin in her hand while she gathered her thoughts. "When you think about it, as important as that memory stick is, it just follows to reason that he would keep it with all the other possessions that were valuable to him."

We all planned to investigate Bull's apartment the next day or so, but an earth-shattering event changed all our plans.

I was working at the Reading Nook, and it was getting close to closing time. Mother and Mrs. Marple had gone to an estate sale to see if they could find any interesting books for sale, so I didn't expect them to come back to the store until the next day.

The door opened, and a tall man with long blond hair strode in. He was impeccably dressed in an expensive suit with his hat pulled low on his forehead. He walked across the bookstore floor with purpose and came straight to where I was standing.

"May I help you, sir?"

He wordlessly dropped a ring onto the counter, and I gasped. It was the ring that I had given Stormy last year. I had found it at a pawnshop earlier that winter. It was incredibly beautiful and quite unique, and I had saved every penny I could for weeks until the glorious day when I finally scraped together enough money to buy it. I surprised her with the ring on Christmas morning. She was thrilled and loved it so much that she hadn't taken it off her finger ever since.

"Where did you get this?"

"So, you recognize it."

"Of course, I do!" Then it hit me. I looked up and was terrified by the hard expression on his face. "What have you done to her?" I whispered.

"Nothing yet. Boss's orders ... for the moment. But if you don't bring us Barron's memory stick, we are anticipating having a great deal of fun before we kill her." His cold smile chilled me to the bone. "To tell you the truth, I almost hope you won't cooperate. She's such a pretty little thing and so *very* innocent. We're going to draw straws to see who gets first crack at her."

Horror paralyzed me. I finally managed to force my vocal cords to work and rasped, "I don't have it. I don't know where it is! We've looked and looked ... everywhere ... but we can't find it."

"Not my problem. I'll be back at closing time two days from today. You better have the stick by then. And, by the way, I don't need to explain what will happen if the police become involved, do I?"

"Please don't hurt her," I whimpered. "Let her go and take me instead."

He burst into harsh laughter as he looked me up and down. "Are you kidding me? Trade you for *her*? Sweetheart, I prefer steak, not hamburger. Now, remember, you've got exactly two days—or else." He laughed as he turned and left.

I stared at the door until my knees gave way, and I flopped down on the floor. It hit me all at once, and I covered my face with my hands and sobbed.

That's where Mutt found me when he came to pick me up. I was crying so hard that he had a hard time understanding what had happened. Once I could finally form intelligible words, they hadn't really made too much sense. I kept on sobbing and all I could say was, "He brought me Stormy's ring."

When I finally calmed down enough to tell him the whole story, he looked grim. Mutt held me in his arms while I shook like a leaf. "Babe, the entire police force is going to work on this, and I'm going to call in everybody who has ever owed me a favor. And since more than likely this involves the mob in Chicago, we'll call in the FBI too. We're going to find her. I promise."

I panicked. "No! He told me not to involve the police. We can't call the police, or they'll kill her!"

He held me even tighter and kissed the top of my head. "Babe, I *am* the police. And now that I know about Stormy's kidnapping, there's no turning back. We'll put out the word that we must keep this operation under wraps. We're all professionals, and we know how to stay under the radar."

When the phone rang, I jumped and just stared at it, unable to move. Mutt picked it up and handed it to me. "Babe, you have to answer it."

My voice was shaking so much I could barely say, "H-hello?"

"Delilah! Is that you?"

"Ivy?"

"Honey," she said. "We've got trouble. Stormy didn't come home this afternoon, and now it's time to go to work and she still hasn't shown up."

I burst into tears again, and Mutt gently took the phone from me.

"Ivy, this is Mutt. I hate to have to tell you this, but Stormy has been kidnapped."

I could hear her scream, "Noo!"

Mutt quickly filled her in and then listened as she spoke to Ebony. She was speaking so loudly that I could hear her voice from where I was still huddled on the floor, although I couldn't quite make out what she was saying.

Mutt said, "Yeah, that might be a good idea, but I didn't tell you that, and you didn't hear it from me, okay? And make sure you and Ebony take extra precautions. I'm taking Delilah to Granny's for the night, and I'll make sure somebody stays with them. Somebody who is armed. I'm not taking any chances."

He hung up and turned to me. "Ivy's going to have Snake put out the word about Stormy. But, for now, we're going to Granny's. We need a real prayer warrior right now, and Granny's the best one I know." He set his jaw. "Then I'm going to work."

Chapter 47

MOTHER STOOD WITH HER ARM AROUND GRANNY'S WAIST AS THEY waited in the doorway. Unfortunately, Ebony had made a hysterical call to tell them what had happened even before Mutt had been able to phone them. When he did get through, both women were panic-stricken. There wasn't much he could say to calm them down, but he filled in Granny about what he knew and told her we were on our way to her house. So, they were watching for us when we pulled into the driveway.

When I got out of the car, my legs were like rubber. I was shaking so hard I could hardly walk, even with Mutt supporting me. As soon as I got into the house, I fell into Mother's arms, and we cried together. She cried for the daughter she never really knew, and I cried for a sister who was more like a daughter. We both cried for the girl we dearly loved.

A few minutes later, a police cruiser pulled up. A female officer got out, and she and Mutt had a short conversation before she came into the house. Mutt introduced her as Officer Beth Williams, and explained that she had been assigned to protect us that night.

When Mutt crossed the room to say goodbye, I clung to him like a frightened child. "It's going to be okay, babe. We're going to find her," he whispered.

I just couldn't make myself let him go until he finally had to peel me off him. Then he was gone. Mother put her arms around me as I watched his car disappear down the road through my tears.

Granny was the first to recover. She clapped her hands to get our attention and headed toward the living room. "Come, girls, we need to pray."

We all stood in a circle and held hands. Even Officer Williams joined us, and we took turns praying for Stormy's safe return.

My faith had never been stronger—or at least that's what I told everybody else. *Ha! I keep trying to beat down my doubts and fears, but think I really needed a baseball bat 'cause I'm not having much luck.* It was like playing Whac-A-Mole. I'd knock one fear down, and another one would pop up. So, I just kept praying, and praying, and praying.

Twenty-four hours down and counting. I was frantic, but Mother and Granny remained calm.

Granny sat beside me and took my hand. "You must have faith, Delilah. Don't you remember how your heavenly Father delivered you from danger, time after time? He knows exactly where Stormy is and what is happening to her—so you must put your trust in Him."

Sometimes it seems like my tongue wraps itself around my brain and holds it captive while the words just fall out of my mouth. I still can't believe what I said to this wonderful woman who had always been so kind to me and who had led me to the Lord. Here she was, trying to comfort me, but I answered her love with hateful words. "How can you believe that? God didn't deliver your son and his wife. He just let them die!"

Granny jerked back as if I had struck her, and I felt the big, bad guilt-gorilla jump up and down on my chest. It sure didn't help my conscience when Mother cried out, "Delilah!"

Tears immediately spilled over and ran down my cheeks. "I'm sorry, Granny. I'm so sorry!"

She closed her eyes for a moment, but when she opened them, they held nothing but love for me. "Delilah," she said, "do you remember when I told you about how I lost faith after my dear Jonathan died? Well, it took me a while to realize that God is God—no matter what happens. There is a verse in the book of Job that says, 'Though He slay me, yet I will trust in Him' (Job 13:15 KJV). Some people can accept this teaching early in their walk of faith, but most of us must journey a long way down the road with Jesus by our side before we reach the point where we can pray, 'Thy will be done. Thy will, not my will, Lord' … and mean it." She took both of my hands and held them tight. "We know He is able to keep Stormy from all harm, but if for some reason that is beyond our human understanding, this may not be His will. We will continue to pray for Stormy's safe return, but if something terrible does happen, we will find comfort in the fact that Jesus was with her the entire time, and then He lifted her up to heaven."

"But why?"

"Shh, child. There are things we will never comprehend while we are still on this earth, but scripture tells us that Jesus promised, 'I will never leave you nor forsake you' (Luke 22:42 NIV). Grab onto that promise, Delilah. Hold it close to your heart. Believe it!"

I spent most of the night in the bedroom, on my knees. Occasionally I'd get up and walk around a bit, but even then, I'd be praying. I knew Mother and Granny were in the living room praying together, but for some reason, I felt compelled to pray alone.

About dawn, I went to join them, and we continued to pray. When the clock chimed, I looked up at it. *Six o'clock in the morning. We have twelve more hours before I have to hand over the memory stick, which I don't have, don't know where it is or who might have possession of it, and don't even know what it looks like.*

That's when it hit me. "Blondie" didn't know what it looked like either. So, if the police could put together some data, something that looked legit, maybe we could buy some time until we found Stormy. I picked up the phone and called Mutt.

Chapter 48

MUTT LISTENED INTENTLY TO MY IDEA, ONLY INTERRUPTING TO ASK A few questions, and then he said, "There's one problem with all this, babe."

"And what's that?"

"We'd have to use you for bait. That mobster will expect you to be the one to hand over the memory stick. If something goes wrong, we may not be able to protect you."

"Do you know where Stormy is?"

"No, but we are doing everything we possibly can to find her, Delilah."

"I know, but you don't have the slightest idea where she's being held and you probably don't have a snowball's chance that you'll find her in time, do you?"

There was silence on the other end of the phone. I could hear him swallow a couple of times before he tried to speak. "Babe, every single one of us ..." His voice broke, and he cleared his throat and tried again. "We all are doing absolutely everything we possibly can ..." His voice was getting tighter. "Delilah ..." he stopped and took a few deep breaths. "Babe, if there is any way possible to find Stormy, I will. I promise you that I won't rest until she's back home."

My heart broke for him, but right then, I had to keep Stormy as my first priority. "But don't you see? We need to have a backup plan. If you can't find her, then we will need a plan B. I'll need your help to put this together so Blondie doesn't get suspicious."

He was quiet for a long minute, and then he sighed. "Okay. I still don't want you to get involved, but I guess we might not have a choice. I'll talk to our techs and see what they can come up with. Okay?"

"Thanks, Mutt."

"Babe?"

"Yes?"

"You know I'm doing everything I can, don't you?"

"I know."

"I love you, babe."

"I love you too, and no matter what happens, I will always love you, Mutt."

His voice broke again. "Thank you," he whispered and hung up.

A couple of hours later, Mutt called back. "Maggie pulled together names, dates, and drug dealings, and at first glance, it looks authentic. She's the best, and it's amazing what she was able to do in such a short time. We'll have an undercover bring it to you. I just hope we won't have to use it."

"I'm going to open the bookstore in an hour. I figure I need to keep everything looking normal."

"Okay, babe. We'll have one of our guys come in as a customer and bring the memory stick. We'll have as many undercover people as we possibly can surrounding you, but we can't get him suspicious and have him bolt."

"I understand. Pray for me."

"Always."

I honestly don't know how I got through the day. Thank goodness Mrs. Marple came in to help because I doubt if I could have made change for a dollar bill on a ninety-nine-cent purchase. Occasionally I spoke to the customers, and attempted to help them, but I'm afraid I proved to be mostly useless. I mainly just dusted, straightened, and restocked the shelves.

About an hour after opening, a woman who I recognized as Susan Collingsworth, one of Mutt's friends and a fellow officer, came through the door dressed in civilian clothes. I think I managed to act naturally as she paid for her purchases. When she handed me her credit card, a memory stick was hidden in her hand. She slipped it to me without a hitch, thanked me, and left the store. I don't think anyone would have noticed the exchange even if they had been watching closely. I slid it into my pocket and continued as if nothing had happened.

According to plan, Mrs. Marple left the store fifteen minutes before I was scheduled to close. I nervously kept an eye to the clock as time crawled by.

At exactly 5:59, Blondie stepped through the door, changed the sign to show "Closed," and turned the lock. My heart was attempting to climb up my throat and escape through my mouth as he strode toward me. "You got it?"

I pulled the memory stick out of my pocket and placed it on the counter. Without a word, he picked it up, slipped it into his inner jacket pocket, and turned away.

"Wait! What about my sister?"

"My boss wants to check this out first. If it's legit, he'll release her."

Panic nearly knocked me off my feet. "But how do I know if he'll keep his word?"

"You don't, sweetheart." He started to head toward the door and then stopped. "By the way, tell that big, bad cop boyfriend of yours if I run into any problems on my way back to Chicago, your sister is dead. And if this memory stick isn't the genuine article, not only is your sister dead but I'll come back and kill you too." Then he turned and left, leaving me shaking.

I staggered to the back room and collapsed into Mutt's arms. "What have I done?"

"It was the only thing we could have done, Delilah. Now we need to find Stormy and then shut down that Chicago operation before they discover that the stick is phony."

"What are we going to do when they find out?"

"Well, we should have a few days before they do. They'll need the password, and I don't think Maggie will be inclined to give it to them." He gave me a grim smile. "Oh, and did I mention that this particular memory stick has an interesting special feature? It's also a tracking device—courtesy of the FBI."

Chapter 49

STORMY HAD BEEN MISSING FOR FOUR DAYS NOW, AND THE SILENCE FROM Chicago was deafening. I heard Mutt and Pete discussing the case when they didn't realize I was in the other room. What I overheard made me sick to my stomach. They were guessing what the odds were that she was still alive. Mutt was afraid they had killed her right after the kidnapping to save themselves the trouble of trying to hide her from the police.

Then Pete mentioned something that made me feel as though someone had punched me in the gut. He said that he was afraid she had been sold as a sex slave. He said that some Chicago gangs were known to run human trafficking rings. That unimaginable possibility drove me to my knees once again, and I begged God to protect her.

I also heard them talk about how the FBI was tracking the signal from the memory stick, but they didn't want to move in until Stormy was safe and sound. I kept my big mouth shut because I didn't want them to find out I had been eavesdropping, but I wanted to scream at them that Stormy couldn't be dead! I had so many questions I wanted to ask them, but I couldn't bring myself to confess that I had been listening. Sir Walter Scott sure hit the nail on the head when he wrote: "Oh what a tangled web we weave when first we practice to deceive." *Yep.*

Granny had phoned Pastor Tim to tell him about Stormy's kidnapping, and he immediately came to the house to pray with us. The next day was Sunday, and he announced what had happened to the entire congregation, and they had a special prayer service for Stormy. Our phone kept ringing with church members calling to encourage us and pray with us. *One thing is for certain: the Lord was being inundated with prayers about Stormy and her kidnapping.*

I felt so sorry for Mutt, and Pete. They both had dark circles under their eyes. I think they were living on nothing but coffee, fast food, and no sleep. Mutt, especially, had a haunted look, and he could barely meet my eyes. I knew he felt like he was failing me, and it broke my heart. The strain was getting to all of us. I couldn't even make myself go to work, but Mrs. Marple was very understanding and said she would take over all my duties until I could come back.

That afternoon, as I was talking to Mutt on the phone, he said, "I've got to go. There's somebody on the other line." He hung up without even saying goodbye. I felt like I was suffocating under a blanket of dread. My gut feeling was he had gotten some news about Stormy, and it probably wasn't good since he would have called back and told me if she had been found alive.

I paced and prayed and prayed and paced for more than an hour, but the phone never rang. I was torn. *Should I try phoning him?* I finally confessed to Granny and Mother what was going on … or at least what I was *afraid* was going on. We all held hands and prayed, or as Granny said, we "stormed the gates of heaven."

It was dark when a police cruiser pulled into the driveway, and Pete got out. Just Pete. I yanked open the front door and stepped out on the porch as he rushed toward the house.

As soon as he saw me, he hollered, "We found her! We found Stormy, and she's okay!"

I fell to my knees and sobbed. "Oh, thank You, Jesus!"

It took me a couple of seconds, but then it hit me. Pete had come alone to tell us the good news. As he helped me to my feet, I asked, "Where's Mutt?"

He didn't answer right away as he guided me back through the door and into the living room where Mother and Granny were waiting. He reassured us about Stormy, but we could see from the expression on his face that something was wrong. Then, Pete took a deep breath. "Well, Mutt's been hurt, but he's gonna be okay."

I grabbed his arm. "What happened? How bad is he hurt? Where is he? And where is Stormy?"

"Now, hold on a minute, and I'll tell you. Mutt was shot during the rescue operation, but like I said, he'll be okay. He's in the hospital, and the doctors are going to take out the bullet tonight."

Once the news that there had been a shootout sunk in, we battered him with so many questions that he finally held up his hands. "Slow down! I can't answer when you all are talking at once." He waited until we quieted, and then said, "Mutt was shot in the chest, and the bullet hit a couple of ribs but it missed all his vital organs. And, no, Stormy wasn't hurt, but those scumbags kept her drugged, so she's dehydrated. That's why she's gonna stay in the hospital tonight. Now if you ladies want to hurry up and get ready, I'll answer all the rest of your questions in the car on the way to the hospital." He winked at me. "You might even get to talk to Mutt before his surgery. He was awake just a little while ago. Would you believe he kicked me out and told me to get my tail over here and explain what went down tonight?" He began to herd us toward the door. "Stormy has to sleep off all the drugs so she won't be awake, but I know you'll want to see her anyway. So, let's get going."

We all piled into the police car, and Pete took off toward the hospital.

Granny was sitting in the front seat, and she turned toward him. "Lead us in prayer, Peter, please."

As I listened to him pray, I realized that Pete was a true prayer warrior. He praised God for rescuing Mutt and Stormy and asked Him to heal them. By the time we swung into the hospital's parking lot, I felt as though I had been to a church revival. It amazed me how calm I was, when I pushed through the doors of the ER and hurried to Mutt's side.

Granny and I stood by the hospital bed and watched him breathe. He was connected to all kinds of machines, contraptions, and IVs. His face was pinched with pain, and his eyes were squeezed shut.

"Mutt?" I whispered.

He opened his eyes and gave me a feeble smile. "Hey, babe. What's a nice girl like you doing in a place like this?"

I was determined not to cry in front of him. "If you weren't hurt, I'd smack you 'long side of the head' for causing so much trouble."

"Babe, you've been around Ebony too much," he murmured.

"Granny's here too."

She took his hand. "You scared the life out of me, Clyde."

"Granny, don't you know by now that I'm too ornery to die?"

"I just worry that one of these days, you'll go faster than your guardian angel can fly." She leaned over and kissed his cheek. "You rest now."

Then nurse came in and injected more medication into his IV. "This is going to make you sleep, Detective Dale," she explained. "When you wake up, that bullet will have been removed, and you'll be feeling a whole lot better."

I could see him drifting away, and I kissed him on his forehead. "I'll see you in a little bit, Mutt. I love you. We all are praying for you."

"Love yah too," he slurred, and with that, he was out cold.

Chapter 50

AFTER THEY WHEELED MUTT DOWN THE HALL TO THE OPERATING ROOM, another nurse came into the room. "Are you Detective Dale's grandmother?" she asked.

Granny dabbed her eyes and nodded.

"I'm Clara, and I'll be taking care of Detective Dale in the recovery room." She patted Granny's arm. "Please don't worry so much. He's going to receive the best possible care. Dr. Anderson is an excellent surgeon and expects him to make a full recovery. I'm sure he's going to be just fine."

We thanked her, and after we finished wiping tears and blowing noses, we managed to get it together enough to leave.

When we pushed through the ER doors, I recognized another one of Mutt's friends, Officer Greg Covington, leaning up against the wall. He straightened up and walked toward us. "How is he?" he asked.

My voice shook a little, but I was able to smile. "He's hurting, and they just took him to surgery, but the doctors expect him to be okay."

"Whew. He sure gave us a scare."

"He gave *you* a scare, Greg?" Granny laughed through a few more tears. "I've aged ten years in the past hour ... and I don't have that many years to spare."

"Yeah, Mrs. Dale, I would imagine that he frightened the daylights out of you." He took her arm and nodded to me. "I'm supposed to bring you two up to Miss Sampson's room. Her mother is waiting there for you."

When we got off the elevator, there was an armed officer outside Stormy's hospital room, but when he saw Granny, he stepped aside so we could go in. In fact, all the cops knew her, and I could see how much they respected her.

Mother was sitting next to Stormy's bed, holding her hand, and when we walked through the door, she looked up.

I just froze and stared at my little sister. It broke my heart to see Stormy lying so terribly still with an IV in her arm, and I was shocked to see how white her face was. She looked so fragile, like a little China doll.

When a sob escaped from my throat, Mother came over to me and pulled me into her arms. "She's just asleep, Delilah. She hasn't woken up since I've been here, but the doctors explained to me that she needs to sleep until the drugs have worked their way out of her system. Don't cry. She's going to be okay, thank the good Lord."

After I finished having my meltdown, I blew my nose and pulled myself back together again and asked her, "Do Ebony and Ivy know?"

"They have already been here. In fact, they got here even before I did. They are waiting for us down the hall, so let's go meet them."

"Wait a minute. We need to pray for Stormy first," Granny said. She reached for our hands. "Let's pray for her and for Clyde."

We bowed our heads, and Granny led us in prayer. When she was finished praying, a deep voice said, "Amen!"

"Peter, I didn't know you were standing there."

"I got to the door just as you started to pray, so I joined in and silently agreed with everything you said." He gazed at Stormy for a moment. "She's going to be all right, but she needs to sleep off all those drugs." He rubbed his face before looking at us again. "Okay, let's go down to the waiting room. I know Ivy and Ebony are anxious and want to hear how she's doing. I'll give the details of what happened to all of you at the same time, so I won't have to keep repeating myself."

As soon as we walked through the doorway, Ivy and Ebony jumped up.

Ebony grabbed Mother's hand. "How's my girl doin'?"

"She's still asleep, but she seems peaceful. The nurse said she'll most likely sleep the rest of the night." Mother glanced at me. "I plan to sit with her until she wakes up."

I nodded. "That's good. And I plan on staying with Mutt after he comes back from surgery."

We sat down and waited for Pete to explain what had happened. He leaned forward in his seat and wiped his hands on his pants leg. Pausing a moment, he stared into space before turning his attention toward Ivy. "I guess we owe Snake an apology, and we need to thank him big-time. Don't know if we would have found Stormy without his help."

Ivy smiled and nodded at him. "I told you Snake was a good man. He would know who to ask and where to look. Not much happens in the hood that Snake doesn't know about."

"What are you two talking about? What does this, uh, Snake have to do with finding Stormy?" Granny asked.

Pete cleared his throat. "Well, Granny, after Stormy was kidnapped, Mutt talked to Ivy on the phone. She told him that her boyfriend, Snake, would look for Stormy 'cause lots of times his street rats know the happenings around the hood long before the cops even have a clue. Then, this afternoon, Mutt got a call from him. He said the word was out that there were some bogus doings going on over at an abandoned warehouse down on Third Street. Snake said he couldn't be sure Stormy was there, but the cops better haul their butts over there, quick like, to check it out."

My jaw dropped. "You mean Snake was the one who found her?"

Pete shrugged. "Well, one of his boys did. Anyway, Mutt sent Greg to do surveillance. When he gave us the green light, Mutt, me, Larry, and George went down there with a warrant and joined him. We kicked open the door, and as soon as we went in, they opened fire. It was like being in a combat zone; bullets were flying everywhere. Mutt got off a couple of rounds before he went down. Luckily, he was the only cop who caught a bullet, but when the smoke cleared, all three of the thugs had been hit. I understand that doctors are digging bullets out of them as we speak … one might not make it, though."

My entire body was shaking so hard that I thought my fanny would vibrate right off the chair seat. Nerves were getting to me, and my voice was shaking as I asked, "But what about Stormy? Where was she during all the shooting? How come she didn't get shot?"

"Well, we found Stormy tied up in a storage room, so she wasn't out where all the bullets were ricocheting around. After I broke down that door and saw her on the floor, it scared the life out of me. She was so still. Let me tell you, I sure was happy when I checked her pulse and felt how strong it was." He turned to Granny. "You probably want to thank Greg. He was the one who kept pressure on Mutt's wound until the ambulance got there." Pete chuckled. "Would you believe that even as the EMTs were heaving Mutt's butt onto the stretcher, he was still giving orders?"

Granny smiled. "Yes, I can believe it."

Pete grinned and sat back in his chair. "So, after we got to the hospital and they got him stabilized, Mutt insisted I go and get you guys. You know the rest."

Granny's eyes glimmered with tears. "Yes, Peter, we certainly do. God, in His mercy, protected them both."

After a while, Pete's wife, Naomi, arrived. She and Pete sat with Granny and me in the waiting room, giving comfort and praying with us. Each time I would lose it, Naomi would hand me the box of tissues, give me a hug, and start praying again.

Greg joined us later with a welcomed tray of take-out cups of hot coffee. As the night dragged on, a constant flow of uniformed and plainclothes cops went in and out, checking on Mutt, but so far, there wasn't a thing we could tell them. I just couldn't stop looking up at the clock as I tried to force the panic back down my throat. Nobody was saying it, but it seemed like the surgery was taking a lot longer than it should.

The hours crawled by, until finally, a woman in rumpled scrubs, a face mask hanging by its strings, and a stethoscope draped around her neck appeared in the doorway. "Mrs. Dale?"

Granny struggled to get out of her chair, and I took her arm as we both stood up. Her voice quivered as she almost whispered, "Yes?"

The doctor smiled warmly at her, and my heart started to beat again. "I'm Dr. Anderson. I just finished operating on your grandson, and I'm happy to say that he came through the surgery with flying colors. We did have a bit of a complication, so it took longer. The bullet shattered when it hit one of his ribs which made the procedure a little more complicated than I expected, but he should make a complete recovery."

Granny clutched at her heart. "Oh, thank You, Jesus!"

Dr. Anderson smiled even wider. "He's in recovery now, but they should be taking him to his room in about forty-five minutes or so. We'll let you know as soon as you can see him."

Granny gripped her hand. "Thank you so much, Doctor."

"You are most welcomed. Detective Dale is a good man, and I'm grateful the surgery went so well. He'll be experiencing a great deal of pain for a while, because of the bullet wound and the broken rib, but I expect he will recover fully and should have no lasting health problems."

Granny's voice shook as she said, "God is so good!"

Dr. Anderson smiled. "Yes, He most certainly is."

Chapter 51

FOR MOST OF THE NIGHT, I JUST SAT AND WATCHED MUTT DOZE. HE would stir and kind of wake up, but then he'd usually go right back to sleep. I could tell he was hurting, but for the most part, the drugs kept him in the twilight zone. A couple of times, he woke up enough for me to help him sip some water, but even then, I don't think he even realized I was there.

I was tickled to find out that Abigail, the same nurse who had taken care of Ivy and then me in the hospital, was now Mutt's nurse. She seemed glad to see me too and gave me a hug. When I told her that both Stormy and I had invited Jesus into our hearts, she shed tears of joy. Throughout the night, she would come in and take Mutt's blood pressure, check his vitals, and stuff like that. Although she was very busy, she always had time to say a prayer for him and give me a quick pep talk. Other than that, it was a quiet way to spend the night.

Granny had gone home after I "honest to goodness, cross my heart" swore that I would call her if there was any change in him at all. She puts on a good game face, but for those of us who know her well, we could tell that she was totally "wore out." It's easy to forget that she's in her seventies and doesn't have the energy she used to. Officer Greg took her home after it was arranged for Bella to meet them there and stay with her.

When he came back from making sure Granny and Bella were safe and settled in, Greg sat in Mutt's room to keep me company for a while.

He explained that Stormy would have a guard stationed outside her room until she was well enough to go home. Well, not exactly home. Greg said she'd probably have to go into hiding until the Chicago kingpin behind her kidnapping was picked up by the FBI. I felt bad for her because I knew what it was like to be stuck in a sleazy little house all by yourself. I decided—right then and there—that I would stay with her. I figured that she sure didn't need to be alone, especially after what she had gone through.

Since Greg was visiting already, I asked if he would stay with Mutt while I zipped up to the third floor and checked on Stormy. He glanced at his watch and said, "Sure, no problem." He settled down on a chair, stretched out his legs, and crossed his ankles. "Take your time. I'm off duty now, so I'll stay here and make sure he stays in line."

After thanking him, I started out the door and immediately ricocheted off the mountain that was coming into the room. Pete grabbed me as I staggered back and kept me from falling. "Hey, girl, where are you heading in such a hurry?"

"I was just going to see how Stormy was doing and ask Mother if she needed a short break."

"Well, since I see you got yourself a babysitter for Mutt, why don't I go up with you?"

"Sure." Even as I answered him, my stomach did a little flip. I had the feeling that Pete wasn't just wanting to stretch his legs when he offered to accompany me. Something was up, for sure. Well, I guess the fact that they were keeping an armed guard outside Stormy's room should have given me a clue. I craned my neck and attempted to look him in the eye, but the best I could do was look up his nostrils. "Is everything okay?"

Pete must have noticed I looked worried because winked at me and said, "Sure 'nuf, little sister."

I gave him a playful slap, and we headed for the elevator.

When the elevator doors opened on the third floor, I noticed right away that the guard was gone and the man standing by Stormy's door looked familiar. I stiffened as my brain gave me a kick-start. *Blondie!*

Pete must have recognized him the same instant as I did. He gave me a shove that sent me flying back though the elevator doors just as they closed, trapping me inside. As the elevator started to go back down, I heard four gunshots in rapid succession.

"Oh, please, God, no!" I prayed frantically. "Please, God, not Pete." It dawned on me that the only reason Blondie was there in the first place was to kill Stormy. I totally lost it and started banging on the elevator doors. After what seemed like forever, but was probably only a few seconds, they opened, and I was face-to-face with a grim-faced Greg. Several other cops were behind him, but in my state of terror, I didn't even recognize them.

Greg grabbed my arm. "What's wrong, Delilah!"

"It's Pete! When we got out of the elevator, the killer was outside Stormy's door. They started shooting at each other!"

The cops all turned around at the same instant, blasted through the door opening to the stairway, and thundered up the steps. I stood frozen, watching them go, until my legs finally decided to function, and then I followed them.

I heard more gunshots, and by the time I got to the top of the stairs and stepped into the hall, the air was hazy and smelled like gunpowder. The door to Stormy's room was open, and a man on the floor was surrounded by a bunch of cops. When I started to run toward them, somebody grabbed me from behind. I started fighting like a wildcat until Greg's voice finally penetrated my thick skull. "Take it easy, Delilah. Your sister and your mother are okay. Slow down and wait a minute until we make sure that guy isn't going to cause any more trouble."

I was gasping for breath, and it was taking all I had to keep from doing a face-plant right in the middle of the hall. "Where's Pete?" I croaked. "Is he hurt?"

He must have heard my voice because he stuck his head out the hospital room doorway. "Everything's okay, Delilah. Your mother is a little shook up, but she's fine—and Stormy slept through the whole thing." He glanced down at Blondie. "You can come in as soon as we finish picking up the garbage."

Chapter 52

I WAITED UNTIL BLONDIE WAS LOADED UP ON A GURNEY AND TAKEN AWAY. I figured he was headed for the operating room and wondered if Mutt's surgeon would be the one to work on him. It would be ironic if the one operating on that hired killer turned out to be Dr. Anderson.

I had to wait until housekeeping finished cleaning up before I could go into Stormy's room, and that took them a while. When I finally got through the door, there was Pete, notebook and pencil in hand, with his infamous recorder sitting on the bedside table, as he finished taking a statement from Mother. When she saw me, she jumped up and pulled me into her arms. "Oh, thank goodness you're okay."

I glanced over her shoulder at my sister. She was still sleeping peacefully in her bed, completely oblivious to the fact that she had nearly been murdered. "I'm fine, Mother," I said. "Pete pushed me back into the elevator, and I missed all the excitement." I turned to him. "Thanks, Pete. I owe you ... again." Something had been bothering me, and it finally dawned on me. "What happened to the cop who was guarding the room?"

He grimaced. "They found him out cold in the janitor's closet. He's got a bad concussion, but he's lucky that Blondie hadn't decided to finish the job. Guess he was in a hurry."

"So, you think he acted alone?" Mother asked.

"Yeah, as far as we can tell. We've swept the entire hospital, the parking garage, and even the parking lot but didn't turn up anything." He glowered at me. "That doesn't mean that they won't send somebody else to finish the job, so you and Stormy are going to do what you are told."

I crossed my arms and glared back at him. "Which is?"

"You two …" He paused as he tucked the notebook in his pocket and picked up the recorder. He glanced over at Mother and then turned to glare at me. "I mean, you *three* are going to a safe house to lay low until we get all this straightened out."

I was about to argue with him when I remembered that Mutt was lying helpless in his hospital bed. I spun around and headed toward the door. "I've got get back to Mutt! He's all alone."

Pete reached out and caught my arm. "Hold on, sister. Wait just a second, and I'll go down with you." He held up his hand when I started to give him some lip. "He's not alone, Delilah. George is down in his room, keeping an eye on him. You don't think I'd let my brother just lay there like a sitting duck, do you?"

I blushed and hung my head for a moment until I had enough guts to look him in the eye, I said, "Of course, you wouldn't, Pete. I'm sorry."

He gave me a quick hug. "It's all good, sister. Now let's go and check on your man."

Later that morning, the drugs wore off and Mutt woke up feeling every single ache and pain. He was not a happy camper, to say the least, and he let everyone within growling distance know about it.

It hurt him to breathe, but when the surgeon came in to check on him, she said that this was normal when you have cracked and broken ribs. He sure wasn't pleased when she told him that they couldn't give him strong enough drugs to block the pain since that might affect his breathing. And then, to top it off, she wrote out an order that he had to exercise his lungs by blowing into some type of plastic contraption to avoid getting pneumonia.

As the day wore on, he must have hurt like the devil because he groused at everybody until Granny walked into the room and straightened him out. "Clyde! You stop snarling like a rabid dog, right now! You know good and well that you should be praising the good Lord that you're alive and Stormy is safe."

He looked like a chastised little boy when he whined, "But it hurts."

"Well, praise the Lord that it *does* hurt because it's *supposed* to. Only dead people don't feel pain." She reached over and tenderly brushed the hair back from his sweaty forehead. "I spent the night thanking God for preserving your life and for keeping Stormy safe. Every time I think about how close I came to losing you ..." Her eyes filled with tears. "I know you are in pain, Clyde, yet I'm so very grateful you are alive to *feel* that pain."

Mutt gave her a rueful smile. "I know, Granny. I'm glad God preserved my life too, but could you pray that it won't hurt so much?"

She smiled and kissed his cheek. "Of course, Clyde." She motioned for me to come closer, and we placed our hands on Mutt as she prayed. After she said amen, I opened my eyes and was surprised to see him sleeping peacefully. Thank God for His tender mercies.

"Let him sleep," Granny whispered. "It's the best thing for him."

A few minutes later, there was a gentle tap on the door. Ebony stuck her head in the room and said, "How's Mutt doing?"

"He's doing okay. He's been hurting pretty bad, but he's sleeping right now."

"Well, since he's asleep and Granny's here, why don't you come up to Stormy's room. She's been asking for you."

Granny said, "You go on, Delilah. I'm planning to stay."

I gave Granny a peck on the cheek. "Are you sure?"

"Go!" She made shooing motions with her hands. "I brought my knitting. I'll be fine."

We got Granny settled on a chair next to Mutt's bed, and when we headed out the door, I was shocked to see who was waiting for us in the hall. "Snake! What are you doing here?"

He glowered at me. "Ain't no reason I shouldn't be here."

Ebony smacked his arm and grinned up at him. "Now don't get your panties in a wad, Snake, or I'll tell Ivy on you." Then she guided me toward the elevator. "Snake is watching our backs, Delilah. He told Ivy there's too much bad stuff going down for us to be walking around by ourselves. He and his boys are keeping us company until this all blows over. And by the way, Pete gave his okay for them to help out."

As he punched the button for the third floor, I turned to him and said, "Thanks for watching out for us, Snake." My voice started to shake.

"Pete told me that you were the one who found Stormy. I can't ever thank you enough."

He just stared straight ahead at the elevator doors. "Ain't for you. It's for Ivy." He glanced over at me. "… And for the girl. Ivy loves her like her own." He set his jaw. "I'm makin' sure ain't nobody gonna hurt her." He glared at me as the doors opened. "Gonna watch over you too. Nobody hurts Ivy's friends."

Snake nodded to the guard, who stepped aside to let us into the room. Stormy was in bed with a folded towel over her eyes.

Pete had already left, but Ivy and my mother stood near her, talking quietly. Mother turned as we walked in. "She has a migraine," she whispered. "The doctor said that all those drugs those goons gave her probably triggered it … not to mention the trauma she's been through."

"Are they giving her anything for it?" I asked.

That's when my sweet little sister lifted the towel and squinted at me. "Delilah? Is that you?"

I reached down to hug her. "Oh, honey, are you okay? I was so scared for you." The next thing I knew, I started to blubber. I couldn't help it. I guess it was because everything piled up together, and then it all just spilled over.

She began patting my back. "It's going to be okay, Delilah. I'm fine … sort of. At least once this awful headache goes away, I'll be fine. Thank God, they didn't hurt me. I was scared, but I kept praying, and God kept them away from me." She started to cry.

I was just so overwhelmed by everything that all I could do was bawl and say, "Thank You, Jesus!"

Mother joined in, and the three of us had a real sob session. Eventually, Ivy and Ebony joined in too.

Snake watched us blubber for a while, and then just shook his head, flopped down in a chair, and clicked on the TV.

Chapter 53

For the next two days, I ran myself ragged going from Mutt's room on the second floor up to the third floor to check on Stormy and then back down again. I know I was driving my various bodyguards to distraction being so pigheaded. But tough, I couldn't help myself, and I just couldn't stay away from either of them. Besides, running up and down those stairs helped burn off some of my nervous energy.

Once all the drugs had worked themselves out of her system, Stormy's migraine faded away and the doctor discharged her. We were just waiting for all the paperwork to get done before she could leave. My heart was torn. I wanted to support Stormy and go with her, but I just couldn't tear myself away from Mutt. In any case, in the next hour or so, I had to decide whether to go or stay.

While I was waiting, Pete and Snake walked over to the empty conference room across the hall and closed the door. I looked over at Ivy, but she just shrugged and went back to helping Mother gather Stormy's things. It's amazing how much stuff a teenage girl can accumulate in just three days, especially when you consider she was asleep for a good part of the time that she spent in the hospital.

I kept my eye on that door, and after what seemed to be forever, the door opened. Pete came out, followed closely by Snake, and they both looked grim. Without a word to anyone, they headed for the stairway. Well, since I'm too nosy for my own good, I chased after them like a hound dog tracking a raccoon. Unfortunately, by the time I arrived at Mutt's room, they had already shut the door. I hovered right outside, you know, just in case someone needed something. I could hear loud voices through the door, and that made my gut twist into knots.

As I was pacing back and forth, the door was yanked open, and a hand whipped out, grabbed my arm, and pulled me into the room.

"Let her go, Snake," Mutt growled. He and Snake glared at each other like two junkyard dogs.

I decided to take matters into my own hands and twisted out of his grip.

Snake glowered at me. "Why you listening outside the door, girl?"

"How did you ...?" *Oops. I just stepped in it.*

He gave me a knowing smile and jerked his head toward the door. "Could see your shadow moving back and forth."

"Oh." I must have blushed fifty shades of red.

Mutt was sitting in bed with his arms crossed, and let's just say that he was *not* putting on a happy face. "Well, Delilah, since you overheard our conversation, what do you think of the plan?"

"Wh ... what plan? Honest, Mutt, I could hear your voices, but I couldn't understand what you were saying."

He sighed and glanced over at Pete.

The big man shrugged and said, "Don't have much choice, brother. Ain't too many options available right now."

Mutt worked his jaw for a moment, stared up at the ceiling, and then looked over at me. "Snake has offered to take us in ... all of us and keep us safe until this business in Chicago is resolved. I've just been informed that the FBI isn't too keen on supplying a safe house for you and Stormy. Their excuse is that the case is winding up, and they plan to pick up several members of the mob today on kidnapping charges. Guess there's been more budget cuts, or something, so they don't want to shell out the bucks. In any case, that just doesn't cut it with me ... or Pete." He paused, glanced across the room, and added, "Or Snake either." He met my gaze. "Witnesses have been known to disappear during trials concerning the mob, and we don't have any intention of allowing that to happen to Stormy or to you."

I managed not to shudder. "Okaay... So, what's the plan?"

"Snake has two empty units in his apartment house that are across the hall from each other, and he's offered them to us. You, your mother, and Stormy will be together, and Granny will stay with me. We figure that Chicago won't connect Snake with you or your sister, and he'll provide a secure place to stay. Snake said that he, with the help of his boys, will guard us." He sighed. "We all know I can't do much to keep you safe until I get my strength back, and since our police force is stretched to the max, they can't protect you 24-7."

I thought, *Wow! Snake owns an apartment building?* For once, I kept my big mouth shut. I turned my attention back to Snake.

Snake cleared his throat and said, "Apartments got furniture, but maybe not what you're used to."

"We girls will be fine," I said. "After all, we used to sleep on a mattress on the floor along with the roaches. But Granny ..."

Mutt said, "We'll bring in a mattress for her. With her bad hip, she'll need a special one that's memory foam." He nodded to Snake. "Other than Granny's bed, we will be cool with whatever furniture you have to offer."

Snake headed for the door. "We'll get everything set up. A couple of the boys will pick up Stormy and her mother here at the hospital. Ivy will make sure they get their clothes."

I touched his arm, and he paused. "Thanks, Snake."

"It's for Ivy," he growled, and he slammed the door behind him as he left.

Mutt's doctor said she would discharge him very soon if he continued to improve—but only if he promised to keep up with his breathing exercises and come back to the hospital for regular checkups. He also had to agree for Granny to oversee his recovery regiment and give his word that he would faithfully follow her instructions.

Those "rules" were kind of comical. Poor Mutt didn't stand a chance against Granny and me. As Granny put it, we would "gird our loins and enter into the battle." I think if he had any idea what fate was waiting for him with us two slave drivers, he might have decided to stay in the hospital. In any case, after arguing a bit, he somehow persuaded me to leave the hospital and go with Stormy. Mutt promised that he and Granny would join us in a few days.

Our escorts, sweet, faithful Jose, and another one of Snake's men named Ralphie, arrived at Stormy's hospital room just as Mother signed the last of the paperwork. Snake was waiting for us in the parking lot with a van, so we all loaded up and headed for our temporary home.

I was pleasantly surprised with our new digs. It wasn't exactly the Hilton, but considering the neighborhood, it was nice. And to be honest, it was a lot better than our own apartment.

When Snake showed us the two units, he said it was up to us to decide which apartment we wanted, and which one would be Mutt's. Both had two bedrooms and were nearly identical, right across the hall from each other. Stormy liked the one in the front of the building the best, and I figured the one in the back would be a little quieter for Mutt and Granny, so everything worked out.

Ivy and Ebony were waiting for us with our clothes and all the paraphernalia we women consider essential. They helped hang up our clothes in the closets, put our other things in the dressers, and stocked the bathroom with a bunch of our shampoos and stuff.

The furniture was old but surprisingly clean and in good shape. The kitchen was already stocked with dishes, and our friends had provided us with all kinds of food.

When Ivy noticed I was looking around, she pulled me aside and asked, "Well, what do you think? Is this good enough for Granny to live in?"

"I'll be honest with you, Ivy. I'm really surprised. It's much nicer than I thought it would be."

"Well, Jose keeps this place up real good."

"Jose?"

"Yeah. He's the building superintendent. Does a bang-up job, too."

"I didn't know Jose worked here for Snake."

She nodded. "Has for years. Snake has high standards, and he's hard to work for, but if you do your job and keep your nose clean, he'll make it worth your while."

I grinned at her. "Well, this sure is a nice place. It's even better than our apartment."

"Yeah. Snake is a good landlord, and he makes sure his tenants have a decent place to live. But he runs a tight ship. You do drugs, drink too much, or cause trouble—and you're out. His apartments are good for families." She smiled. "And he don't let nobody tear up his place neither." She got serious, and our gazes locked. "He's a good man, Delilah. He's just a little rough around the edges, and he don't follow all the rules sometimes."

I thought about it for a while before I asked, "If this is Snake's building, how come you didn't move in here after you were attacked? I mean, I'm glad you live with us, but why did you say you didn't have any other place to stay?"

She glared at me. "I didn't say that ... Ebony did. Besides, I don't take charity from him, and I sure ain't gonna ask Snake for nothin'. He offered a while back, but I told him I was happy where I was. Didn't want to put him out none."

That's when it hit me. "You are in love with Snake, aren't you?"

Ivy snorted. "Of course, I love him, but not in that way, Delilah. He's like a brother to me."

Yeah, sure he is.

Chapter 54

It didn't take us long to get settled into our new place. Once Granny's mattress arrived the following day and we got her bed set up in their apartment, we were ready for them to arrive.

A couple of days later, I was looking out the window when I saw them pull up. I watched Jose help Mutt out of the car and keep a tight hold on his arm as they walked up the front steps and into the entrance. I waited at the head of the stairs until they finally reached the second-floor landing. Let me tell you, it took all I had not to burst into tears when I saw how white and pinched Mutt's face was.

As we started to take Mutt into his apartment, Granny started fussing up a storm—and we turned to see what was going on. Snake came striding up the stairs with Granny in his arms.

She was waving her cane in the air, kicking her feet, and generally making a ruckus. "I am perfectly capable of walking up a flight of steps, young man," she squawked. "Put me down immediately!"

"I ain't got all day to wait on you, woman. 'Sides, you might break your neck falling down these here steps with that cane of yours, and I ain't got no insurance for that kind'a thing." Snake deposited her in front of the apartment door and turned to me. "You're in charge of keeping her in line." He had pasted a grim expression on his face, but his eyes were dancing. I'm sure that anybody with a little less willpower would have burst out laughing. But he just nodded to Mutt and trotted back down the stairs.

By the time we got Mutt into bed, he was bathed in sweat and I was concerned about how rapidly he was breathing.

We gave him his pain medicine, and then Granny tucked him in. He closed his eyes and started to drift asleep until she crooned in his ear, "You rest a while, Clyde, and then we'll do your lung exercises."

His eyes popped open. "Don't you think going up those stairs exercised my lungs enough for today?"

"Now, Clyde, you promised the doctor that you would do those exercises four times a day without fail, and I intend that you do."

Mutt squeezed his eyes shut and groaned.

Granny gave him a peck on the cheek. "Sleep tight, Clyde," she whispered. She turned to me. "Well, now that we've gotten him put to bed, would you show me the rest of the apartment?"

After I gave her a tour of the place, she grinned at me. "This kind of reminds me of our first apartment when Jonathan and I were newlyweds. Our decor was five-and-dime store, and the furniture was similar to this: plain but sturdy." After she walked through the entire apartment, she turned to me with a big smile. "Yes, this will do quite nicely."

Even though I knew it was best for us to hide out in the apartment until the Chicago gang was put in prison, I couldn't help but worry about my job at the bookstore. Mrs. Marple had assured Mother and me that our jobs were safe. She said she would hold them open for us "until the cows come home and start milking themselves," but I was still worried. In the meantime, she and Mr. Marple had come out of their semiretirement, and she assured me that they enjoyed "putting the old harness back on, at least for the time being." So, I felt a whole lot better about the situation.

To tell you the truth, it was kind of nice to just relax and do nothing for a change. Stormy and I had always worked hard for most of our lives, trying to keep our heads above water, scratching and clawing just to stay alive. I had never experienced downtime before until my run-in with Willie Nelson's pickup truck, and now we both had time to put up our feet and chill.

From my perspective, the best part of our exile was that I was seeing Mutt more than ever before. We really enjoyed our time together but could have done with a little more privacy for some occasional cuddling and smooching, if you know what I mean. But no such luck. Granny was always vigilant, plus we had plenty of visitors dropping in too, so we were always well chaperoned.

One afternoon, Ivy dropped by our apartment, but Ebony wasn't with her, which was unusual. She seemed to have something on her mind, and when she asked if Granny could come over too, I knew something was up. She asked us to sit down, but then she got up and started to pace.

Finally, Granny snared her hand as she motored past her and gently pulled her down onto the sofa. "Now, this is not getting us anywhere, dear, and our heads are about to explode waiting for you to explain what is going on. So, why don't you just tell us what's bothering you?"

Tears began to trickle down her scarred cheeks, and I handed her a box of tissues.

She wiped her eyes, got herself together, and said, "Granny, do you remember telling Ebony and me the Bible story about that prostitute, Rahab?"

"Of course, I do, honey."

"Do you think that story is true? Do you honestly believe that she's Jesus's great-great-way-way-back-grandma?"

"Yes, I do, dear—with all my heart."

Ivy twisted the wad of tissues in her hands while we waited. I was holding my breath, and so was everybody else in the room. I'm sure we were all hoping and praying for the same thing.

"Well, I've been thinking about it ever since that day." She began to sob. "Do you think Jesus would really want somebody like me?"

Granny pulled her close and wrapped her arms around her. "Oh, honey, I know He does. He's been waiting such a long time for His prodigal daughter to come home." She began to tell the same Bible story that Pastor Tim preached when I had attended his church that first time and ended up answering the altar call.

Granny is a great storyteller. She told us about the son who had acted like an absolute bum when he insisted that his father give him his inheritance early. Then he went off and soon blew it all on wild living. In the meantime, his father had been watching and waiting for his youngest son to return. Eventually, the young man decided to come crawling back home with his tail between his legs. Yet while he was still a long way off, his father saw him and ran to welcome him. When his father reached him, he threw his arms around his son and kissed him. The son offered to work as a servant, but his father refused his offer and instead dressed him in expensive clothes and threw a big banquet in his honor.

The entire time Granny spoke, Ivy's eyes never left her face.

Then there was absolute silence after Granny paused and tenderly took our broken friend's hands in hers. Her voice grew strong and clear. "Ivy, your heavenly Father has been standing at the gate, waiting for you, and now that He sees you coming down the road, He's running toward you with His arms open." She lovingly wiped the tears from Ivy's face. "Will you allow Him to take you into His arms and hug you? Will you surrender to Him? Will you accept the unconditional love He is offering you?"

"But … what do I have to do?"

Granny smiled. "Just hug Him back, Ivy. And then give Him all the pieces of your broken heart and let Him put it back together again so you can become whole."

So, there we were, in the living room of one of Snake's apartments, as we all knelt in prayer. Granny led Ivy in the Sinner's prayer as she accepted Jesus as her Lord and Savior.

When she said she wanted to be baptized by Pastor Tim, Granny phoned him with the news. We could hear his joyful shouts of praise all the way across the room.

After we had a big ol' group hug and finished blowing our noses, Ivy gave us a wobbly smile. "Okay, all we have to do now is to convince Ebony to take the plunge too." She laughed. "Maybe we could make it a twofer."

Chapter 55

As it turned out, it happened exactly that way, and then some. I guess Ebony didn't stand a chance between Ivy and Stormy. As brand-new Christians, they sure weren't shy about sharing their faith. Granny said that the way they were so willing to share about the Lord put her to shame. Pastor Tim called them his "uber-evangelists" and said he wished he had a bunch more like them in his church.

Speaking of church, that's the one thing that Granny refused to compromise on. She said that she doubted that the gang from Chicago would be looking for us in church, but she didn't care if they did. She said God would protect us, but if it came right down to it and something did happen, what better place was there to meet our Lord? So, anyway, she expected that we attend services, and Mutt agreed with her. As it turned out, because of their stubbornness, some amazing things happened.

For one thing, since they insisted that we go to church, and Snake was so determined to protect us, he grudgingly came along. So did several of his men, including Jose and his wife, Maria.

At first, Snake would just sit there with his arms crossed over his chest, looking like he wanted to kill a rock. But as time went by, he gradually became more relaxed and more attentive to Pastor Tim's preaching. It was much later when Snake told us he and the preacher had secretly met a couple of times a week to discuss the Bible. He said that those discussions became quite lively at times. I bet they did.

Once Ebony decided to join the church, she explained how she came to make her decision. She told us that she had thought about how Mother and I escaped being murdered by Bull and how Stormy wasn't hurt the whole time the kidnappers held her captive. And then there were the times when Stormy and I had been kidnapped by Barron's gang, when "Willie Nelson" had tried to kill us, and how Mutt had survived after getting shot twice.

She described her conversation with Pastor Tim: "I asked the preacher a bunch of questions. Then I told him I guessed for that whole hot mess to happen and for all them people to survive okay, just weren't no coincidence. I told him that I tried to figure a way around it, but just couldn't 'splain it. It really messed with my head, you know? I finally decided that it had to be a God thing. Ain't nothing else it could'a been. So, I told him that I decided to throw in the towel and join up."

I doubt if there was ever a baptizing like Ivy's and Ebony's, and I'm pretty sure there won't ever be another one quite like it, either. Ebony, being Ebony, dressed up for the occasion. Thank goodness her friend Makena Branson had convinced her to wear traditional African dress instead of her usual flashy outfits. This church practices what I think is called "full-immersion baptizing," so she was a little put out that she had to wear a robe during the actual baptism.

There's a big ol' creek conveniently located right behind the church building where they have the ceremonies. Back when I was baptized, it was just a small affair with a few of my friends along with Stormy and Mother and, of course, Granny and Mutt. Stormy's was a bit bigger. I mean, with her outgoing personality, she has a lot more friends than I do, so between her friends from the diner and the ones she had made at church, there was quite a crowd.

But with Ivy and Ebony ... wow! I believe the entire congregation turned out. I guess some of it had to do with curiosity. After all, Open Door to Grace had never had the likes of those two enter their midst before. But, just as Pastor Tim had promised, everyone had welcomed them with open arms.

Dressed in their baptismal robes, Ivy was the first to go in. Pastor Tim gently tilted her backward into the water until she was completely submerged. When she came back up, the only way to describe it was that she was radiant. She just stood there, eyes closed, with her arms lifted towards heaven and the most beautiful expression on her face. Snake was there to watch, and I was amazed when I saw him wipe a few tears from his eyes.

Jose and Maria came forward next and asked if they could be baptized too. Pastor Tim talked to them for a while, and I guess he asked them questions about their beliefs and stuff, but then he gave them both a big hug and led them to the water. I was really choked up watching them. The more I came to know Jose, the more I appreciated him. He's a good person, for sure, and even though I don't know his wife all that well, I have no doubt you can say the same thing about her.

Then it was Ebony's turn. Granny always said God had a sense of humor and, she said, if you didn't believe it, all you had to do was to look around at the people He created. I agree with her and I'm sure He enjoyed what happened that day.

When Ebony came up out of the water, she was so excited that she started jumping up and down, praising the Lord. But the creek bottom was covered in small, slippery rocks, and the next thing we knew, she cannonballed back into the water, knocking Pastor Tim right off his feet in the process. They both came back up spluttering, and when the preacher tried to help her, Ebony slipped, and they both went down again. Several of the deacons waded in to help, but the next thing we knew, they were all floundering around in the water too. I mean, it was like watching *Jaws* meets *Animal House*.

They all started to laugh, and the more they laughed, the harder it was for them to stay on their feet. At first, we spectators were trying to remain pious and all, but with the scenario that going on in the creek right in front of us, nobody kept it together for very long. By the time Ebony finally made it to shore, we were all weak from laughter. And there's no doubt in my mind that the Lord had real good belly laugh that day too.

CHAPTER 56

Poor Mutt was ready to climb the walls. The doctor had yet to release him for work, and when he pressed her about, it all she would say was, "We'll see." To top it all off, she said that once she did release him to go back, he would have to hold down a desk job for a while. He wasn't too pleased about that, but he finally decided that at least sitting behind a desk would be better than being stuck in the apartment every single day—except for Sundays when we went to church.

So, all he had to occupy himself was to sit in the apartment and complain, until even Granny lost patience with him. She finally kicked him out of the apartment and told him to go walk around inside the building and get some exercise. That's when Jose took pity on him. He let him tag along while he did the maintenance work in the apartments. Then, after a while, Snake began to join them on their rounds. When Pete was added to the mix, whenever he was off duty, it became quite an interesting intermingling of the intense personalities of these four very different men.

We could hear them laughing and joking around all over the building. I swear they acted like a bunch of big kids. So, while us girls were "cooling our heels," as Mutt put it, the guys spent a lot of time together and eventually figured out that they really liked each other. Even though I knew that they had become good friends, it blew me away when Mutt told me he had decided to move into the apartment permanently. He explained that it was more convenient than where he was living now, and it was "much nicer digs."

Several days crawled by before Mutt finally got the phone call we had all been waiting for. The tracking device embedded into our bogus memory stick had led the FBI right to the gang's headquarters in Chicago. They rounded them all up, and they were even able to grab the kingpin: Nelson Blackburn. I guess he must have been a real nasty piece of work since the feds seemed particularly pleased that they had nabbed him.

From what the agent told Mutt, when Blackburn was arrested, he couldn't give a reasonable explanation as to why the memory stick was found in his private office, locked inside one of the drawers of his personal desk. Imagine that.

The FBI only arrested them for Stormy's kidnapping for now, but they hoped the indictment would eventually be expanded, to include the charge of murder. Apparently, the two thugs who kidnapped Stormy and survived the shootout with the cops, were singing like birds. I guess the feds planned to prove the kidnapping charges since Blackburn had the memory stick that was used as ransom in his possession. More charges were pending.

Mutt was worried that even though the members of the Chicago gang were behind bars, Nelson Blackburn's influence wasn't just confined to inside the prison walls. He reminded us not to let our guard down since Blackburn still could put out another contract on us. And this time, Mutt warned, the killer might be successful. So, it wasn't over yet,

He felt that it was even more urgent that we find the original memory stick with the information copied from Stanley's computer, so Mutt wanted to "go through Bull's apartment with a fine-tooth comb." He just had to find a judge who would reissue the search warrant.

I let him know, in no uncertain terms, that he best not even try to go without me. After all, before all this ugly business happened, he had invited me to go, and I still wanted to snoop through those books. Finding that cursed memory stick had become real personal to me.

And then, of course, there was the matter of Stanley Barron. Nobody had seen him since the day I found Mother in the old farmhouse cellar, but we knew he was out there somewhere.

Mutt was suffering from cabin fever just sitting around in the apartment. So, of course, he took his frustrations out on us, until we wanted to run screaming out the door.

But then the following week, the doctor gave Mutt the okay to go back to work on light duty. Thank goodness! I was worried about him going back too soon, but Pete pulled me aside and said, "Don't you worry, sister. He ain't gonna be doing nothing foolhardy 'cause if he even thinks about doing too much, I'm gonna sit on him."

You know, the idea of that mountain of a man sitting on top of Mutt so he doesn't get hurt kind of defies logic, doesn't it? In any case, I didn't have a say in the matter. But I guess if I was honest with myself, it was good for Mutt to return to duty.

I swear, the day he returned, Mutt must have grabbed the phone the moment he walked into the station. He got ahold of the judge and had the search warrant for Bull's apartment reissued. Then he called me right away, and Mother and I met him there a few hours later.

When the super let us in, I was surprised to see how nice it was. It was the typical upscale bachelor apartment with nice furniture and paintings on the walls. I would never have guessed that a man like Bull would have lived in a place like this. But maybe he had a split personality or something, and this apartment was where his "other half" ... the Clarence Murphy half ... lived.

Mother and I made a beeline for the floor-to-ceiling bookshelves and started pulling out books, but Mutt stopped us in our tracks. "Whoa! Wait a minute. We need to be organized and have a system. This isn't just a lark so you can satisfy your curiosity, you know. We're on official police business."

We decided to begin searching the bookshelf behind the couch and found a small stepladder stashed in a corner. We started at the top and worked our way down. I stood on the ladder and handed the books a few at a time to Mother, and she gave them to Mutt while he sat at the dining room table. He flipped through each one, and then stacked the books he was finished with in a pile.

Once we went through one shelf, we would return the books and begin the next section. After an hour, we had completed the first bookshelf and moved to the next one. We were halfway through the second bookcase when I came across an odd book. It was a classic Nancy Drew mystery. It's very strange for a man like Bull to collect juvenile fiction.

I must have stopped and stared at it for a while because Mother asked if I was okay. I showed it to her, so she could read the title: "The Clue In The Diary." We exchanged glances.

Mutt got up from the table and joined us. "What have you found, Delilah?"

I silently handed it to him, and we held our breath as he opened the cover. He looked up at me and grinned. "Well, well, well. Looks like our man had some unusual reading habits." He angled the opened book so we could see the memory stick, safely cradled in a perfectly hollowed-out hiding place.

Mother gave Mutt an exuberant hug. "Well, praise the Lord, we found it!" she said. She waited until I climbed down off the ladder, and then we did a little victory dance, much to Mutt's amusement.

"I need to get this to the FBI as soon as possible. Let's get going" Mutt turned and started toward the door.

"Hold it right there, buddy." Mother stood with her hands on her hips. "We are going to put the rest of these books back before we leave. They are too valuable to be left just laying around. Hopefully, this collection will eventually be donated to a library or a college."

It didn't take us long to replace the books and have the building superintendent lock the apartment door. After we secured the crime tape across the doorway, Mutt headed for the police station to deliver the memory stick to the FBI. Then Mother and I went back to the apartment to tell Granny and Stormy the good news

It took a several days before we got the all-clear from the FBI, and then we were finally free to leave the apartments in Snake's building. A bunch of Pete and Mutt's fellow officers got together and helped move us back to our respective homes. Mutt decided to stay and planned to finish moving the rest of his things from his old apartment once he had time to heal a bit more.

It's amazing just how much stuff we had accumulated in the few weeks we had lived there, but the guys didn't complain as they toted everything down the steps and into the van. First, they went to Granny's house to get her, and my mother settled in, and then they stopped at our apartment to drop off Stormy and me.

When I walked through the door of our apartment, I slowly turned in a circle so I could take it all in. It felt so good to be home.

Chapter 57

"How could he just disappear into thin air?" Mutt paced past my chair for the umpteenth time, muttering to himself. He had been obsessed with the disappearance of Stanley Barron ever since we got to the hospital's maternity waiting room. Mutt couldn't have been more nervous if *he* was the expectant father instead of Pete.

I knew it wouldn't do any good to ask him to sit down since I had already tried that a whole bunch of times. Keeping his mind on police work instead of worrying that his best friend's baby was about to be born was his way of keeping it all together, but this attempt at coping wasn't working too well, and he was about to lose it.

"How long does it take to have a baby anyway?" He rubbed his face and looked at me. "It's been hours. Do you think something's wrong?"

I managed not to laugh at him. "These things take time. I'm sure Pete and Naomi have things under control."

That didn't calm him down very much at all.

The next thing I knew, he had waylaid one of the poor, overworked nurses going down the hall. "How is Mrs. Tanner? Why hasn't she had her baby yet?"

I guess this nurse was a veteran at dealing with nervous fathers because she stared him down, and that's not an easy thing to do to a cop. First, she made a point of glaring at her arm until he dropped his hand, and then she kind of drew herself up to her full height and asked, "And you are?"

"I'm Detective Dale, Detective Tanner's partner. He's been in there for hours with his wife. They were supposed to have a baby."

"How long has Mrs. Tanner been in the labor room?"

Mutt glanced at his watch and looked a little wild-eyed when he saw the time. "It's been over six hours!"

I could see the twinkle in the nurse's eye. "Only six hours? I take it this is her first?"

Mutt nodded frantically.

"Well, Detective Dale, you may as well get yourself real comfortable because she's only getting started. Most first babies take their time getting here, so you are in for a long night. In fact, I've known some babies that take twenty-four hours or more before they make their appearance." She patted his shoulder and then continued down the hall, leaving poor Mutt, just staring after her, slack jawed.

That's when I decided that changing the subject might be helpful. The only other thing that seemed to hold his attention was Barron: "Did the FBI find much dirt in the information that Stanley stored on the memory stick?"

That seemed to finally divert his mind onto a different track.

"Oh, yeah. Would you believe that back in the day, ol' Stanley had quite an operation going? A sort of small-town Murder, Inc. with connections to the Chicago gang. He was involved in stuff like drugs, prostitution, protection money, and every other kind of dirty business you can possibly think of. Apparently, if somebody got in his way, it didn't turn out so good for them. The lucky ones got their kneecaps broken, but if that didn't solve the problem, they just disappeared. I don't know what happened over the years, but things slowly went downhill until Stanley gradually lost his grip on his little enterprise. Chicago kept slicing off pieces of the action and then finally took over the whole pie. Only a few crumbs remained but after his stroke, what little he had left, slipped through his fingers, leaving him holding nothing but dust."

"So, the cops can't use the information to convict him because it's too old?"

"Oh, there's no statute of limitations on murder, so they can charge him with a bunch of them. That memory stick was a gold mine."

"Well, if that's true, why in the world did he keep all that incriminating evidence?"

"Who knows? Apparently, he transferred all the information to his computer a few years ago and then saved everything. Maybe it was an ego thing, and he wanted to have a permanent record of his glory days. Anyway, there was also a detailed record of his dealings with the Chicago syndicate ever since he began his criminal career, including his association with Nelson Blackburn for the past fifteen years. The FBI will be able to use all that information to put the entire organization behind bars for a long time."

A lump lodged in my throat, and I couldn't seem to swallow it. "Then, do you think the boss from Chicago ordered Stanley's elimination? Is that why you can't find him?"

Mutt shrugged. "Could be. Especially if they thought they had the real memory stick. He could have been using it for blackmail, and then once they thought they had it in their possession, there wouldn't be any reason to let Stanley live."

I could feel the blood drain from my face as the full truth hit me. "You mean, I signed Stanley's death warrant when I concocted that scam?"

Mutt stopped his pacing and pulled me into a hug. "Babe, this isn't your fault. It was Stanley's decision to play with scorpions when he tried to blackmail a crime syndicate, and as a consequence, he got stung. Not too smart on his part. Besides, we don't know if he's dead or not. For all we know, he could be sitting on a beach in the Bahamas, getting a suntan, and enjoying a drink."

Someone cleared their throat, and Mutt and I jumped apart. A nurse was standing in the doorway. "Detective Dale?"

"Yes?"

"Detective Tanner asked me to inform you that according to the doctor, it could be several more hours before the baby is born." She smiled, put her hand on her hip, and mimicked Pete's voice. "He said, 'Tell them to get something to eat 'cause this here kid is as stubborn as her daddy and won't come out until she's good and ready. And she ain't ready yet.'" She grinned at us. "It will be a while, and no matter how much you two wring your hands and pace, it's not going to speed up the process."

We both laughed and thanked the nurse.

Mutt took my hand and grinned. "Come on, babe. Let's go eat."

We came back with a take-out bag for Pete. After we talked to the nurse and got the okay, I changed places with the expectant father, and then Mutt practically dragged his friend out of the room so he could eat. I visited Naomi for a while, helping with the breathing exercises and generally keeping her calm until Pete came rushing back into the room.

Naomi smiled and said, "For goodness' sake, honey. You must have swallowed that burger whole."

He took her hand and tenderly kissed it. "Don't take me long. Ate my burger, made a pit stop, and scrubbed up again. Didn't want to miss anything."

"The way things are going; I think you would have had time to eat a six-course meal." She groaned softly as another contraction clamped down.

That's when I decided to hightail it out of there.

As I left, I could hear Pete saying, "Breathe in through your nose, breathe out through your mouth. That's it, sweetheart. You're doing great."

Mutt and I spent the next few hours sitting in the waiting room chatting, watching TV, and reading old magazines. I must have finally dozed off for a while because I was jerked awake by Pete's booming voice.

"It's a girl! Eight pounds, fourteen ounces. Got lungs like an opera singer. Looks like her Mama, thank goodness. She's beautiful!"

The two friends locked themselves into a bear hug and pounded each other's backs. When they pulled apart, I was surprised to see tears running down Mutt's face too. "The nurse said they had to clean her up and then take her to Naomi in her room. Then you guys can meet her."

"What's her name, Pete?" I asked.

"Well, it sure ain't Gaylord." He grinned and then turned serious. "Her name is Rosa Harriet Tanner. Figured we needed to name her after somebody she could look up to, so we named her after Rosa Parks and Harriet Tubman. Both of those ladies were smart, courageous, independent. They knew what they wanted and how to get it. They were both strong women and had plenty of guts."

Mutt slapped him on the back. "Well, you and Naomi couldn't have picked anyone better to name her after than those two."

Pete's eyes filled with tears again. "My little girl's gonna have a better life than me. She's gonna have a *good* life. I'll make sure of that." Then, after giving me a joyous, nearly rib-cracking hug and one last back-slapping bear hug between the guys, Pete hustled down the hall toward Naomi's room.

After the nurse told us that Naomi and Rosa were ready for visitors, Mutt and I, armed with balloons and a teddy bear, paused in the doorway and watched as the new parents became acquainted with their daughter.

When Pete glanced up, he was just beaming. He motioned to us. "Come on in and meet the future president of the United States."

We tiptoed over and peered down at the precious little bundle. Of course, we oohed and aahed until Pete stood up and said, "You want to hold her, bro?"

Mutt nodded, and as he cradled Rosa in his arms, he just stood there with a silly grin on his face. When he handed the baby back to her mother, he smiled. "You did real good, Naomi. Especially since she doesn't look like her daddy."

We all laughed, and then it was my turn. I gingerly took her from Naomi and studied Rosa's tiny face. She took my breath away. I held her in my arms and marveled as she curled her tiny ebony fingers around mine and gazed up at me with gorgeous brown eyes. For some reason, my eyes filled with tears as I looked up at her parents and whispered, "She's perfect."

Pete puffed up like a peacock. "Well, did you expect anything less than perfection? After all, she *is* my daughter."

Naomi smiled and looked up at him with a loving expression. "That's right, and I pray that Rosa will always have the same sweet, gentle spirit that her father has."

Wow. It must be wonderful to have such a loving relationship like the Tanners. I glanced over at Mutt, and he gave me a sweet smile that made my heart soar. *I sure hope I'm not reading more into that smile than I should.*

Chapter 58

AFTER LITTLE ROSA WAS BORN, I WOULD GO TO BED AT NIGHT AND START dreaming about babies. When I would wake up and realize it was just a dream, I'd feel kind of … I don't know … sort of empty or something. Up until the moment when I held that precious child in my arms, I had never pictured myself becoming a mother. After all, considering my own broken childhood and the fact that I had had the overwhelming responsibility of raising Stormy when I was so young myself, I guess I figured I'd had more than my fill of diapers and colicky babies to even consider having one of my own. I suppose I viewed motherhood as something to avoid at all costs. That is, until now … until I met little Rosa.

I was never one to daydream since I always had to grapple with reality, fighting and scratching just to keep my head above water. Then, of course, I had to take care of Stormy too. It never occurred to me that better days might be ahead, and I guess I was always afraid to think otherwise. *Maybe that's why I kept Mutt at arm's length for so long. I just hope I didn't overplay it. It would break my heart if he gave up on me now.*

A couple of weeks ago, Snake was quietly baptized with a few of his close friends as witnesses. He and Pastor Tim had been meeting for months before finally he made the decision to accept Christ as his Savior. Let me tell you, Ivy was over the moon, and the rest of us were thrilled for him too.

So, when those two walked into our apartment, grinning like two fools, I should have known what was going on. I should have been prepared for it, but to tell you the truth, I was blindsided. I saw Snake take her hand, and when Ivy looked up at him with such a loving expression, I'm ashamed to say that I felt spinach-green envy rise up and fill me so full that I thought it might start oozing out of my ears.

We were all staring at them when Ivy turned to us with the happiest smile you ever saw and said, "We've got something to tell you guys."

Ebony stood up, practically vibrating with anticipation. "Come on, girl. Out with it!"

Ivy and Snake exchanged glances, and then her voice squeaked with emotion as she announced, "We're getting married!"

Ebony let out with a war whoop that rattled the windows, and Stormy rushed over and engulfed Ivy in a big old hug, but I just stood there, glued to the floor. When I finally managed to walk over to hug her and give Snake's arm a friendly pat, I hoped that the smile I pasted on my face looked genuine. I was happy for them. Really, I was. Afterall, if anyone ever deserved to be happy, it was Ivy. I knew I should be thrilled for my dear friend, but that fifty-pound weight on my chest made me face up to the fact that I was green-eyed jealous, and there was no getting around it.

Mutt came over and pulled Snake into a big old bear hug, and they slapped each other on the back. Never in my wildest dreams did I ever think they would become friends, and now those two, along with Jose and Pete, were practically inseparable.

Ebony grabbed Ivy's hands and began jumping around, dancing, and hollering, "When, when?"

After things settled down a bit, they explained that Pastor Tim was going to marry them next Friday night.

Ivy was just beaming as she and Snake made goo-goo eyes at each other. "Can you believe it? Not only am I getting married, but I'm getting married in a church!"

Mutt was grinning at the two of them as he slipped his arm around my waist and pulled me close. "That's great news guys! Are we invited to the wedding?"

Snake smiled. "Of course, brother. It wouldn't be official without you, Jose, Pete, and your women there."

I managed to ignore the crack about being Mutt's "woman" and just smiled and nodded.

It was a sweet ceremony. Only a few of us were invited, and then we followed Granny back to her house. A nice buffet was waiting for us with all kinds of fixings. We had a great time laughing and stuffing our faces while we celebrated with the bride and groom.

During the party, I had a shock when I saw Jose and Maria talking to Pastor Tim and I noticed Maria's thickening waistline. I'd always heard people talking about how a pregnant woman "just glows," yet I hadn't really believed it until I saw Maria's face. *Yep. No doubt about it. She and Jose are expecting a little one.* Once again, jealousy grabbed me by the heart and nearly yanked me off me feet.

What is wrong with me? These are my friends, and I should be happy for them! Well, I am happy for them, but still ...

That night, while we were sitting on Granny's porch swing, Mutt seemed deep in thought. He would start to say something and then stop and shake his head.

Finally, I couldn't stand it anymore. "What's going on, Mutt? Is something the matter?"

He sighed and stretched out his legs and crossed his ankles. "I was just thinking ..."

"About?"

"About Ivy and Snake. They sure seem happy."

"Yeah, they sure do."

"And did you know that Jose and Maria are going to have a baby?"

"I noticed Maria's belly after the wedding, and I figured they were."

He sighed again and turned so he could study my face. "Do you think you'll ever be ready, Delilah?"

"Ready? For what?"

His smile faded and he stood up. "Never mind."

I panicked and jumped up. "Wait a minute Mutt, please ..."

He stopped and turned to me with a serious expression. "What about Stormy?"

"Huh?" I sure didn't expect that question. "What about her?"

"Will you ever be willing to let go of her?"

"She's only sixteen!"

"Delilah, she just turned seventeen, and in a few months, she'll be going to college."

I guess the horrific thought of losing my baby sister to the big, bad world must have crossed my face.

Mutt gently hugged me and said, "Babe, you know Stormy's been studying her brains out for the past few months to pass the entrance exams. She earned that scholarship, and now that the church has decided to pick up the rest of her expenses, she'll be able to enter State this fall." He grasped my shoulders and gazed at my face. "You need to let her go. She's ready."

My bottom lip quivered. "I know she's ready, but I don't think I am."

"I don't think any mama is ever ready, not even when her 'little bird' is perched on the edge of the nest and flapping its wings." He gave me a loving smile. "Babe, you have got to let her fly so she can soar."

Tears started to trickle down my cheeks. "I know, but it's just so hard. It's probably the hardest thing I've ever done."

"I would imagine it is, babe, but you are strong enough to do what is best for Stormy."

I nodded and leaned against his chest.

"Babe?"

I looked up at him.

"Once Stormy is settled, would you consider something?"

My heart started to pound. "Consider what?"

He paused, and then with a husky voice, he whispered, "Us."

It took a moment for my brain to process what he had said. When it finally sank in, I leaned forward to answer him with a big old kiss.

At first, he seemed a bit surprised, but to say that he recovered quickly would be an understatement.

I just melted into his arms, and I wanted to keep on kissing him forever. Of course, we had to stop before we went too far, and I'm kind of embarrassed to admit that it was Mutt who put on the brakes; not me.

"Babe!" He was breathing heavily. "We have to wait. I sure don't want to, but I respect you too much."

I was straightening my clothes when his words finally sunk into my thick skull. "Wait? Wait for what?"

Smiling as he took my hands, he lovingly searched my face before softly asking, "Delilah, would you marry me?"

Chapter 59

I felt like I was caught up in a whirlwind. Granny and Mother were thrilled with our news, but our small little wedding was morphing into a gigantic mega-event. Once they started to make up the guest list, I guess they went a little over the top. Apparently, the entire congregation of our church was going to attend, not to mention all members of the police force, our friends, acquaintances, any person I had ever said hello to, and everyone else who happened to populate our fair town. They were all going to be invited. *Good grief!*

Mutt finally stepped in and brought those two back to earth. After a heart-to-heart talk, the four of us compromised. Our wedding would be larger than we had originally planned, but smaller than Woodstock. I was already getting nervous, and we were just getting *started* with the plans and preparations. *I'll be so glad when it's all over with, and Mutt and I can move into our own apartment in Snake's building and begin our life together.*

At first, I was worried about Ebony. After all, she would end up alone in our old apartment and be responsible for paying the rent by herself. But as luck would have it, a couple of weeks before Mrs. Blakely's original lease was scheduled to be up, Ebony found out that Snake had a one-bedroom apartment available. So, instead of renewing the lease at our old apartment, she decided to move into in the same building we would be living in. *I guess we'll be just one big, happy family … I hope.*

Then, in the middle of getting ready for Stormy to leave for college and attempting to conquer the never-ending, ever-expanding list of all the "I absolutely need it and besides, all the other kids will have it" things needed to properly launch my baby sister onto her college career, plus planning a wedding that rivaled Charles and Diana's, we also had to help Ebony move into her new apartment. So, why not? We sure didn't have anything else to do.

We decided that Stormy and I would bunk at Ebony's new apartment until Stormy left for school and I got married. There was a sofa bed in the living room for us to sleep on, and since goodness knows that we all were used to living together in tight quarters, the lack of personal space wouldn't be a problem. Of course, that apartment was a whole lot nicer than our original fifth-story walk-up apartment that we all shared; a time that seemed like a lifetime ago. We figured that once Mutt and I were married, Stormy could stay in our second bedroom whenever she came home from college.

During the process of moving Ebony, I noticed a real hunk of a guy working his tail end off, toting endless pieces of furniture and boxes up the stairs and into her apartment. When he paused to rest a moment, Ebony introduced him to us as Rob Martin. He seemed like a nice guy and a decent kind of person. I especially liked how respectfully he treated her and had a sneaking suspicion that he was sweet on her.

Later, Ivy pulled me aside and told me that those two had been an item for months. I guess I had been so involved in everything else that had happened lately that I hadn't even noticed what was going on with Ebony. Ivy told me that they had met at church and hit it off immediately. She said Rob knew about Ebony's former life but was willing to accept it as something that had happened in the past. *So, maybe we'll be celebrating another wedding in the near future. Who knows?*

Oh, yeah, another thing happened. Wonders of wonders. Ebony got a new job! Her friend from church, Makena, told her that a nearby trendy boutique was looking for a salesperson. Ebony interviewed for the job and was hired on the spot. The pay was a whole lot more than what she was making at the diner, and it was located within walking distance of her new apartment. She is so excited, and I bet she'll do well. Thanks to Makena's patient teaching and guidance, she has developed a real eye for fashion

SHARON JOHNSTON BACON

and colors, and with Ebony's flamboyant personality, I'm sure she'll be a big hit with the customers.

I've gotten back into my old routine too. It felt so good to return to the bookstore, and Mrs. Marple seemed relieved when I finally got back. She said she enjoyed working again, but she was even happier to return to her semiretirement.

Mutt fully recovered from the gunshot wound and went back to full-time duty. I can tell that he's glad, but to tell you the truth, I'll always worry every time he leaves for work. Nowadays, you never know what might happen. It seems like war has been declared on cops—even in our little town.

Anyway, I'm glad things have settled down. I just wish we could find Stanley Barron. I know that Mutt and Pete are tearing their hair out, but so far, nothing. It's like the earth opened and swallowed him.

But then, it was just a few days later, after I had decided that his whereabouts would never be discovered, we finally found out what had happened to him.

Chapter 60

As soon as Mutt walked into the bookstore with an expression that would sour milk, I knew something was up. When Pete came in right behind him with the same solemn look on his face, I set the books I was shelving back into the carton and gave them my full attention.

Mutt glanced around the store that was empty of customers for the moment and then asked, "Can we go in the back and talk?"

Panic grabbed me by the throat. "What's wrong? Is everybody okay?"

He gave me a grim smile, took my arm, and gently guided me toward the break room. "Everyone you care about is fine, but Pete and I have something to tell you."

I paused and looked back at the showroom.

Mutt said, "Don't worry. We'll keep the door open and keep a watch out for customers. Besides, we'll hear the bell if someone comes through the door."

I led the way to the kitchen area, and we sat around the break table. My body was stiff with tension, and I clasped my hands together in white-knuckled anticipation.

Mutt cleared his throat and leaned forward. "Okay, here's the thing. We found Stanley Barron."

I searched his face. "And?"

"He's dead."

I let out a big sigh of relief. I just couldn't help it. "How?"

He cleared his throat again. "Well, you know the day that you found Shirley and rescued her?"

"Of course, Mutt. How could I ever forget?"

"You said you were making your getaway when you met Stanley's car on the road, heading back toward the farmhouse."

"Yeah …"

"And you told us that you noticed he started to chase you, but you were able to outrun him, and after a while, you lost sight of him. After that, you never saw his car again."

"That's right …"

"Well, a highway crew found his car today. It had gone off the road, down a steep hill, and into a grove of trees. You couldn't see it from the road. It wasn't found until one of the crew members glanced down the hill and saw the sun reflecting off the rear window. No one had ever noticed it before."

"Oh."

"Apparently, he missed a curve while he was chasing you. When the car went down the embankment, it got wedged between two big pine trees."

I shuddered. "So, he was killed in the wreck?"

"Not immediately." Mutt looked especially grim. "It looks like when the car hit the trees, it damaged the engine, and it stopped running. The power windows wouldn't open, and the trees were blocking the doors."

The full horror of it all hit me. "So, he was trapped and couldn't get out."

Both men nodded.

"And nobody found the car until today?" I looked from one man to the other. "How do you know he wasn't killed right away?"

Pete shook his head. "There were signs that he tried to get out." He seemed to be choosing his words carefully. "He didn't die easy, Delilah. It probably took several days."

Mutt stirred in his seat. "The coroner will be able to tell us more after he's finished with the autopsy."

A bunch of different emotions went through my mind. Of course, I was relieved, but the sheer awfulness of how he had died haunted me. I just sat there, nearly paralyzed by all my thoughts, until I managed to pull myself together enough to ask, "Do Mother and Stormy know?"

Pete stood up. "Not yet. I'm going over to where she works to tell Stormy now. Where is your mother? We thought she would be here working."

"She and Mrs. Marple went to some estate sale to check out the book collection. They should be back around lunchtime."

Mutt checked his watch. "I'll stay here for a while to see if she comes back in the next little bit."

Pete looked at us both and nodded. "Okay, bro. I'll pick you up on my way back to the station."

"Sounds good."

Mutt followed me back into the showroom, and I retrieved the box of books and started shelving them. I guess I just needed something to do while I processed everything. I must have been too quiet because Mutt put his hands on my shoulders and gently turned me so that I faced him.

"You know it wasn't your fault, don't you, babe? After all, he was bound and determined to kill you and your mother. I think the Lord intervened and kept you two safe."

"Yeah, I know. It's just ... you know, to suffer like that. I wouldn't wish that on my worst enemy."

He smiled and pulled me into a comforting hug. "I know, babe. That's one of the things that I love most about you."

When Mutt told Mother what had happened, she had the same reaction as I did. Stormy took the news a little more calmly though, and she said he had gotten "what he deserved." But after she thought about it for a while and prayed about it, she apparently changed her mind. Later, she commented that it was too bad he ended up dying like that.

When the coroner's report came back, it sickened me. He estimated that Stanley had probably lived for at least three days after he crashed. Granny said she hoped that he used the time to reconcile with God and ask for His forgiveness.

They say there's always the hope that a sinner will turn to God before they die, although in this case, I seriously doubt Stanley did. But then again, you never know. And, besides, who am I to judge?

Epilogue

Today is my thirtieth birthday, or at least we figure this date is close enough since Mother still can't remember exactly when I was born or, for that matter, Stormy's birthday either. We have accepted the fact that we both have bogus birthdays, so that's no biggie. Anyway, that's what we tell ourselves.

As I stared out the window, little Hannah was latched onto my breast like a piranha, nursing hungrily. This girl is no shrinking violet, that's for sure. Kind of like her mama, I guess. Mutt is playing with our twin boys in the backyard. With all the babies being born in this apartment house, Mutt says it must be something in the water. Including the other tenants, we're up to a whopping even dozen kids. We parents decided that a play area was sorely needed. We worked our tails off hauling away all the junk, seeding grass, and installing a swing set. Snake also planted a garden, and I can see him picking some of the veggies with "help" from his little Ricardo and Jose's two boys. I'm amazed at Snake's patience, especially when it comes to little kids.

Hannah's finished nursing, and I patted her back until I was rewarded with a belch that would do her daddy proud. We grinned at each other and headed to the bedroom for a much needed diaper change. In between the baby talk, while I cleaned my daughter's little buns, I think about what these past few years had brought, and about the changes that are coming.

Mutt and I will probably be moving soon. We've been scrimping and saving to make a down payment on a house. I've got mixed feelings about that. Our apartment is getting too small, and we need a house with three bedrooms, but I hate to think about leaving our friends. Of course, we won't be going too far away, but it won't be the same. We are both active in Helping Hearts, and at least our new home will be close enough that we'll be able to continue working with the kids. I can't help being amazed how Mutt's protégé, Eddie, turned his life around. Can you believe that he attends college, and once he passes the bar exam, he'll be a lawyer?

Mutt and Pete are still partners. The Brenville Police Department remains small, but our small city is slowly growing. I'm not sure it's for the best. I think I'd rather it remains the sleepy little town I remember as a kid, but I guess you can't stand in the way of progress.

Pete and Naomi's Rosa and little Martin Luther are growing up so fast. Pete told us they quit the baby race once our twins and daughter were born, but maybe not. I've noticed Naomi's growing belly, and I don't think it's from her eating too much. I've counted on my fingers, and my best guess is the baby will arrive sometime during summer break, so that should work out well. Naomi won't miss too much time before she gets back to her first-grade class. She's a great teacher, and I can't wait until our boys have her. Of course, that will be in a few more years.

I'm working part-time at the Reading Nook. We need the extra income, and I need to get away from dirty diapers and snotty noses sometimes, you know? Now that Mother is manager of the bookstore, it's easier to keep my schedule flexible. Luckily, I've got plenty of babysitters available, and we usually take turns watching each other's kids, which works out well.

A few years ago, I never would have dreamed that Ivy and Snake would be heading the youth church at Open Door to Grace. They make no bones about their former lives and how the Lord delivered them out of that toxic lifestyle. I guess their honesty helps them have a great rapport with the teens, including the ones involved with gangs. Pastor Tim is thrilled with their ministry and how they have led so many of the kids to Christ.

Rob and Ebony have taken it a step farther. They moved to Atlanta and work in an urban ghetto at a mission sponsored by our church. I worry about them and the baby that is due soon, but I guess the good Lord is big enough to keep them safe.

My baby sister is finishing up courses in order to earn her master's degree in social work. I am so proud of her. Stormy has started working as a children's advocate intern. She's determined to prevent another child from slipping through the cracks like we did when we were growing up.

I can't help smiling when I think about Granny. She's still going strong, although she's slowed down a bit with that arthritis in her hip. You know Granny. She won't let anything keep her down. And, oh my, how she enjoys her great grandkids. Since she considers all our children as her great grandkids, that makes eight and counting.

Bella and the dogs have moved in with Granny and Mother. They all get along together remarkably well, and Mother enjoys Bonnie and Clyde. Guess there is no accounting for some people's taste.

Well, my quiet time is over when the door burst open, and two sweaty little boys explode into the room. "We're hungry, Mama!" they say in unison. It never fails to amaze me just how those two are synchronized in just about everything they do.

Mutt gave me a quick peck on the cheek. "Come on, boys. First, we wash our hands and then we'll figure out what to have for lunch." He is a great dad, but that's no surprise, since he's such a wonderful husband. I'm so blessed.

After we finish eating, Mutt and the boys decided to bake me a birthday cake. After much laughter and a whole lot of mess, I was presented with their masterpiece. It was lopsided, kind of caved in at the middle, and had icing oozing off its sides and onto the plate. It was beautiful. I told them it is the most beautiful birthday cake ever created. And I meant it too.

That night, we had a party, and everybody was invited. My biggest surprise is that Rob and Ebony drove all the way in from the city to be there. "Girl," she said, "You didn't think you could celebrate the big 'three-oh' without me, did you?"

We had a wonderful time, catching up on all the news, telling stories, and reminiscing about the years gone by. After everyone left, and we finally got the kids settled down, Mutt and I headed for bed.

In the darkness of our room, we started to smooch. We were really starting to get it on when the quiet was shattered by Hannah's wailing. Mutt sighed, threw off the covers, and slipped on his robe. "Stay in bed. I'll get her."

Mutt came back in a few minutes and handed me a nice, clean, freshly diapered baby and then watched with a sweet smile as our daughter nursed.

When I was younger, I had never even dared to dream that I would be so happy. After suffering through a deprived childhood and a miserable life, who would believe that I would end up with such a wonderful family? God has been so good to me, and now it seems that the sky's the limit.

And there's no doubt in my mind that, God willing, the best is yet to come.

Printed in the United States
by Baker & Taylor Publisher Services

Printed in the United States
by Baker & Taylor Publisher Services